Jane Caro is an author, columnist, broadcaster, advertising writer, documentary maker and social commentator. She has published ten books, including a memoir, *Plain-Speaking Jane*, as well as *Just a Girl* and *Just a Queen*, the first two novels in the Elizabeth Tudor trilogy. *Just Flesh & Blood* is the third and final book in the series.

Jane appears frequently on *Q&A*, *The Drum*, *Sunrise* and *Weekend Sunrise*. She has created and presented three documentary series for the ABC's *Compass*, with another in production. A frequent ad hoc columnist, she writes regular columns for *Sunday Life* and *Leadership Matters*.

Jane divides her time between Sydney and a cattle property in the Upper Hunter. She is married, with two daughters, a grandson and a granddaughter.

@JaneCaro

Also by Jane Caro

Just a Girl

Just a Queen

Unbreakable: Women Share Stories of Resilience and Hope (Ed.)

Destroying the Joint: Why Women Have to Change the World (Ed.)

Just Flesh & Blood

JANE CARO

UQP

First published 2018 by University of Queensland Press
PO Box 6042, St Lucia, Queensland 4067 Australia

uqp.com.au
uqp@uqp.uq.edu.au

Cover design by Jo Hunt
Author photograph by David Hahn
Typeset in 11/16 pt ITC Galliard by Post Pre-press Group, Brisbane
Printed in Australia by McPherson's Printing Group, Melbourne

The University of Queensland Press is assisted by the Australian Government through the Australia Council, its arts funding and advisory body.

ISBN 978 0 7022 6001 8 (pbk)
ISBN 978 0 7022 6118 3 (pdf)
ISBN 978 0 7022 6119 0 (epub)
ISBN 978 0 7022 6120 6 (kindle)

A catalogue record for this book is available from the National Library of Australia

University of Queensland Press uses papers that are natural, renewable and recyclable products made from wood grown in sustainable forests. The logging and manufacturing processes conform to the environmental regulations of the country of origin.

I dedicate this book about the past to
my grandchildren, Alfred and Esther Howard.
They represent the future.

Prologue

ANNE, MAY 1536

Her hair was cut short for the first time in her life and the chill on the back of her neck was unfamiliar. It would be a warm spring day, but the hour was still early and the sun had not yet had a chance to do its work. She could feel the cool air moving around her, not strong enough yet to be a breeze; more like a breath.

She had not many breaths left.

She stifled the impulse to put her hand up to her neck and stilled the accompanying bubbles of panic that had risen in her stomach. She must not think about her neck if she was to maintain her composure.

To distract herself she turned towards the people gathered below the scaffold to watch her die. There was a multitude. They were silent and their faces solemn. Then she heard a woman call out from the back of the throng. She spoke with the harsh accent of the common people of London and her shrill voice carried across Tower Green.

'Tis a pity good Queen Katharine did not live long enough to see your head upon the block!'

Queen Anne remained motionless, but the woman's words hit home. She had thought the death of her great rival, Katharine of Aragon, just a few weeks before, only a good thing, cementing her own legitimacy as queen. Even in her extremity, she had to repress a wry smile at the thought of her own foolishness and at the irony of one queen's death following so hastily upon the other.

A ripple of murmurs ran through the crowd in response to the woman's insult, whether in approval or disapproval she did not know, although she could guess. Nevertheless she looked down from the scaffold at the people closest to her. She recognised some of the upturned faces: men and women she had once known well and had thought of as friends, but she did not see any kindness in their eyes. She did not see kindness in any of the thousand pairs of eyes that watched her so intently and for that she was grateful. Their hatred helped. It made her feel defiant. She could not have borne any sign of pity.

She had rehearsed this moment ever since they told her the timing of her execution. She had gone over and over it in her mind, imagining what she would see, forcing herself to feel what she would feel so that it might not undo her when she was compelled to face the reality. Composing her final words had helped steady her. She knew what she must do in her last act on earth. She must do everything she could to safeguard the fate of her little daughter.

Elizabeth would be standing up in her cot at just this moment, Anne thought, arms outstretched to her nursemaid. The vivid image brought tears to her eyes. She had to swallow hard to hold them at bay.

'Time to get up! Time to get up!'

Anne remembered the child's imperious demands and impatience. How eager the little girl was to get up and get out into the world. How the child's tone had made them all – queen, ladies and attendants – laugh with pride and delight at her forwardness. Elizabeth did not speak like a baby, although she was not yet three. Her words were clearly articulated and her piping voice already carried a note of command. She spoke in complete sentences with all the words in the right order. Anne's heart swelled with pride at the thought of her child. Henry did not realise the jewel he had in this daughter of theirs. Anne must do all that she could to send her safely into the future.

She knew her words must speak no insurrection, no excuses, no defiance. She must not be seen to criticise the justice of her sentence. She would not admit guilt, nor would she claim innocence. Her words must be calm, conciliatory, humble and loving. They would be written down, they would be reported and they would be remembered. She must die quietly and unprotesting so that her infant daughter might live and prosper and all Anne's hopes and ambitions not be in vain.

'Elizabeth.' She spoke her daughter's name so quietly that none could have heard it but God. The people watching saw her lips move and assumed she was praying. They were right.

'My Lord Constable, may I speak to the people assembled here?' She was relieved that her voice sounded so steady. It raised her spirits a little. She turned back to the crowd below her. They had surged forward in anticipation, the better to hear what she had to say.

'Good Christian people, I am come hither to die, for according to law ...'

It was good that all through the long and sleepless night she had rehearsed the words she would say. She knew them so well they flowed unbidden from her lips, leaving her mind free to take in everything about her. The air she breathed was sweet, the scent of the flowers blooming in the Tower gardens causing her a pang of regret. The crowd was so silent as they strained to hear her words that she could hear the distant roar of the lions and tigers from the Tower menagerie as they anticipated their next feed.

'... for a gentler nor a more merciful prince was there never and to me he was ever a good, a gentle and sovereign lord ...'

She could feel rather than see the crowd relax as

she spoke. It was clear that she would say nothing that would shock or accuse. She would go to her death mildly, causing far less trouble in her demise than she ever did in her life.

'If any person will meddle of my cause, I require them to judge the best. And thus I take my leave of the world and of you all, and I heartily desire you all to pray for me. Oh Lord, have mercy on me! To God I commend my soul.'

She turned and scanned the stony faces of the people standing with her on the scaffold. 'Who among you is my executioner?'

'He will be here presently, my lady.'

But the words of the Lord Constable did not deceive her. She knew he was one of the men standing behind her.

Lady Kingston stepped forward and removed Anne's mantle. Then the condemned queen was given a linen cap which she tied over her shorn hair. This time she could not resist placing her hand protectively over her neck. The skin was cool to the touch and she could feel little goosebumps pimpling her flesh. Whether from the unaccustomed exposure or from fear, she could not tell.

Now a French-accented voice in her ear. 'Will you forgive me, Your Grace?'

'Willingly, good master executioner.'

But she did not turn around. To see him would undo her.

'Kneel and pray, my lady.'

'Will you give me a little more time, good sir, so I may make my peace with my God?'

'I will.'

As she prayed, they put a blindfold across her eyes and the bubbles of panic in her belly fizzed and burst, forcing open her eyes against the dark, so that her eyelashes brushed the linen that shut out all sight of the world. Her ears strained to hear the approach of the executioner, but what she heard was the thump of her own heart and the pant of her now frantic breath.

The executioner had removed his shoes so he would make no sound as he approached. But she heard the collective intake of breath by the assembled multitude as he raised the blade and she knew.

ELIZABETH, MARCH 1603

'You must go to your bed, Your Majesty. The doctors insist upon it.'

Robert Cecil looms over me in the dark. He startles me. I have been thinking about my mother's death. Imagining myself in her skin, in her brain and her heart. I have tried to feel what she must have felt, see what she must have seen. I know, better perhaps than anyone who was actually there, every action she took, every gesture she made, every word she spoke, minute by minute. When I was young, I insisted that those who were present tell me every detail, sparing me nothing, until my mother's last moments were imprinted on my brain. Yet still I was unsatisfied. Try as I might, I could not live her death – only she could do that. Anyway, it is my own last moments that press close upon me now.

I stir myself on my cushions and rub at my eyes, trying to bring them back into focus. I clear my painful throat and peer up at the man who stands over me. I remain silent until I am once again in possession of myself. Only then do I speak.

'Little man, little man, the word "must" is not to be used to princes. If your father had lived you durst not have said as much.'

I have been reclining on a pile of cushions all this afternoon and into the night. I have been unwell for days with aches and pains and an agonisingly sore throat. I have struggled on with my duties regardless, doing everything while standing, sitting only occasionally in a chair. I could not shake the fear that the minute I gave in to my illness I was giving in to death. The longer I could stand, the longer I held the spectre at bay.

'Your Grace! Your Grace!'

But I could not stave off the inevitable forever. As my mind drifted, my knees went from under me and I began to swoon and looked to fall. Hands clasped at me quickly, preventing me from tumbling to the floor.

'Fetch cushions, bring as many as you can find!'

My head was spinning, but I could see my ladies scurrying about, bringing mounds of cushions from chairs and divans and piling them up about me. Once they were in place, my ladies lowered me gently to the floor.

'Will you not retire to your bed, Your Majesty? You will be so much more comfortable there.'

Philadelphia Carey, granddaughter of my mother's

sister, knelt beside me, her face filled with concern. I knew she meant only to do me a kindness, but a terrible dread took hold in my belly. The only bed left to me was my deathbed and I was not ready for that – not yet. There was still work for me to do. Not perhaps as a queen, but as a woman. I would not die if I could help it while that work remained undone. I flinched away from the girl and nestled deeper into the cushions.

'No, no. I will stay here a little while and catch my breath. I will be back on my feet ere long.'

Facing death, I am more my father's daughter than my mother's, it seems. I turned my face away from my attendants and closed my eyes. I would rest a little and perhaps then I would be my old self again. And then I remembered that my father's last words were of just such a false hope. When asked if there was any 'learned man' (by which they meant a man of God) he would speak with, he said, 'If I had any, it would be Dr Cranmer, but I will first take a little sleep and then as I feel myself, I will advise upon the matter.'

The thought made me snap my eyes open. I am dying, but – like my father – I am not quite ready to be dead yet.

I am the last, the very last. There will be no Tudors after me. The dynasty my grandfather risked his life to establish, and my father his immortal soul, has not survived more than three generations.

All my friends are gone. All my peers. All those whom I loved and who grew to adulthood beside me have died. Elizabeth who was the first of her Christian name will also be the last of her surname.

But all is not lost. The Stuarts will follow me and Tudor blood runs in their veins. England and Scotland will be united without any blood being shed, royal or otherwise. Whether this new nation will be for good or ill, I do not know. That challenge is for future monarchs to struggle with. My race is run. I will have done what I can for it just by dying.

'May I fetch a doctor, Your Grace? Perhaps they can relieve your pain.'

Robert Cecil is hovering nearby. It is a symptom of my decline that fear of me has faded. I am no longer Elizabeth the queen, mighty and dreadful. I am Elizabeth a dying woman, soon to have no more relevance than a memory.

It hurts so to swallow – yet swallow I must, before I can speak. 'A pox on your doctors, Master Secretary! They will only torture me with their blood-letting, their cups and their leeches.'

Ah, but my voice is so hoarse! I can no longer bellow in the way that made my attendants jump and tremble in their shoes. Nevertheless, the force of my emotion makes my secretary bow and scrape and back away into the shadows. I have kept the doctors at bay for a little while longer at least.

As I fail, I lose their respect. The mantle of monarchy begins to fall from my shoulders, revealing the wrinkled and haggard flesh of an old woman, long past her prime.

I have lived too long. It may have been my great gift to my people, but it has come at a great cost to myself. There are few alive today who remember an England that was not Elizabeth's. My long reign has given my people the stability they needed and that stability has brought with it prosperity. At least I can die knowing that I have left my kingdom in much better shape than I found it.

The child turned his neck towards me. The scrofula that infected him bloomed like hideous, twisted flowers around his ear, down his neck and onto his shoulders. It took all of my will to stop myself recoiling at the sight.

'Bless you, my child,' I said as I leant forward and laid my fingers upon the horny protuberances. 'May God in his grace cure you of this evil.'

Swallowing hard, I ran my fingers gently over each of the wens as I had been shown. I smiled at the boy, who looked at me with eyes that shone with hope. I felt humbled by his belief in my ability to cure what the common people called the King's Evil. I had only been queen for a few months and it still felt strange. Unlike the boy, I could not believe that I really held the power to cure him in my touch.

The next sufferer was an old woman, her chest hideously swollen with the disease. After her, an old man, then a girl and, most shocking of all, a baby.

Dutifully, I stroked each disgusting sore, made the sign of the cross above each sufferer's head and said the words I had been taught. Earnestly, I hoped that they would be cured. Secretly, I did not believe they would. But it was not just the disfiguring disease that shocked me about the people who queued up to receive my blessing. It was the rags they wore, the bareness and filth of their feet, and how thin their bodies were. I might not be able to cure their sores, but I swore then and there that I would do what I could to return my kingdom to prosperity so that even the least of my subjects were a little better off under my reign than they had been under my sister's.

I could hear the wet coughing from consumptive chests of many of those who waited for my supposedly healing touch. I could see others who rested on crutches and hobbled forward on misshapen legs, all of them humble, patient and respectful. I felt ashamed of my rich garments and full belly.

Eventually, over the years, I grew used to the Maundy Thursday ceremony and familiarity made touching the scrofula less distasteful to me. I almost began to look forward to it, especially when my physicians assured me that most of those I touched did indeed find themselves cured.

Whether God worked through me to cure the scrofula, I do not know, but I do know that I have been a thrifty housewife. I have restored my realm to good order. I have repaired and rebuilt my little island when it was battered by storms and inclement weather. I have not allowed dust and dirt to accumulate in dark corners. My hearth is clean. The windows sparkle. Vegetables and fruits grow in abundance in my gardens and the chickens are all good layers.

Not that it was such a great task to pass on a kingdom in better shape than I found it. England was in disarray when I inherited it and not just for the poor. It was a country rent by religious strife and the instability that followed five monarchs in a little over a decade. Merely by remaining alive I was an improvement on my predecessors.

But how will history judge me when I am dead and gone? Will it be as kind to me as I am being to myself? I once said to my parliament that I would be content with an epitaph that read: 'Here lies Elizabeth who ruled from 1558 to such and such a time (1603, it would seem) and who lived and died a virgin.' Yet, now that the event I once thought was so far in the future is fast upon me, I find such a judgment is not enough. I wish to be thought well of. I hope my labours have not been in vain. Is this pride? If it be so, then it is just another sin that can be added to my long list.

*

They say my father sent for a Frenchman called Jean Rombaud to come to London with a fabled sword honed from the steel of Toledo. The Frenchman's task was to separate my mother's head from her body. To send for a skilled swordsman instead of using the brute force of the axeman was a gesture of mercy – a sharp sword being more likely to deliver an instantaneous death than a blunt axe. I hope it was my father who sent for Rombaud. Sometimes I worry that it may not have been the king who felt an impulse towards mercy, but his secretary, Thomas Cromwell. They tell me Cromwell was friends with my mother until she fell from grace.

Certainly someone couldn't bear the thought of such a barbaric instrument mutilating my mother's slender neck. It must have been my father's decision, surely. He had loved the woman to distraction for almost two decades, he had rent asunder God's Christian church just to gain access to my mother's person. He must have kissed that same neck with passion and delight many times before his love turned sour. Surely it was my father who could not bear to see my mother's soft white skin hacked at by a clumsy axe. Unless Thomas Cromwell also carried a torch for her. If my father's suspicions were correct, he would simply have been one among many. Or was it just simple kindness? Is it possible for a man to feel pity for a woman without any accompanying desire? That is for men to answer, I suppose. I do not know that I have ever seen it.

My mother was not accompanied by any friends when she went to her death. The women appointed to attend her in the Tower were not from the ranks of the ladies who loved her, but rather from the ranks of those who did not. Blanche Parry saw my mother lose her life – it was from her lips that I so often begged to hear the horrible tale – but she watched from the crowd below the scaffold, not as an attendant upon it.

According to Blanche, it was Lady Kingston who cut my mother's hair. She was the wife of the Constable of the Tower, sent to spy. I hope the woman had enough pity in her to use the scissors gently and with care. They cut my hair when I was recovering from the fever of smallpox, to help save my life. They cut my mother's to facilitate the headsman and so hasten her death.

Blanche also told me how beautiful my mother's hair was and how they loved to brush it to a shine.

'Gently, Blanche. Gently!'

'Forgive me, Your Majesty. There was a knot!'

'A lover's knot, perhaps?' Only Mary Boleyn had the cheek to tease Queen Anne so, according to Blanche, and the queen tolerated such behaviour from her older sister. This time, however, she did not laugh, but instead became strangely solemn.

'Alas, no, Mary. I have not been called to the king's bedside for some time now.'

'Perhaps he has not fully recovered from his fall at the joust.'

‘Perhaps he worries that you have not recovered from … well, from … your recent loss.’

My mother had miscarried what might have been my brother only a few weeks before. How different both our lives might have been if that longed-for prince had been born.

‘I do not know and I have not seen him in a situation where I could ask him. He seems strangely distant, ever since his fall.’

‘All have remarked on his change of temper. Perhaps his head pains him still.’

‘Perhaps.’ And my mother sank her small chin onto her hand in a melancholy aspect.

‘Your hair is very beautiful, Your Grace.’ Blanche held up the mirror. ‘I have never seen hair shine like yours.’

‘It is your skill with the brush, Mistress Parry.’

‘Nonsense, Your Grace. I can brush my hair from now until kingdom come and it will never shine like yours.’

‘The king used to love to stroke my hair and wrap strands of it around his fingers and watch it slip through them – like spun silk, he’d say. Sometimes he’d sink both his fists into it and tug at it gently.’

‘He will do so again.’

‘I hope so, Blanche. I hope so.’

I wonder if my mother grieved over being shorn of her hair. Or if the terror of losing her head made such a loss seem small by comparison. It is a ritual humiliation for a woman to have her hair taken from her head. Unless such drastic action is needed to cool her during a fever and so save her life – the loss of a woman's hair is the mark of her shame. Was my mother ashamed when she went to her death? She did not say so. I know every word she spoke on her scaffold but there is one sentence of her brief oration that always brings me to tears.

'... He was ever a good, a gentle and sovereign lord ...'

She said these words out of love for me, perhaps. I like to think her last thoughts were of what she could do to protect her little daughter, left alone as an infant in a hostile world. If she accused my father of killing her for spurious and manufactured reasons, she made me more friendless and more vulnerable. By speaking well and fondly of the king my father and the king her executioner, she gave him no excuse to look upon me any more harshly than he already did.

Of course there was a bitter irony to her words. How could a gentle and a merciful prince be about to cut off her head?

It makes me want to weep to think of the careful words she sent out into the world on my behalf with what must have been almost the very last of her breath.

They say the swordsman made a little game to distract her from what was about to come. They say that after she had signalled she was ready, he said loudly so that she could hear him, 'Now, where is my sword ...?' As if he did not have it already in his hands raised above her quivering neck. He did this as a kindness, I warrant, so that she did not anticipate the sword until it had already fallen and she was beyond anticipation of any kind. (Perhaps men can feel pity for women, after all.)

I am dying slowly, by inches, and I am aware of every last moment of it. I cannot help but wonder if, when I die I will see my mother at last. I thrill at the thought of such a reunion.

'*When will you pay me?*
Say the bells of Old Bailey.'

I am a small child again, in the nursery at St James's Palace. My nurse, Kat Champernowne (she is not yet married to John Ashley), is giggling and holding hands with Blanche Parry, their arms raised to form an arch. Other ladies stand in line, doing the same, including a woman more grandly dressed than the others, who I think must be my mother. She is laughing the hardest of all. I am stepping through the arch of their arms, chanting the rhyme with them. I am breathless with alarm and excitement.

'*When I grow rich*
Say the bells of Shoreditch.
Pray when will that be?
Say the bells of Stepney.'

I have played this game before and I know what is coming. I am almost bursting with anticipation. The women build the tension, slowing down the chant.

'I'm sure I don't know,

Says the great bell of Bow.'

And now the rhythm changes and I begin to giggle nervously.

'Here comes the candle to light you to bed …'

I shriek and begin to run out of the human arch but – too late – the women are moving their arms up and down fast in uneven waves and I must dodge and weave to avoid them. I laugh with delight.

'And here comes the chopper to chop off your head!'

Fragrant, velvet clad arms sweep me up from the game and hold me close, kissing the top of my head instead of chopping it off. But I do not want to be held. I want to play. I wriggle and squirm against her embrace until the woman puts me down.

'Again! Again! Let's play it again!'

'Oh, *enfant bien-aimé*, you have worn us all out with your playing.' And to emphasise her exhaustion, she plops herself down on the floor with a great pouff of skirts. I am not impressed. I can see by her amused expression that she is not really tired at all.

'Pooh! Get up! Get up! I want to do it again!'

I go over to the dark-haired woman with the elegant gown and grasp her long fingers in my small hand. I pull her with all my might. She plays along so that when she suddenly rises I fall backwards onto my bottom. It does not hurt, but I do not quite know whether to cry or to laugh. The women around me burst into laughter and the force of it frightens me a little. My face must have crumpled, because the elegant lady with the French accent sweeps me into her arms again and holds me close, kissing my forehead and soothing me with soft words. 'Do not cry, *ma petite*, do not cry. You are always safe with me. No harm can come to you.'

And then she begins to sing another song to me and my heart beats faster with delight, all frustration forgotten. It is my favourite game of all.

'*Rock-a-bye baby on the tree-top,*
When the wind blows, the cradle will rock,
When the bow breaks, the cradle will fall
And …'

At this point the French lady flings me upside down until my head hangs down among her skirts while she holds tightly to my legs.

'*DOWN will come baby, cradle and all!*'

Then she sweeps me up again and throws me into the air and I laugh and laugh and hug the lady tightly when I land safely back in her arms. It is the happiest I can remember ever being.

No matter how old we become it seems we never outgrow the need for our mother. Yet I also shrink from the idea of seeing her again in the afterlife. I cannot help but wonder whether she will judge my actions here on earth as not worthy enough to have made up for her sacrifice and the terrible foreshortening of her life. I have felt the need to do right, to atone for her death, all of my days. I knew I had to survive and succeed to make up for what she had lost.

I do not think she went to her death accompanied by guilt or by shame. I think she knew she was innocent of all the crimes with which she was charged. I think those who watched her die knew she was too, although they would never have dared say as much. My father died consumed by guilt and shame. My stepmother Catherine Parr told me that he screamed at phantoms as he lay on his deathbed and claimed that ghosts gibbered at him from its foot. I do not doubt that one of the ghosts he saw there in his delirium was the headless spirit of my mother. Perhaps she pointed at her wound and made him look at the ghastly mess he had made with his Toledo steel.

I wonder – if her spirit did sit at the foot of his bed tormenting him – did she carry her head under her arm or had God put it back where it belonged? Will Mary of Scotland's ghost carry her head? Is it she who will greet me at the gates of heaven and cast me out, pushing me hard so I plummet downwards to suffer in the everlasting fires of hell? Or will my mother greet me and gently ask me to sit once more at her side?

How will I know which one is which? Aye, there's the rub, for I never saw Queen Mary's face in life and have no clear memory of my mother's. She died too soon for me to fix her face in my recollection and portraits are a poor substitute. And both may have no head. What if I mistake one headless phantom for another?

These are feverish imaginings. Nevertheless I look around me quickly in search of gibbering ghosts that point accusing fingers. I see nothing from an unearthly realm, just a clutch of apothecaries who dare not come closer, and behind them my ladies who pray for my immortal soul. I hope they pray hard. I think it is not possible to rule over men and not commit many sins. Yet, I was not bloodthirsty. As God is my witness I did all that I could to avoid the shedding of blood. I hated going to war and shifted and shied so skittishly when pressed to do so by my ministers that they cursed me and agreed among themselves that my equivocation was proof that women are not equipped to rule.

'Your Grace, will you take a little refreshment?'

It is Philadelphia Carey, my first cousin Henry Carey's daughter, granddaughter of my Aunt Mary Boleyn, one of the few who will dare approach me in my extremity. Her gentle entreaty is to no avail. Despite my thirst, I clamp my lips together like a child refusing its pap and shake my head. Let us hasten to the end.

Philadelphia rises up from her knees with a rustle of silken skirts and many heavy sighs. She turns to the assembled doctors and shakes her head sadly. I close my eyes. I know what they are thinking. That I should hurry up and die.

But perhaps I am unfair. No doubt they are afraid of the changes that will come after me. I may have infuriated my ministers and attendants, but they know me well. I am the devil they know. My cousin James is the most feared ruler of all: an unknown one. I have never met him, but from his letters to me and from what my ambassadors say, he appears to be a bloodless little man – close-lipped and tight-faced. Although he is married and has been blessed with three children, there are rumours that he is fonder of boys than he is of women. Ah well, it is a common enough vice and best ignored. He, like me, like all of us, will one day have to give an account of himself to God and face a reckoning for all his abominations. The Stuarts must make their own future just as the Tudors made theirs. And the future is no longer any business of mine.

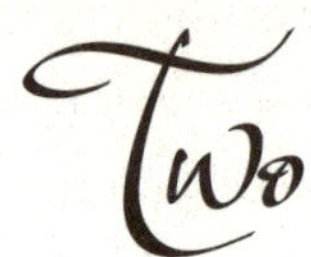

There are flowers on the mantel. I can see them through the gloom because they are lit by a candelabra someone has hastily placed by their side.

The flickering light is not enough to show their true colours and they are shadowy and darkened, but I can still make out the pink of the roses and the deep blue of the hyacinths.

They fill the vases in my private apartments with fresh flowers daily, but I have rarely taken much notice. Now, the beauty of this simple posy – even in this restless shadowy light – hits me with an intensity that almost hurts. I would rather look at the flowers than any of the faces staring at me from the gloom. The roses hang so heavy on their slender stems they droop and blush before the straight-backed hyacinths. One flower turns its head up; the other angles it down.

*

'Robin! You cannot expect me to be impressed by the gift of my own rose, grown in my own garden by my own gardeners.'

Robin had given me a flower. If we walked in the garden he would often search the flower beds for the most perfect specimen, neither too tightly furled as a bud, nor so overblown it had passed its prime. When he found what he was looking for he would pluck the rose then fling himself on one knee and offer it to me with an exaggerated flourish. I loved him best when he was playful and self-mocking. It was at those moments that I felt less like a queen and more like a flesh-and-blood woman.

I was laughing at his teasing face.

'Will you not take my humble offering? This rose in the pink of its fragile beauty?'

'I will take it, if you insist, but it is my own, so it is a gift from myself to myself.'

'Everything I own is yours, Your Grace.' He remained on his knee as I tucked the rose into my kirtle.

'No, indeed, sweet Robin, if this gift is any guide, it seems everything I own is yours.'

A petal falls from a rose in the vase on the mantel and I feel it like a blow.

There – in my mind's eye – is my Robin's handsome, laughing face with his neatly trimmed beard set off by his perfectly starched and laundered white ruff.

As he kneels before me, I am looking down on his green hunting cap that sits rakishly atop his auburn curls. It bears a scarlet feather that bobs up and down as he throws back his head in delight at our banter.

How I loved him. To take my ease with him at the end of the day was reward enough for all my labours. To ride with him – my master of horse – was the highlight of my calendar. To resist him was the trial and discipline of my life.

Now, at this the last, do I regret that I never succumbed? That I never allowed myself to fully know his body as is common for men and women?

Robin's face was very close to mine and his eyelids were heavy and low. I could feel his breath against my cheek. I sat motionless, afraid that any movement on my part might break the spell. He came closer still and his hands were suddenly around my waist. Then his lips were on mine and I thought my heart might burst through my chest and, although I knew what I ought to do when a man (actually he was still a stripling) took such liberties, I did no such thing. Instead I threw my arms around his neck and kissed him back most heartily.

We were very young, not yet fifteen, I think. We were both at the court of my brother, King Edward, who was already ailing. Robin's father was busily protecting his position as regent and I was of no particular interest to anyone, being a distant second in line to the throne. Such was the chaos in the court that those who should have been watching us were easily distracted and we had taken full advantage to sneak away. We had been racing one another through the park, enjoying the sunshine and the opportunity to stretch our limbs and fill our lungs. Then we had dropped – out of breath – onto the grass beneath the shade of a spreading oak. It was as we were half-sitting, half-reclining together, catching our breath, that a new mood had overtaken us. We who were never alone were suddenly quite alone and we were young and beautiful and the sap of youth ran urgently through our veins.

We kissed each other passionately over and over and we took other liberties, exploring one another in ways that should have made us ashamed, but did not. No one could see us, of that we were certain, but somehow I still kept a rein, my clothing stayed on, even if a few buttons were undone and a few ribbons loosened. Eventually, strangely peaceful, we sat quietly, my head upon Robin's chest, his arms around my shoulders.

'I shall marry you when I am old enough.'

'Why aren't you old enough now? Your brother Guildford is younger than you and already betrothed to Lady Jane Grey.'

'That's my father's doing, not theirs. I will only marry for love and I love only you.'

'I love you too,' I said, shyly. 'But I can't marry you.'

'Why not?'

'Because I am of royal blood and they will not let me

marry the one I choose. They will want to marry me off to some foreign prince or potentate who will be ugly and smelly and beat me with a stick.'

'We could run away!'

I just shook my head. 'If we tried that they'd have you up for treason and chop off your head.'

'But I can't let you marry an ugly, smelly brute of a foreigner who will beat you!'

'Don't worry. If I can't marry you – and I can't – then I won't marry anyone and they cannot make me.'

'You can be my mistress, then, and I will keep you in a fine house and visit you whenever I can—'

I stopped him talking nonsense by kissing him again and thrilling once more to the touch of his hands as they roamed about my person.

'My Lady Elizabeth!'

We sprang apart, but we were fortunate. It was Kat, my loyal governess, who had happened upon our hiding place, sent to search for me when my absence was finally noticed.

'I'll thank you to keep your hands to yourself, Master Dudley. Honestly, the pair of you, carrying on like wantons! Count yourself fortunate that it was me who found you and not someone else! You could have landed in the Tower for this, young man and' – Kat turned to look at me – 'as for you, you deserve a whipping!'

She grasped me tightly by the hand and pulled me away from Robin. I followed her willingly enough, knowing she would take the matter no further. As she hustled me away, I turned and blew a kiss to the boy I loved – still love, to this very day. All I could think then, giddy girl that I was, as I hurried across the grass after Kat was that Robin Dudley loved me and wanted to marry me. For that brief sunlit moment it was all I cared about in the world.

Far too quickly, real life intervened. My brother died. Robin and his father and brothers (poor Guildford) landed in the Tower. My sister Mary claimed her throne and I became the next in line. Never again was I to be so unimportant or so free.

All these long years later, I regret that I could not marry Robin and experience the delights of the flesh, yet I am also grateful that I could not. I did not surrender to my desires (not even beneath that oak tree) and so I remained – not just master of myself – but master of my destiny and my kingdom. Our roles were reversed. He was the Delilah to my Samson. If I had given in to him I would have been drained of all my power. No wonder I regret and I do not regret in equal measure.

'Philip of Spain would not invade if all his military effort achieved was merely to put the crown of England on the Queen of Scots' head. We have done his work for him by getting her out of his way.'

William Cecil, now Lord Burleigh (father of Robert who stands at this moment in the corner), was back in favour after having been banished from court for his part in the unauthorised execution of my cousin. It had taken me months to recover my equilibrium after the death of Mary, Queen of Scots and I had not thought any year could be as fraught as 1587. When the new year at last dawned, I was filled with relief and hope. I thought I had put my troubles behind me. How naive I was.

Perhaps it was no coincidence that the execution of my Catholic rival was so closely followed by the threat of invasion. It was what I had feared and one of the reasons I had kept alive that woman so many called the 'viper at my bosom'. I remember explaining as much to Cecil when we heard warlike rumblings from our old enemy Spain.

When we received the news of King Philip's great enterprise I could not resist reminding Cecil of the responsibility he bore. He was, as always, equal to my challenge.

'You may be right, good madam, but while the Queen of Scots lived, plots against you would be fomented and there were many in England who would have rallied to her cause, if she had looked like she might win it. There are none in England who wish to live under the Spanish yoke. Nay, not even the Catholics among your subjects. We lived under Spanish rule during the reign of your sister and none recalls her time with affection. When the King of Spain attacks, you will find no traitors in your ranks.'

He had a point and indeed the English rallied around their queen with an enthusiasm that touched me.

Still, as God is my witness, I did all I could to stave off the threat of war. I would not allow Admiral Drake to burn all the Spanish ships after his daring and successful raids in Corunna and Cadiz. I hoped our victory would convince Philip that we were not to be tangled with. When Drake towed home their great treasure ship – the *São Filipe* – I thought the loss of so much wealth might also make the Spaniards think twice. I was wrong. Nevertheless, I was no longer a new queen. I had been to war before and I had learnt from that experience. I was determined not to make the same mistakes. I would not relinquish control of my army or my treasury again, not even to the man I loved.

'I will not give you the powers you seek, my lords.'

Hawkins and Howard, the captains of my fleet, were furious. I could see it in the high colour of their cheeks and in the way they clenched their fists and stood so straight and tense before me. I cared not. We had been arguing up hill and down dale for hours. At first they had spoken to me gently, in tones reserved for a novice. This had not helped their case.

'Do not speak to me as if I have no understanding of what confronts us! Have I not proved to you yet, over these many years, that I put the safety and fortune of my kingdom above all other considerations?'

'All marvel at your wisdom, Your Grace.'

'Nonsense! Do not flatter me with honeyed words. You think like all others of your sex that war is not the business of females. Well, I tell you what is my business as your queen and that is the health of my treasury. You would drain it, my lords, and ask me to grant you permission to do so. What a great fool you must think me.'

'Penny-pinching and war have no place together!' Admiral Howard had raised his voice in frustration. He was standing with his back to the fireplace and took a step towards me. I did not take a backward one. I flashed a warning look and stood my ground, but I forgave him his passion. Indeed, I matched it.

'Aye, it is easy to spend that which does not belong to you. I have no desire to win a war only to find I have saved a bankrupt kingdom. If fight we must – and I still parley with the Duke of Parma, so all hope of peace is not yet lost – then I will watch the cost with a close and rigorous eye. I, and I alone, will decide how much we spend and on what.'

Admiral Hawkins opened his mouth to protest but I raised my hand to stop him. 'Enough, my lords! If and when we go to war we will speak again – and be assured that I have no intention of letting the King of Spain take my throne from under me. In the meantime, get my fleet into readiness and we will wait to see which way the wind blows.'

The two great naval captains left my presence with

barely concealed bad grace. I could well imagine what they would say about me once they had left my palace, but I did not care. If I could avoid war with Spain, I would.

I failed in my quest for peace. The Spaniards were determined to have my crown and cared not how much blood they spilt in the getting of it. I was true to my word, however. I kept account of every penny my commanders and my admirals spent on preparations. I approved every decision and every appointment. I might be a woman but I was the ruler of my kingdom and I was not – not for one single moment – going to let any man-jack of them forget it.

Howard and Hawkins had control of the fleet, Lord Hunsdon was my general on land. My Robin was lieutenant-general; it was his forces that would face the Spaniards first when they made landfall. I wanted to be with my troops as they awaited invasion. If we were to be victorious I wanted to be part of that victory. If we were to be defeated I wanted to die among them. I may have prevaricated while there remained hopes of peace, but once my attempts to avoid war had failed, my blood was up. I was excited, exhilarated and I felt no fear. I sent word to Robin that I would set up camp with my troops at Tilbury, but he refused to hear of it. He arranged for me to stay a mile off in the house of a Mr Rich and from there I could visit the camp.

There was an eerie quiet over the military encampment as I made my way by horseback to dine with Robin in his tent. As it was August, the sun was still high despite the late hour. Sunlit or not, the men were subdued as they settled in around their cooking fires. As I rode through their ranks, I could hear the murmuring of quiet conversations and the occasional shout of laughter. The men tended to their meals, or played at cards or simply lay quietly, stretched out in the mild summer evening.

As I threaded my way I was reminded of another night such as this, many years before. I sensed the same tension in the air that I had witnessed the night my sister Mary made ready to fight for her kingdom against the usurper Lady Jane Grey. I thought of the young soldiers from that long ago army who would now be grey bearded and sitting at home by their firesides, waiting for news. All England held its collective breath in the summer of 1553, just as they did again in August 1588. It is odd to realise now that neither of those great armies ever drew (or shed) a drop of blood. But we did not know that night what the dawn would bring.

'I find I am impatient for the fight. It seems I may have the heart of a warrior, after all.'

I was dining with Robin in his tent. I was in a strange mood. There was something exciting about the novelty of eating a meal at a table on rugs thrown across the bare grass. No doubt it was also the whiff of impending invasion that was so stimulating. Danger concentrates the mind.

'It will come soon enough—' Then Robin groaned and clutched at his belly. He had been doing this often of late.

'Are you quite well, my lord?'

'It is nothing: the grippe. Too much rich food. I have never been able to curb my appetite.'

'But you have merely picked at your meal. You have made me look greedy.'

And indeed I had finished my pigeon pie, even polishing off the very last of the crust, using it to sop up the gravy. War made me hungry. It had the opposite effect on Robin. His pie was crumbled into bits, but I could not tell whether he had tasted any of it.

'You are growing thin. You need to keep your strength up.'

'I can afford to lose a little of my girth so such a loss is more to the good than otherwise.'

Robin had grown a little portly as he had aged, but I did not like to see him fading. His health mattered to me, more than that of anyone else in my kingdom.

'Have a care, old friend.' I took his hand in mine. 'I cannot do without you.'

Suddenly there was a kerfuffle outside and a messenger hastened into our presence. He gave Robin a note. As my lieutenant-general read the parchment, its contents made him swear great oaths under his breath. I stood up and walked around the table so I could read it over his shoulder.

'What is it?'

'The Duke of Parma has embarked all his forces and is even now crossing the Channel.'

My heart pounded in my chest. The moment was almost upon us, but still I did not feel fear. Only exhilaration. I turned towards the entrance of the tent and made haste to leave.

'Stay, Your Grace. They will not land before daybreak and I would rather the men got their rest. I will wake them and ready them before the dawn, but for now, let them sleep.'

'And you must sleep too.'

'Little chance of that. I will make plans.'

'May I speak to the troops in the morning before the battle is begun? I have brought with me the white horse Robert Cecil gave me for the purpose.'

Robin gave me a long look. I could see that he was weighing the possibility of risk to my person and the problem of delays against the benefits of such a proposal. I remained silent. I would do whatever it was he wanted me to do. He was my general, but I hoped he would allow me to give my soldiers Godspeed.

'It is a good plan, Your Majesty.' And he nodded his assent. 'Soldiers go better into battle when their hearts are as stout as their forearms.'

The next morning, very early, I left the house of Mr Rich and rode once more towards my troops at Tilbury. Despite lookouts having been posted since first light, there was still no sign of the Spanish Armada, and, as the day was clear, we would see them on the horizon long before they made landfall. Notwithstanding my feather bed, I had not slept. Instead I had gone over and over in my head what I intended to say to my troops. In the darkest hours of the night I had also wondered what might happen to me if the Spanish won the impending battle. The thought of what they might do to me if they took me alive was horrifying. I could not get the tales of the humiliations suffered by King Richard III at the hands of my grandfather on Bosworth Field out of my mind.

In the morning I hid a dagger in my garter. If I were captured I would kill myself with it. I hoped I might take a few of the scoundrels with me, withal. It is fortunate my skill with such a weapon was never tested. As I think back upon it now, I almost laugh at my foolhardiness. I doubt I could have killed myself, let alone anyone else. I had no idea then how hard it is to die.

I dressed with care. I wore a silver breastplate and carried a silver helmet resplendent with white feathers. I dressed as a warrior queen. My white horse was brought to me, saddled and bridled. The beast's coat had been brushed to a shine and its long grey mane and tail fluttered in the cool early morning breeze. I mounted the horse and it ducked its head and snorted as it felt my weight on the saddle. I patted the animal on the neck as it sidestepped a little and fought the bridle. Perhaps my barely restrained excitement had communicated itself to the creature.

'Whoa ... whoa,' I whispered into the mare's ear as its hooves clattered on the flagstones. 'You are my battle-charger. We will face whatever the day brings together.'

My quiet words and firm hand on the reins did their job. The horse settled down after a few tosses of its magnificent head and we were able to ride calmly towards the battlefield.

As we drew closer to the encampment, another of my generals, Henry Norris, rode out to greet me. He was accompanied by a phalanx of soldiers. Once our paths crossed, they immediately surrounded me. I pulled up.

'How now, Sir Henry? Why the armed guard?'

'It is to protect you, Your Majesty, as you ride through the rough soldiers.'

'Oh no, my lord, I will not appear as if I am afraid of my troops. They will be fighting for me on this day and I will not insult them by requiring a guard. I do not wish to keep my distance from them, nor to have them kept distant from me. We will live and die together this day, so we will speak together as friends, as comrades, as equals before God. Dismiss your guard.'

I rode among my troops unguarded, as I wished. Robin walked beside me, holding my horse. Norris and Robin's stepson, the Earl of Essex, walked beside me on the other side; nevertheless I was alone.

The troops stepped back and made way for us until we reached a little rise. I stopped my horse and looked about me. The day was fine and clear and as yet there were still no shadows on the horizon. A soft breeze blew across the headland, tossing the white feathers in my helmet and ruffling my horse's mane. I stood in my stirrups and looked at the men around me. Many of them fell to their knees and most removed their headgear – helmets if they had them; caps and bonnets if they did not. I motioned for them to rise and looked down upon their honest English faces.

'My loving people, we have been persuaded by some that are careful of our safety to take heed how we commit ourselves to armed multitudes for fear of treachery.'

I could not help glancing at Norris as I said this and he had the grace to look away.

'But I assure you, I do not desire to live to distrust my faithful and loving people. Let tyrants fear. I have always so behaved myself that, under God, I have placed my chiefest strength and safeguard in the loyal hearts and good will of my subjects, and, therefore I am come among you, as you see, at this time, not for my recreation and disport, but being resolved, in the midst and heat of battle, to live or die among you all, to lay down my life for my God and my kingdom and for my people, my honour and my blood, even in the dust. I know I have the body of a weak and feeble woman, but I have the heart and stomach of a king and a king of England too, and think it foul scorn that Parma or Spain, or any prince of Europe should dare to invade the borders of my realm. The which, rather than any dishonour shall grow by me, I myself will take up arms, I myself will be your general, judge and rewarder of every one of your virtues in the field. I know, already for your forwardness, you have deserved rewards and crowns; and we do assure you, in the word of a prince, they shall be duly paid you. In the meantime my lieutenant-general shall be in my stead.'

Now, I paused to look at my general, my Robin. His head was down yet I could see that he – like all of us comrades in arms – was overcome with emotion. I took a deep breath and continued.

'A more noble or worthy subject no prince has ever commanded, nor do I doubt your obedience to my general. Judging by your concord in the camp, and your valour on the field, we shall shortly have a famous victory over those enemies of my God, of my kingdom, and of my people.'

I looked down once more at Robin and saw that he had tears coursing down his cheeks. I had never loved him more. The troops set up a hullabaloo the like of which I have never heard and threw all their caps and helmets into the air, then caught them and threw them up again. I could feel their love and their ferocity vibrating in the air. I had never felt more like a queen than I did at that moment and I had never felt more like a woman as I watched Robin weep. It was, I know, our finest moment.

We did not know then that there would be no fight with the Spanish that day, no, nor any day while I sat upon England's throne. We did not know till sometime later that Drake had seen fit to send fireships to put the fear of God into the Spanish fleet. Or that God, seeing his work, had in His turn seen fit to send a fierce storm to scatter the Spanish Armada and help my brave captains in their endeavour to protect the sovereignty of my kingdom and my crown.

We had a great victory and we did not have to fight. Men may have regretted the lack of glory, but, for me, it was the perfect triumph.

Three

The door into the chamber opens. It brings with it a draught of air. I open my eyes and see a messenger enter and take a few long strides towards Robert Cecil. My secretary rises from his stool and the messenger hands him a sealed document. Once I might have wondered what it contained. No longer. Yet, for reasons I do not immediately understand, I feel dread.

Suddenly, I have left this darkened room stinking of stale air, and I am back in the Presence Chamber at St James's Palace. There is an odour of wood smoke in the air, not from the fire in the hearth – the chimneys all draw well at that modern and comfortable building – but from the bonfires that were burning all over England to celebrate our miraculous and bloodless defeat of the Armada. Church bells were ringing too. I can hear them again now, reverberating through the streets and alleyways and across the Thames. They had been ringing on and off for weeks. I am standing by an open window, enjoying the exuberance of my capital. If I could escape from my palace and roam the streets among my people, I would, but the closest I can get to them is through this window. I stand and catch snatches of conversation from those who come and go past this great house.

'It was Drake that beat the Spaniards! I'd have given anything to be on his flagship – watching the Armada turn tail and run in the face of his fireships must have been a sight!'

Two workmen dawdle in the quadrangle below. One of them trundles a wheelbarrow; the other totes rakes and long-handled spades.

'Not if you were one of the Spaniards terrified of burning to death while surrounded by the ocean!'

'They shouldn't have tried to invade England, then, should they? We'd have left them alone if they'd left us alone.'

'Aye, they say the queen's not over-fond of war.'

'Stands to reason. She's a lass, after all.'

'But they say she had the blood well and truly up at Tilbury, sitting on her white horse, ready to fight and die like any common soldier.'

Then the two men leave the courtyard and I can eavesdrop no longer. It takes me a moment to get over being called 'a lass' but I am pleased my words at Tilbury are being repeated.

I remain so exhilarated by the triumph that I am easily distracted from my work and drawn away repeatedly from my desk, back to the window to see what is happening below. I catch other conversations.

'They say Drake captured a great treasure ship …'

'My nephew was at Cadiz. He said he'd never seen a sight like it!'

'Think I might run away to sea …'

William Cecil is not as flighty. He is at his desk. Then a door opens, bringing with it a draught of air. A messenger enters and approaches Cecil. My secretary rises from his desk and the man hands him a sealed document.

I remain at the open window. I do not even turn my head.

I have not forgotten those last few carefree seconds: the smells in the room, the sounds from the streets, the way the sunlight was falling through the open window, spilling itself onto the Persian carpet at my feet, illuminating the interwoven reds and browns. I have also not forgotten how I felt: light-hearted, unburdened, confident of the future that lay in front of me.

Another snippet of vivid memory bursts upon my mind's eye. It is as if even now, all these years later, my brain skitters away from the tragedy of which I was about to be informed. My meandering brain hurries backwards through the years of my life to a moment the evening after my coronation. I see it unfold in front of me as if it were happening here and now.

*

'A toast! A toast to our new queen!' Robin stands before me, shining with youth and vigour. His cap is awry and he has had rather more of the fine wine than he should, but he is filled with exuberance and holds aloft his goblet for the umpteenth time.

'Another one? Surely, Robin, our fine company has had their fill of toasting my health and I rather suspect you have had your fill as well.'

He looked so tipsily crestfallen at my gentle scold that I had to laugh.

'Oh, very well, my lord, let us have another toast to my health and prosperity, if you insist.'

And the gathered company of lords and ladies rose as one and raised their cups and shouted in unison.

'God bless Queen Elizabeth! Long may she reign!'

Then Robin very slowly listed sideways, his face suffused with a silly grin, until he toppled over completely and landed noisily upon his neighbour, spilling his wine as he fell. The grin never leaving his face.

I laughed at him heartily and from the sheer delight at being alive, being safe and – at last – being queen. I had no conception then of what it really meant to rule.

The next time I was to feel so sure of myself and the future was in those few seconds at the open window of St James's Palace, as I savoured my victory over the Spanish and my growing international reputation as a formidable queen.

I continued to look out of the window and paid little heed to the messenger who had entered. William Cecil took receipt. I still paid no attention. If the message was important I knew that Cecil would waste no time telling me of its contents. If it mattered little, he would make his own judgment in his own time. It was part of his job to protect me from trifles.

I had forgotten the messenger by the time I became aware that Cecil was standing close by. I looked up and when I saw his face my exuberant mood evaporated. So sombre was his expression that a cold dread took hold of my heart. It was so soon after our triumph over the Spanish that my first thought was that our euphoria had been premature.

'What is it, my lord? I knew our time of peace and triumph could not last so very long. Has Spain mustered another Armada?'

'No, Your Grace. The Spanish are still licking their wounds. This news concerns the Earl of Leicester, your lieutenant-general. I am sorry, Your Grace, I fear that this is very bad news indeed – and I can think of no kind way to say what must be said. The Earl of Leicester – has died.'

Cecil's lined face displayed great kindness and pity. He took the liberty of putting his hand on my shoulder by way of comfort, if only for a moment. In some part of my brain I registered this act of *lese majeste*, however kindly meant, but most of my wits were concentrated on trying to absorb the meaning of the words that my old friend had just spoken. I had seen his lips move, I had heard what he said, I knew the language he spoke, but I could take no sense from his words.

'How say you? Robin – *my* Robin?'

'Aye. He has succumbed to the low fever that had him ailing these past few weeks.'

I was silent. My brain felt as if it had struck an insurmountable obstacle. Its mechanism had stalled. I now knew what my old friend had said, but still I could not comprehend it. 'Succumbed? When, Cecil, when did he succumb? And where? Who was with him? Was he alone?'

Perhaps there had been a mistake. Someone else had died and they had mistaken him for Robin. Cecil looked down at the message he still held in his hands.

'It says here he died on the fourth of September at Cornbury, en route to Buxton. His attendants were with him. Those are all the details I have.'

Still I had not given up hope that this was some strange error. 'But he wrote to me, only days ago. Here, I still have his letter on my desk ...' And I took it from the pile of papers where it lay. I waved it at Cecil as if its existence would somehow prove that the man who wrote it also still existed.

'He says – he said – he was feeling better, that the physic I gave him had restored him. He says that he is once more himself. He wrote it from Ricote, my lord, where I have also stayed so many years ago … where I stayed on my way to Woodstock. See? See here—'

And I pointed to Robin's signature and read the words he had written beneath.

'See? See what he says: "from your old lodging at Ricote, this Thursday morning ready to take my journey." He was going to Buxton to take the waters …'

And then it struck me that the journey he had been ready to take had turned out to be an entirely different one, one that would take him wholly away from me – and the thought undid me. The gears in my brain lurched forward and I began to sob.

Cecil reacted as he always did to my tears: anxiously, clumsily, making haste to stem them. 'I am so sorry. He was your oldest and dearest friend.'

My heart and soul were wholly caught up with my own pain – I was only just beginning to feel it as my brain made sense of the world again and it was already overwhelming.

'I thought *you* would die, Cecil, long before I had to part with *Robin*.'

Wise Sir William merely nodded at me silently, hands clasped behind his back. He understood that I was lashing out more from grief than anger. 'Indeed, as did I. I am many years his senior and the ague eats at my bones and warns me of the grave regularly.'

This set me to sobbing even more violently. I could not contemplate losing Cecil as well as Dudley and the thought made me realise that all the men and women I loved and cared about were ageing and likely to die. Our time was drawing more rapidly to a close than any of us had expected. It was Robin's death, so untimely, that first brought me face to face with the fact of my own mortality.

I left the chamber and fled to my private apartments. I wanted to be alone to absorb the blow, which I now felt had the force of a broadsword. I wanted to remember, to imprint my memories of Robin on my brain so that while dead he might be, alive he would always be in my memory.

'Here, my Lady Elizabeth, catch this!'

Robin and I met when we were eight years old, when he and his brothers began to take their lessons in the royal classroom under the tutelage of John Dee, a gifted teacher who made us all long for his praise. Robin was the cleverest of the Dudleys, but he was no match for me and I was no match for my cousin Lady Jane Grey. The three of us led the class and our rivalry was intense. But 'the little nun' (the name Robin and I gave to Jane behind her back) was the one who most often received the fairest of our teacher's words, and her success annoyed us both. It was in teasing her that Robin and I began our first alliance.

That morning Dr Dee had praised extravagantly some work of Jane's and said nothing at all about mine.

Now out in the garden, I was still silently sulking over the slight when Robin snatched Jane's book from her fingers and threw it over her head.

'Got it!' I cried before I actually had. I ran forward and leapt into the air, deftly catching the spinning volume. 'Come on, Jane!'

I laughed as my cousin clumsily attempted to run towards me. 'You'll have to do better than that!' It was the phrase my teacher had said to me that morning and his words still rankled.

I hoisted up my skirts and kept my distance. I knew that I could outrun her easily, but I stayed just out of reach to torment her. She tried to jump up and grasp the object, but she was too short and too clumsy.

'Give it back! Give it back! That is no way to treat the works of Erasmus!'

Her protests were to no avail. It soothed my jealous feelings to see her so helpless. Just as she came close enough to reach up for the book in my hands, I raised it higher above my head and threw it back to my fellow tormentor. 'Robin! The works of the great Erasmus are about to hit you in the head unless you take care!'

But he was too nimble and, leaping forward, snatched the hurtling book in mid-air. 'Guildford!' he cried as he threw the book away from an almost weeping Jane. But Guildford had not been paying attention and the book flew over his head to land in a puddle.

'Look what you have done! That is Master Dee's own

book and he will be furious with you, Robin Dudley!' Jane picked up the book and tried vainly to dry it off on her skirts, but merely succeeded in getting her dress muddy in the process.

'It was Guildford's fault. He failed to catch it.'

'No, do not blame your brother. It was you who caused the book to be treated with so little respect and you who will be punished for it.'

'It was just a bit of fun. No one meant for the book to be damaged.'

'What did you think would happen? But then you don't think, do you, Robin Dudley? That's your problem.' Sometimes Jane Grey sounded more like an old woman than a child. It was just another thing that annoyed us about her. I am very sorry now for my cruelty to my brilliant cousin. Hers was a short and sad life. Her shining intellect did her no good at all.

But all that was in the future. At that moment, in the sunny gardens at Hampton Court, she was just an irritating younger schoolmate whose only fault was to be too obviously our intellectual superior.

Robin pulled a face at her retreating back as she took her precious book and went in search of our teacher so she could tell him her tale.

I laughed. 'You will get another beating, Robin.'

He shrugged and then winked broadly at me. 'Well, then, you must give me a kiss afterwards to make me feel better.'

I blushed and laughed at him, shaking my head. 'You'll have to catch me first!' I was already bolting away from him, but there is no denying my heart skipped with pleasure at his words.

When he was alive I could only ever see him as he was, how he looked when he stood before me. But with death, it seems, comes an eternal youth. Now, so many years after he died, I see his face as it was when he was young. By dying, he conquered the humiliations of old age, in my memory, at least. There is no one left alive now who will remember me as anything other than the wizened old crone I have become. It is no pleasure to outlive one's friends.

Robin's face was always alive with mischief and expression. His moods were like quicksilver and while he was not the oldest of our classmates by any means – his brothers John, Ambrose and Henry had that honour – he was our leader. We all turned to him for guidance when no adults were nearby.

When Robin perceived that he could not best Jane or me in the classroom, he decided to move the competition to a different field of endeavour. It was Robin who invented the games we played and what tricks we visited upon the attendants tasked with watching over us.

This was a clever tactic and I enjoyed physical activity much more than my studious cousin. Even when the sun was shining and the size of the gardens made it easy to avoid adult eyes – especially if we were fleet of foot – Jane would choose to sit on a bench with her nose in a book. She was small of stature and short of sight. When she read she held the book right up close to her eyes so that her nose almost touched the page. The combination of these defects made her poor at games of catch or shuttlecock or bowls. She was slow-moving and cautious. She avoided physical risk – much good that it did her – and lacked confidence away from her desk.

But I wanted Robin's good opinion more than anyone else's except, perhaps, my father's. I think I have lived all my life wanting my old schoolmate's good opinion, and relying upon it too, even when he betrayed me, which he did, not just once but many times. I forgave him, though. Always forgave him. The bond we forged in childhood was stretched on occasions, but never broken. Perhaps it was because we shared not just our games and our mischief, but times of great difficulty and danger. The strongest alliances are usually forged under duress.

It was Robin who tried to comfort me on the dreadful afternoon in the long gallery at Hampton Court as we watched Queen Katherine Howard run for her life, because she was about to be arrested for treason by my father, her husband. We were but nine years old at the time and I think the terror of that doomed young queen taught us both in a few moments just how harsh life could be. I remember we clung together in an ante-room, trying to make sense of what we had seen. I also remember that it was me who ended the embrace. That was another pattern throughout our lives – until he took it upon himself to die so prematurely, of course.

He grew from harum-scarum boy to confident stripling. He swaggered a bit as a young man, a little too sure of his own worth, perhaps. I remember how pleased he was with himself at his first wedding, although he very quickly came to rue the day.

'I am an old married man now, Elizabeth, with a fine young wife eagerly awaiting me in my bed.' He watched me carefully to see how I might react.

'Well, you must do your duty by her, sir, and not tarry any longer with me.'

I was not about to let him see how unsettled I was feeling.

'Duty! Is that what you call it?'

'I call it nothing, my fine married friend, for I am but an ignorant young virgin and happy to stay that way. It is you who must perform now, my lord, not me.'

And just for a moment, I could see he was nervous and my heart softened towards him, but before I could say another word, he had gone. I turned to my Bible, grimly determined to keep my thoughts on things spiritual. I did not succeed.

I watched him grow and mature and gain wisdom as life refused to bend itself to either his charm or his will. No doubt he observed the same changes in me.

I never approached the future with the same gusto and optimism as did the young Robin Dudley. It was one of the things I loved best about him. No matter what life handed out, he never quite lost his enthusiasm for it. He was not half-hearted, he was not cautious. He could find enjoyment even at the worst times. Yes, he was vain and cocksure, attributes that did not endear him to other members of my court. He was too fond of worldly praise and favours and I had to knock him down many a time because of it, but he was never daunted. Back he came, throwing himself once more into the fray, speaking his mind, boasting, telling ribald stories, seducing pretty women (aye, I am neither blind nor a fool), showing off. He entertained me, he made me laugh and I knew he sincerely loved me. Partly because I was his queen and it served him well to love me, but partly because he knew me as no others did, as Elizabeth the woman. Despite his fair words I was never Gloriana to him. I was no mythical creature in his eyes. I was mere flesh and blood. It was a relief to see the reality of my human frailty reflected back to me. It meant I could relax with him as I could with few others and no other man.

Our fortunes rose and fell together too. We were both prisoners in the Tower at the same time. My mother was executed on the Tower lawn by my father. His father and his brother (poor Guildford) were executed there by my sister, Mary. Along, of course, with our old schoolmate and victim – poor Jane Grey, the nine days' queen. We survived, but we knew what it was to live in daily fear of our lives. Yet still in the face of great loss and much danger, Robin made merry quips when we saw each other within the prison's grim confines and his dauntless cheek raised my spirits.

Once we were released and our fortunes turned for the better as my poor sister's health declined, he remained my loyal servant. When she finally died, Robin was one of the first to ride helter-skelter from London to Hatfield to tell me that I was now queen.

'Long live Queen Elizabeth, the first of that name!' Robin knelt before me, his head bowed. I was not used to being treated as a queen and it felt even stranger that the friend of my youth, the boy who had never hesitated to tease me, should be making his obeisance so solemnly.

'Thank you, my lord …' And then I paused. I wanted to make a joke to return to our old, easy ways with one another, but I glanced at the stern faces of the great men around me and my courage failed. We passed an awkward few moments with Robin still on his knees. 'Will you walk with me?' I spoke abruptly.

As I rose, so did he, and the men who surrounded us stepped forward as if to follow.

'No, my lords. I would walk alone with Sir Robin. We will remain in sight.'

I already knew that I must be careful with my reputation. I did not speak, however, until we were out of earshot.

'Surely you have some quip to make? Some tease about the silliness of me being your queen?'

'Oh no, Your Majesty. I only wish to swear to you that I – among all your subjects – am the most loyal. You are the queen of my heart and my soul.' He put his hand on his heart as he said the words and had such an earnest look upon his face that I could not help but laugh.

'Oh Robin, don't treat me like a stranger. I am the same girl I was before I wore a crown. It is my estate you must worship, not me. I will need a friend in this great task. I will need an advisor who will speak the truth. I will need a companion who will amuse me and help me leave the affairs of state behind. You know me best – I want you to be that friend. Will you be the same to me as you have ever been?'

'I will be of service in whatever way I can.'

I could see he was still in awe of my change of station and I sighed. 'You can be my master of horse. You are a good judge of horseflesh and look well in the saddle. I cannot think of better qualifications for the man who will hunt with me whenever the weather is fine.'

'I have other gifts too, Your Grace. I am a fine swordsman.'

'I have no need of a sparring partner, unless it is in conversation. Set your mind upon that.'

Throughout my reign he was with me. An irritant sometimes – when the Dutch made him their governor-general; a source of grief at others – when he married Lettice Knollys. He broke my heart when he married a second time, and such a pretty young woman, the daughter of my dearest friend. That made the betrayal doubly hard. He was my greatest solace and my bitterest temptation. I have cried more tears over him than I have over anyone and I cannot now think of a better tribute.

As we aged, the passions that often disturbed our relationship in our youth passed and we entered calmer waters. I knew that I could rely on him for disinterested advice and that my safety and success were always central to his thoughts. He showed that superbly at Tilbury.

It was only a few short days after that moment of our greatest triumph that I saw him for the last time. I wish I had known it was to be our last ever meeting, but I had no inkling of it. Perhaps I should have known. He was not well. He had not been well for some time, but I took his strength and his vigour for granted. I took his continuing presence as a given. If only I had known he would be gone so soon there are many things I would have told him, not least that I loved him and that my greatest regret was that I could not marry him. As it is, I remember our final conversation word for word.

'You say we had a great victory, but it was a symbolic one. We did not really get to prove our mettle against the Spaniards.'

'It is the foolishness of youth to wish for the

vainglory of war. We are again secure in our kingdom without spilling a drop of blood. Our enemy has been vanquished and humbled. Thanks to the courage and skill of the captains of our fleet and to the glory of God. You are only chagrined because no credit for the victory can go to you.'

'That is unkind and unfair, Your Majesty! You said yourself that you thought it foul scorn for the Spanish to dare to invade your kingdom. I just yearned to rub their noses in it.'

'I am glad you did not. I do not like to think of you in any danger. Your safety matters to me. Speaking of which, your appetite does not seem to have improved.'

We were dining together, in St James's Palace rather than a tent, but once again he had hardly touched his meal.

'No, my stomach still troubles me, and I find I have no taste for food.'

'That is not like you. The strength of your appetites has always been one of the qualities I value most about you.'

Robin gave a great hoot of laughter and I was pleased to see some colour return to his cheeks. 'Aye, Your Grace, but I am not getting any younger and the appetites of a man my age are mere shadows of their former selves. Indeed, there are some that can barely rise to the occasion at all.'

'Come, come, my lord, you have a lusty young wife.'

'Yes, Lettice makes little secret of her boredom.'

'Well, you would marry her.'

'I have never been much good at choosing wives. I am much more skilful at choosing queens – particularly of my heart.'

'It is not your heart we speak of now, but your stomach.'

'Well, *you* may have been speaking of my stomach—'

'Hush, Robin, it is your health that concerns me. I have no interest in your other parts.'

'Aye, as you have always made very plain.'

'Have you consulted a physician?'

'The doctors tell me I still have a touch of the low fever.'

'I am only just recovered from it myself. It gave me much trouble and you are correct: it made even the daintiest morsels taste like ashes in my mouth.' I cut another slice of plum cake. 'But, as you see, the malaise has left me, and food has regained its flavour. You should take the waters, my lord. I have heard great reports of the healing power of the waters at Buxton.'

And then I saw him turn pale and grasp at his belly as I had seen him do before.

'But you are in pain! Perhaps this is more than the low fever?'

'No, it is wind only. I have always been a martyr to wind.' And with that he released a great fart. 'See, Your Grace! I feel much better already!'

'No wonder you have always made such an excellent master of horse. You have so much in common with them.'

'I will always be your master of horse, but what about the post of lieutenant-general of England and Ireland that we discussed?'

'Ah ha! So that is why you are complaining about the lack of a battle at Tilbury! You see the title slipping away from you?'

And we squabbled affectionately over his love of grand preferments late into the night. I did not see him grasp his belly again, so when I left him I was well contented that his complaints were all minor.

It was a pleasant evening, like so many others we spent together, but nothing that mattered was said. I did not know, never even imagined, that the malady in his stomach and bowels would prove fatal – and so soon.

Four

As my old friends aged and – far too often – died, I turned to the new generation. Not from choice but from necessity.

Robert Devereux, Earl of Essex, stepson of Robin Dudley, was tall, athletic and handsome. He was all movement and activity. He could no more sit at a desk and pore over state papers than he could sew a fine seam. He despised Robert Cecil, son of William Cecil, for his physical incapacity. The younger Cecil had been born with a twisted spine and the hunch in his back made him many inches shorter than his athletic peer. Nevertheless, although Essex would never have admitted it, he also envied the hunchback his brilliance. Robert Cecil had no natural charm. Robert Devereux was nothing but charming. I was fond of Devereux. I respected Cecil. The two rivals did share one attribute. They were both consumed with ambition.

After Robin Dudley died, in my bereavement I turned

towards his stepson Essex, the boy he had loved as his own. When Robin was alive, I showed Essex favour for his sake. Once Robin was dead, I continued to do so. After a time, I became fond of the young man in his own right.

'May I tempt you with a sugar-plum, Your Majesty? They are the finest I have ever tasted.'

'No thank you. I find that I have no appetite for sweet fancies.'

'Shall I play for you? Or read to you? One of Master Shakespeare's sonnets, perhaps? Or Spenser's *Faerie Queene*?'

'No, I have no appetite for fine rhymes either. I am sorry to be such dull company.'

The faces I see as I revisit the past in my imagination are all young. And, in my memory, so am I. It is delightful to travel back in time, not least because it makes me forget the fire in my throat, the stiffness in my limbs and the choking sensation in my lungs. For whole moments at a time, the years fall away, and I am young again and full of vigour.

'Good shot, Your Majesty!'

I lowered the bow as the members of my court clapped, their applause elegantly muffled by the leather gauntlets they wore to protect themselves from the icy cold. I squinted at the distant target.

'Not a bullseye, I think.'

I could see the arrow and it was a little to the left.

'But such a shot and on the ice, Your Grace. It does your skill and concentration much credit.'

It was the winter of 1564 and I was in my prime. Others may have found the intense cold hard to cope with, but I found it invigorating. No doubt the thick Russian sables I wore helped my enjoyment. Even so, my breath was as visible as that of everyone else as we stood on the frozen Thames.

When the great river had frozen completely over I seized the advantage and ordered that archery butts be dragged out onto the ice. We would have a fine, straight and virtually endless trajectory for our sport – a hard thing to find in my increasingly crowded capital. Then I challenged my courtiers to a tournament. The appointed day had dawned fine if icy but – full of the excitement and vigour of youth – I was not discouraged; nor were the younger members of my court. I caught a glimpse of Cecil dutifully standing on the sidelines, but he did not look well pleased. He was stamping his feet on the ice and blowing on his gauntlets like a walrus. But the young men and women competing lined up across the span of the mighty river, heedless of the temperature as they concentrated on getting as many arrows home as they could.

I loved the feel of pulling back on the bow. The slight creak of the yew as it bent to my command, the answering twang of the bow-string. I liked the tug on the muscles of my arms as I stretched the string and arrow into place. Then the moment of intense concentration as I narrowed my eyes and focused on the tiny red dot at the centre of the butt many yards away across the ice. At that moment, I could see my breath, hear my heart beat – it was important to keep them both calm and steady. In my experience, a racing heart meant a lousy shot. I inched the arrow back just a little further, then I stood completely still and took a deep breath. As I exhaled I let the arrow fly. Time seemed to slow as I watched its tail-feathers twist and turn through the air. These were the precious seconds that I enjoyed the most, watching the small missile speed towards its destination. The arrow was me at that moment and I was the arrow. And when it went home there came a moment, the exquisite moment, when I held my breath waiting to see if my aim had been true.

'The winner of the Royal Thames Archery Tournament, Your Grace, is Sir Henry Lee, with three bullseyes!'

My factotum's clarion call carried across the ice.

'Well done, sir.'

Sir Henry Lee was my champion and armourer and the strongest and most vigorous man in my court. The result was hardly a surprise and so the muffled applause was a little less than enthusiastic.

'Second place goes to Sir Robin Dudley, with two bullseyes.'

‘I’ll beat you yet, Lee! I’ve set up a practice range in Leicester House just for the purpose.’

‘And third place, and first among the lady competitors, goes to Your Majesty, with one bullseye.’

My delight may have been a little disproportionate to my triumph, but it was wonderful to get out from my desk, away from ink and paper and the complications of statecraft and find that I could beat every other woman of my court with the strength of my arm, the power of my concentration and the accuracy of my eye. And even if, as I sometimes suspected, some of my ladies let me win by doing rather less than their best, I had hit the bullseye. There was no disputing an arrow in a target.

For long moments now, I forget the present and return to the past, leaving my ailing body behind. I have forgotten where I am and the ordeal I am facing. Then a shadow falls across me, bringing me back. My eyes – having, it seems, some life left in them – flicker open to see who it is that comes close. To be brought back to the present is hard. My pain once again imposes itself. As my eyes focus I half expect to see Death’s head peering at me from under his black hood, but I am not so fortunate. No, it is Robert Cecil venturing as close as he dares to see whether I still breathe.

‘I am not dead yet, my lord, but do not be impatient. I will not tarry much longer.’

I hear a mutter sweep through my attendants and sense rather than see Cecil bowing repeatedly as he steps backwards into the shadows. I look at the members of my court gathered around him and what strikes me forcibly is their vivid youth. I blink a little to clear my vision – are these yet more phantoms from the past, or flesh-and-blood creatures of the present? When did my court change from one generation to another? When did I become so much older than everyone around me? It was not always so. When I first came to my throne as a girl of twenty-five, I was one of the youngest at court. Now, at nigh on seventy, I am one of the oldest. What happened to all the years in between? How have I allowed them to slip by me so quickly?

My motto is '*semper eadem*' – 'always the same' – and I have lived up to it, particularly when it came to the men and women who made up my court. Once appointed, they would be with me for life. Aye, and there's the rub: almost none have had a life as long as mine. Where I could, however, I replaced the father with the son, the mother with the daughter.

Seeing Robert Cecil (albeit through hazy and unfocused eyes) reminds me of his father, William – my old friend and most valued advisor. He has been dead these five years or more and I have missed him every day. His son, through no fault of his own, is a poor substitute. In my experience, children always are.

Robert is as wily as ever his father was and as

conscientious, but he is not wholly my creature. He has his eyes fixed on the future and has been looking towards it for all the years I have known him. I was his father's future, right enough, but I am not Robert's.

William Cecil did not die suddenly as Robin did. He'd been ailing for years and when he became too ill and infirm to carry out his duties, he sent his clever young son Robert to deputise for him. Robin had also increasingly brought his stepson, the young Earl of Essex, into my court. It was no accident that Essex was one of the three noblemen who escorted me through my troops at Tilbury.

As I had with their fathers, I used the two young men for different purposes. I relied on the younger Cecil to give me advice and to carry out my commands quickly and efficiently. I turned to Robin's stepson to keep me entertained and amused.

It was loneliness, I suppose, that made me start inviting Robin's stepson to dine with me on occasions or join me in a game of cards after supper. At first, I did not seek amusement – I was too deep into grief to want that. What I sought was someone with whom I could talk about the man I had loved and lost, forever this time.

'My stepfather would have kept you amused, I do not doubt. I am sorry I am such a poor substitute.'

'Ah, Robbie, it is not your fault. Your wit and charm are justly renowned.'

'Do let me sing to you, then. A song is one thing my stepfather could not provide. He famously could not carry a tune.' With that he began to imitate Robin's hoarse and tuneless attempts at singing and, despite my grief, I could not help but laugh.

'He had so many other talents I suppose it was only fair that God kept one or two from him.'

'Aye, Your Grace. He could ride like the wind and no one could tell a better or more amusing story.'

'And he was utterly loyal, none more so.'

'He was a very fine father to me, even when his own small son was still alive.'

'That loss was a very hard one. I never saw him struck so low.'

Robin and Lettice had lost their only son when he was but an infant, less than four years old. It was a devastating blow.

'I did my best to make up for it. And it is my privilege to try to do the same for you.'

'That you did. And Robin was grateful for it – as I am for the comfort you now offer me. He loved you as well as any son of his own body. He never tired of telling me about your latest accomplishment.'

'He taught me everything I know, and I miss him sorely every day.'

'As do I. As do I.'

Essex pulled a sympathetic face and picked up the lute by his side. He was only a serviceable player, but he had a fine, sweet tenor voice, well suited to the songs fashionable at court. He began to sing one of the melancholy ballads composed by Master John Dowland:

'I saw my lady weep,
And sorrow proud to be advanced so,
In those fair eyes where all perfections keep.
Her face was full of woe,
But such a woe, believe me, as wins more hearts,
Than mirth can do with her enticing charms.'

Essex may not have been brilliant, but he was no fool. His choice of melody was as tactful as it was sympathetic. It suited me well to just sit back and listen. His song soothed me, even as it drew from my body great sighs. It was in hope of more moments like this that I began to spend more and more of my time with Robin's charismatic stepson.

Essex saw his chance and gave me as much flattering attention as he could. It was pleasant to be admired by such an attractive young man and he was skilled at offering me the compassion and understanding that his stepfather had provided. He also flattered me as a queen and, when I let him get away with it and as he grew bolder, as a woman. It was a game I knew well and had always enjoyed. Essex made me feel young again, he soothed me, he filled the gap of playmate, confidant and friend, at least to a point. Poor Robert Cecil laboured under the disadvantage that his father was still in the land of the living.

For the sake of their fathers, both alive and dead, I gave Essex and young Cecil full rein to prove themselves, but – truth be told – I had come to secretly favour one ambitious young man over the other. I knew Essex was impulsive and liable to go off half-cocked, but I put that down to the naivety of youth. I knew he was vain and often imperious, but his arrogance amused more than annoyed me. I enjoyed indulging him. It gave me pleasure to give him pleasure and I ignored the small signs of petulance and hot temper he occasionally displayed. Even against my better judgment, I began to give him opportunities.

In allowing my heart to rule my head, I broke the habit of a lifetime and I was to bitterly regret it.

'Only three hundred and fifty of the more than one thousand lords you took on this ill-fated venture have returned, my Lord Essex. By any measure that must be counted a debacle.'

The Earl of Essex had disgraced himself by leading some ill-conceived raids against the Portuguese, undertaken without my say-so. Perhaps he had grown bored with being the late-night confidant of an old woman and, impatient for more masculine glory, had taken advantage of my favour to launch a foolhardy enterprise.

'The Portuguese are lily-livered cowards, Your

Majesty, and refused to join us in the fight against their new Spanish overlords! We thought they would flock to our standard!'

Essex's colour was high. I could see he was shocked by my tone. Inwardly, as I berated him, I was berating myself for allowing him to assume that in my eyes he could do no wrong. A high price had been paid for my indulgence of this young aristocrat and not by me, either.

'Well, you thought wrong, my lord, grievous wrong, and the blood of good Englishmen now runs in the gutters of Lisbon.'

'It wasn't our fault. We believed the promises of Antonio, Prior of Crato. He assured us that his countrymen would support his claim to the throne over that of the usurper Philip!'

'He is as big a fool as the rest of you!'

I was furious with Essex, Francis Drake, Antonio (Pretender to the Portuguese throne) and all the other hotheads of my court who were so quick to disobey orders and take matters into their own hands. They had attacked the Portuguese capital without permission. The raid, they told me, was meant to be a pre-emptive strike to harry and weaken Philip of Spain and protect us against any chance of another Armada. All it had managed to prove was our relative weakness and ineptitude.

'Your reckless adventure has made my kingdom *more* vulnerable – not less! Philip must be laughing behind his hands.'

I saw Essex's handsome young face go red with anger. I suppose he was all of twenty-three at the time and young men can never tolerate being laughed at. I held up my hand to prevent a further outburst. 'Do not presume on your closeness to me in blood.' The Earl of Essex was my Aunt Mary Boleyn's great-grandson. 'Or on the love I bore your late stepfather. You are always keen to impress upon me the excellence of your talents, whether it is on the tennis court, the battlefield, at my council table, or in song and you do indeed have much potential. But, my headstrong young lord, you must also learn to take responsibility for your weaknesses as well as credit for your strengths, as I am sure your stepfather would have told you had he been alive.'

The memory of the times Robin had launched foolish, vainglorious enterprises made me soften my tone. Although not related by blood, the two men had much in common.

I think I did see Essex as the son that Robin and I might have had if the world had turned out differently. I knew that the partiality I showed to Essex made people talk. They took my obvious favour to mean that I was in love with him as I had been in love with his stepfather. (Interestingly no one ever spread such rumours about my relationship with Robert Cecil, even though I was careful to pay an equal amount of favourable attention to him.) No matter. I was not in love with either man, whatever my court believed. I did not see the handsome young man in front of me as a possible lover; I saw him as a substitute son.

Now I watched him pout and flush. I even thought I caught the hint of a tear in his eye. He really could not bear to be publicly berated and Robert Cecil was standing in the corner of the chamber, still as a statue but very much present. I knew the younger Cecil was enjoying his rival's humiliation and the idea annoyed me. I liked to keep the young men evenly matched. And, old fool that I was, I felt pity for the impetuous young lord.

I stepped forward and gently slapped Essex on the cheek with my hand. It was more a caress than a smack and I could see by the light that leapt into his eyes that he had read the gesture as such. Indeed, he grasped my hand as it rested on his cheek and kissed it rapturously.

'I must chastise you, my lord, so that you can learn salutary lessons. But like a good governess, I must also forgive you and understand that your failures – like those of your stepfather before you – are due to an excess of zeal.'

The young man dropped to his knee at my words and began to swear great oaths of loyalty. He was always theatrical, and his gestures were more suited to the stage than my privy chamber.

'Away with your protestations of loyalty. It is deeds I want from you, my hotheaded lord, not words. But you may come to my chamber this evening after supper and we will play cards and put this unfortunate event behind us as good friends must.' I waved my hand to dismiss him. 'You may leave us.'

And Essex rose nimbly to his feet – how I envied him that ease of movement – and bowed his way from my presence.

'Until tonight, Your Majesty,' he said as he reached the doorway – held open for him by a manservant – so others beyond it might hear. He sounded like an eager lover and I knew that was his intent.

'Aye, aye, but not until after supper.' In contrast to him, I sounded gruff and impatient, like an indulgent grandmother trying to hide her feelings. As Essex left the room I signalled for Cecil to approach me. 'How does your father, my lord? Did he enjoy the inhalations I sent him?'

'Aye, Your Majesty, he was most grateful for them, but the gout sits upon him heavily and he suffers great pain from his teeth. He hopes to be back by your side when his aches and pains recede.'

'I always miss his wise counsel, but you may tell him from me that his son makes a fine replacement. You have inherited the skills of both your mother and your father.'

William Cecil's current wife, Mildred, was a woman of great learning, and I was particularly fond of her. She was very much a woman after my own heart. Perhaps it was why William Cecil and I made a formidable team. He was one of the few men I have ever met who genuinely enjoyed the company of women whose wits could match his own. 'My poor talents, such as they are, must suffice, until my father is well enough to reclaim his place.'

'Such modesty, my Pygmy, is becoming but not convincing.' I tapped him playfully on the hand with my ivory fan and I saw him wince. Not because of the gesture, but because of my use of his nickname. It was not a kind moniker and he did not much like it, but he also knew that few were granted the privilege of a pet name, and, like it or no, I had one for him and none for his rival. His father was my 'Spirit' and Essex's stepfather my 'Eyes'. Why I had not granted Essex a pet name I do not know. Perhaps it was simply that one did not spring to mind, or perhaps I sensed that such an intimacy with a man of Essex's impulsive nature might be dangerous.

William Cecil was ailing, but the old man was made of sterner stuff than many of his younger colleagues. The next of my intimates to die was the man I nicknamed the Moor.

Sir Francis Walsingham died complaining about his finances (a common theme) at his house in Surrey surrounded by his wife, last surviving daughter (who was also the long-suffering wife of the Earl of Essex) and grandchildren. I received word of his death just before I was to dine with William and Mildred Cecil at their house in London. I knew that my old friends would be grateful to hear of my spymaster's demise first-hand from their queen, however, I waited until I was seated and the wine was being poured before I broke the news.

'Sir Francis has died, my lord.'

'I am sorry to hear that, but it is not entirely unexpected. He has been ailing these past weeks.'

'Aye and yet the news has shocked me and knocked me off kilter. He always seemed so indestructible.'

'Alas, none of us is.'

'Allow me to give you a glass of this fine Bordeaux, Your Majesty.' Mildred Cecil signalled her servant to bring the decanter.

'It is the curse of ageing that our peers slip away so easily and so frequently.'

'There are many curses of ageing, my lord, and yet the alternative remains worse. Don't wish your life away.' I took a long draught of the fine red wine. The taste of it on my tongue comforted me; the warmth of it in my throat was an even greater comfort.

'Yet if the old never died, there would be no room for the young.' William Cecil nodded meaningfully at me. I knew what he meant. The loss of my secretary of state left a vacancy that a younger man could fill. There was only one younger man who could do so.

'There is no need to wink at me, old man. I know

that Sir Francis's death creates an opportunity for your son.'

'Your Majesty, please forgive my husband, he does not mean to be so forward.' Mildred shot her husband a stern look. 'Or so heartless.'

'Sir Francis was a good and noble servant, but I am not ashamed to admit I never warmed to him as a human being. I am far too old now to pretend otherwise, however much that may offend you, my dear.' Cecil grinned at Mildred and leant forward to fill his own glass with the excellent wine.

'He was a hard man to like. I cannot recall a time when he actually managed a smile. Do you remember when that poor supplicant – I can't remember what favour he was asking for, can you, Cecil? – bowed so deeply he burnt his buttocks on the fire guard? He jumped about three feet in the air and you had to douse the flames with a jug of water! You and I managed to hold our laughter until the poor man had left the room, but then we collapsed in a heap. Walsingham never changed his expression.'

'Indeed, and he looked at the pair of us as if we had taken leave of our senses.'

We were both laughing again now at the memory.

'It was a property dispute, I believe.'

'What was?'

We were both beginning to regain our self-control.

'The favour the poor man was asking for ...'

'You mean he came about his seat, good my lord?'

And we were off again, leaving Mildred to look at us as if we had lost our minds. But it was good to laugh with Cecil and to reminisce. I miss him so much.

When at last our hilarity had passed – perhaps it was disrespectful to Sir Francis, but it was not meant to be – I continued to muse on how good a servant the stern old man had been.

'But I trusted my welfare to Walsingham and he fulfilled that trust completely. No man better. Your son will have large shoes to fill, my lord.'

'Puritans such as Sir Francis rarely make good company despite being such loyal servants.' It was Mildred who spoke, her characteristic dry manner had returned now that she knew her husband had not offended me.

'They are a stern brotherhood. Yet I find myself saddened by his loss, not just because he did me good service, but because he is another of my old companions who has gone.' My voice faltered a little as I said this, and I took a long drink from my goblet. The fire crackled cosily in the hearth and I felt glad to be with my two old friends. Then a fearful thought took hold of me. 'You must take great care of your husband, Mildred.'

And I leant forward and took her hand in mine. It was as wrinkled as my own. 'I could not bear to lose him.'

'Nor I, Your Grace. But William is stubborn. He will not rest although the doctors tell him that he must take more ease. I think he means to die on his feet, reading state papers over your shoulder.'

'You must sit, my lord, and not stand!' I grew agitated, jumping to my feet and pacing in front of the fireplace. I felt guilty. Mildred's remark had hit home. I knew I asked much of the elderly Cecil. I knew that his advice was as necessary to me as breathing – more so now that both Robin and the Moor were gone – and I knew that by taxing him I might also be shortening his life. I could not bear to think of it. 'Every day that he attends me I will fetch him a stool, no – with my own hands, from this day forward and indeed, my lord—'

Cecil was about to speak, but I silenced him with a gesture. 'I forbid you to stand in my presence. You must always be seated and with a blanket over your knees and a fire at your feet. Whatever you require I will fetch it.'

'So, I will become the master and you the servant? And how will that look, Your Grace, to those about us? The rumours will fly across Christendom that Lord Burleigh is about to die and has the queen for a nursemaid.'

'Perhaps they will accuse me of being in love with you too. It sometimes feels to me that I only have to smile at a man and the whole world then fancies me in love with him.'

'You speak of the Earl of Essex.'

'Yes, him among others.'

'There is no fear of rumours about me. I am not

young nor am I beautiful, nay, nor ever have been. Perhaps that is why I have never been accused of dallying where I should not.'

'And yet you have been lucky in love.' I smiled at his wife who, in truth, I valued almost as much as her husband.

Cecil took Mildred's hand a second time and gave her such a look that I could not help but envy. Their marriage was one of the few I have seen that was granted uninterrupted happiness.

'That I am. There is no doubt of that.'

We paused for a while and thought our own thoughts – of the past and of the future, but, then, as always, I returned restlessly to the present.

'We will miss the Moor as a spymaster, whatever we may think of his charms as a person. What will we do to maintain the eyes and ears we have all over Europe?'

'I have kept a record of all his informants. I will write to them directly and make sure they continue to be useful to us. Indeed, in recent years I have encouraged them to write to me as well as to Sir Francis so that we both had a relationship with them.'

'This is why I value you. You think of what may be as much as of what currently is. It is a trait few possess.'

Yet, despite our plans, a seamless transition was not to be. Essex also saw an opportunity. To my surprise, it was Essex who took charge of Walsingham's informants. He did so by using his charm to befriend Anthony and Francis Bacon, long employed by the Moor as his trusted lieutenants. It also aided his ambitions that, as Walsingham's son-in-law, he could claim the Moor's power base by right of inheritance.

It amuses me to think how the death of the old creates possibilities for the young. How they gather and scheme and manoeuvre themselves to fill the space left by the grim reaper. It will be the same when I shuffle off this mortal coil. James VI of Scotland has been impatient to become James I of England. He will not have to wait much longer. Well do I know the feeling of teetering on the brink of destiny, impatient for the glorious tomorrow. It is impossible not to secretly wish for the death of the person who stands in your way. I know this because that is how it was for me when my poor sister died. Decay is followed by renewal – it is the natural way of things.

Look at the young people in this room now – my 'loyal' servants, clustered over there in the corner, watching me, waiting with gathering impatience for whatever comes next. The night has fallen and they light candles. Some leave, to eat their supper, I'll be bound, to keep the life in them so that they can be ready to grasp whatever opportunity my death may bring. Change is frightening and unsettling, but it also carries with it new chances.

It is not just the young who look at the old with

impatience, however. It works the other way around as well. As the years went by and I grew older, my advisers grew younger and knew less. I grew impatient as they said the same things that others had said many times before. The young see each new thought as a revelation. The old know that there are no new thoughts, just new thinkers. I could forgive them their enthusiasms. After all, the old know what is to be young, but perhaps because the young do not yet know what it is to be old, I could not forgive them their arrogance. They would patronise me. So many of my youthful advisers assumed that because I was old (and a woman), I knew little.

It was not very long ago, just before I fell ill, in fact, that one young upstart, I think his name was Brown, presumed to advise me loftily on the state of affairs in the Netherlands. He spoke to me as if I was the child and he was the adult, as if he was the king and I was his servant. I allowed him a sentence or two, but such was his self-satisfaction, I could bear his tone no longer.

'Tush, Brown, I know more than thou dost.'

He looked affronted, but held his tongue. He went back to the pile of papers in front of him, banging them loudly in a way that communicated his disapproval. He was a bumptious young man, not easily deflected. Only a few minutes later he raised his head and attempted to pontificate about the situation in France, presuming once more to enlighten me about something I already knew. I wanted to bellow at him furiously, but for once

I held my temper. I am not sure why; perhaps it was his youth. He had, as yet, hardly as much as a hair on his chin. Instead, I eyed him witheringly and through gritted teeth, repeated myself.

'Tush, Brown. As I have already said to you, do I not know?'

Once, at the height of my powers, none dared to treat me with so little respect. It seems everything changes – even that.

Five

'I have just arrested your Portuguese doctor, Your Majesty!' Essex burst through the door unannounced, his face flushed with excitement. It took me a moment to work out who he was referring to. I had many doctors, some of them were foreign but I had never enquired about their country of origin. 'Dr Lopez?'

'Aye, Your Grace.'

'On what charge?'

'Treason. I discovered the plot while I was investigating the Portuguese traitors who surround the Prior of Crato and who are selling secrets to the Spaniards.'

Essex had been obsessed with the Portuguese ever since his disastrous escapade when he lost so many good men in Lisbon. Now that he had access to Walsingham's network of spies, through the Bacon brothers, he could indulge his desire for revenge to the full. It seemed he had wasted no time.

'God's death! That man has caused me almost as

much grief as the Queen of Scots ever did. How I wish I had not made Antonio welcome in my kingdom!'

'I have found no evidence directly against the Portuguese pretender, but he is in need of funds and that always makes a man vulnerable to temptation.'

'Tell Antonio to go to France. Let him make mischief there. I have had my fill of him.'

'Indeed, but it was as well we investigated Antonio's household, or I would never have discovered a traitor with such intimate access to your person.'

'What exactly is Lopez accused of?'

'He was plotting to poison you, Your Majesty.'

'But why? To what end? My demise would gain him nothing. Rather the opposite.'

'Who knows why Jews do as they do? Betrayal comes as naturally to their race as breathing.'

'Dr Lopez is a good Protestant. I have often seen him in church.'

'Outwardly only. In private he is a Jew.'

'As long as he obeys the law, I have no interest in what he believes in private. And he is a good doctor. He has eased my pain on many an occasion.'

'All the better to win your trust. But he could not outwit me.'

I was annoyed at his assumption of superior discernment, but I let the flash of irritation pass. Instead I spoke to Essex gently, soothingly. I hoped to dissuade him from persecuting the poor doctor. I had no doubt that Essex was motivated by a desire for revenge in return for his own humiliation in Lisbon at the hands of the doctor's countrymen.

'You do not have to prove anything to me. I know you have only my welfare at heart and that any errors you may have made in the past sprang from only the best intentions. You were young and inexperienced, and the Portuguese adventure is not merely forgiven but forgotten. Why bring it to the fore again?'

The earl's expression changed in an instant. His face took on a surly, mulish quality and his eyes narrowed to slits. 'This has nothing to do with that, and it is cruel of you to think so. I have found evidence of treachery, just as Walsingham used to. It is my duty to act accordingly just as it was his.'

I had done my best to dissuade him from his crusade against my Jewish doctor, but if Essex had evidence of treachery, who was I to say nay? I knew only too well that plots against my life sprang up as thickly as weeds and in the most unlikely places. I remained suspicious, however. I was worried that poor Lopez was too convenient a scapegoat. I could see how well it suited the earl's purposes to distract from his recent military failure by winning glory as the man who foiled treason. But I did not want to confront Essex. His purpose was to amuse me and make my life easier, not more difficult. I decided I would wait to see how events unfolded.

Minutes after Essex had departed, to boast of his

triumph no doubt, Robert Cecil stepped forward and indicated that he wished to speak to me in private.

'There is no evidence against Dr Lopez, Your Majesty.'

'Why would Essex arrest a man against whom there is no evidence?'

'He has already gained much praise by doing just that. Lopez is a foreigner and a Jew, and the people love to have their prejudices against such outsiders confirmed. And now that Antonio is penniless and has no longer any hope of gaining the Portuguese throne, Lopez has no powerful friends. He is an easy target.'

'It seems we have the same concern. It troubles me that the Earl of Essex would so easily sacrifice an innocent man.'

'The earl is ruthless in your service.'

'Do you hate him so very much?'

Now it was Cecil's turn to flush. He stood in silence for a moment or two, the better to regain his composure. 'I do not hate him. I merely have respect for evidence and the law. I am not the one filled with hate.'

I looked at Robert Cecil and thought I understood. Unlike Essex, he was a man who had to overcome prejudice. His misshapen body not only made him the butt of jokes and cruel remarks; it also made him an object of fear and suspicion. Despite his ever-increasing power, he was a lonely figure around my court, especially when his father was absent – as he was increasingly often. Those with an ugly exterior are often thought to be ugly all the way through, just as outward beauty is believed to indicate inner virtue. I have lived long enough to see the lie in both.

Despite his parentage, Robert Cecil was an outsider, like poor Lopez, and being an outsider had given him a greater understanding of others who survive on the fringes. As a woman, a virgin and a queen, I also knew what it was to be isolated.

'There is to be a banquet tonight, Mary. What should I wear?' I was excited. Our life in the royal nursery was predictable and humdrum. I was desperate for something different and for some attention.

'Don't be foolish, we are not invited.'

'But I have not seen my father for such a long time.'

'No longer than me. We have both been ignored in this out-of-the-way wing of the palace.' My sister sighed and put her embroidery to one side. She rubbed her face hard with both her hands, leaving her skin and eyes quite red. Never pretty, she now looked plain and sad.

But I was only five years old while my half-sister, Mary, was seventeen, and it was my own disappointment that interested me. Mary continued to try and explain, indifferent to my mulish expression. 'The king is not interested in us since our brother Edward was born, and we will simply have to entertain ourselves.'

I pouted and stamped my feet. 'What's so special about Edward, anyway? He's just a baby and never does anything interesting but mewl and puke!'

'Hush, child, he is a boy, a prince, the heir to the throne – and we are just girls.'

'And not even princesses anymore! I hate Edward!' I was whipped for speaking so violently, as no doubt I deserved to be, but I felt my isolation at least as much as my bruises.

Essex, pampered from birth, adored and admired by all who saw him, had no such understanding of the insecurities of those who do not belong. Instead he both shared the general prejudice and, it now seemed, was prepared to exploit it for his own purposes.

'Are you saying that the Earl of Essex hates Dr Lopez because he is of the Hebrew faith?'

'Many good Christians feel the same, Your Grace.'

'But you do not?'

'I prefer to judge a man on his merits.'

'Maybe it is his Portuguese nationality that inflames the earl?'

'Or perhaps a combination of both. I cannot tell another man's motivations. All I know is that there is no evidence against the poor doctor.'

I turned to my attendant. 'Fetch and tell him to come here.'

Within moments the most popular man in my

kingdom was back in my privy chamber, but the smile died on his face when he saw who else was in the room. I took two steps towards him and leant forward before I spoke.

'Cecil says there is no evidence against the doctor.'

'Nonsense. He has been plotting against you for some time.'

'How do you know this?'

'I have my sources, as you well know. They are the same informants that my father-in-law trusted implicitly. Why would we begin to doubt them now?'

'Do you have any documents? Letters? Any statements that can be sworn by witnesses?'

'I am sure they will be found in time.'

'In other words, you do not. Men like Lopez are vulnerable to malicious accusations, my lord, as I am sure your predecessor knew only too well. You need to tread carefully and gather solid evidence before any action can be taken against a man who may well be innocent. The trouble with persecuting an innocent man is not simply the injustice that is done. It means the real traitor goes undetected.'

I thought I had plucked the unfortunate Israelite from out of danger's way, but Essex was not so easily thwarted.

'Dr Lopez has confessed to his crime.'

It was some days after our initial interview about the

doctor and Essex was once again standing in front of my writing table. I was caught at a disadvantage and I knew it. A wisp of grey hair had escaped from under my wig. I knew he would notice. I knew that it pleased him to see signs of weakness in others.

I looked up from my inky labours and tried to tuck the wisp of hair away. I failed.

'He has admitted that he plotted to poison you, and so has been condemned to death.'

'I say again, my lord, to what end? Who did he work for? Was he doing the bidding of Philip of Spain?'

'Yes, that is it precisely and the Jew was being paid handsomely for his treachery – and in gold, not the mere thirty pieces of silver that satisfied Judas Iscariot.'

'You have proved your point, it seems.'

'My only point, Your Grace, was to protect you.'

Poor Dr Lopez. There is no doubt it can be very dangerous to get too close to power.

Essex was loved by the people and he gloried in their admiration. It was hard for me to blame him for that. I know only too well how heady such attention can be. However, what is right and proper for a monarch can be dangerous for one of her subjects. Essex had many talents and much about him that was endearing. He could not hide his feelings. His face displayed what was in his heart. He had the spontaneity of a spoilt and adored child – a child who has not yet learnt to be wary of the world. His mother, my second cousin (and erstwhile romantic rival), Lettice Knollys, had adored her only surviving son and he had grown up secure in her constant good opinion. He also grew up unable to cope with any correction or criticism. Just as praise and triumph lit his face up instantaneously, so any thwarting of his will, any hint of disapproval, brought a thunderous scowl. At first, I enjoyed his company and, like his mother (and his grandmother), I indulged his childishness. Perhaps because I had controlled my feelings so rigidly for such a long time, his spontaneity warmed something inside me that I had felt was long dead.

But, as is so often the case, my obvious fondness for Essex not only increased his own opinion of himself, it made him enemies. They waited in the shadows until they saw an opportunity. They did not have to wait for long.

I find it makes me uncomfortable to relive my experiences with the Earl of Essex, unlike the pleasure I feel when I remember his stepfather. My unease brings my mind skittering out of the past and back into the gloomy chamber of the present.

It is still dark outside and the ranks of the courtiers awaiting my demise have thinned. Some are weary. Some are hungry. No doubt some are bored. I think that I may be drifting in and out of consciousness, for sometimes I cannot quite distinguish memory from the here and now. I feel as if I am actually travelling in time, reliving my life, returning to ghosts from the past who seem to grow more substantial the closer I get to joining their spectral company.

I am in a strange grey place, between this world and the next. The living, breathing human beings in this room feel ghostly and insubstantial. Yet, as I drift in and out, it seems to me as if Essex still lives. I can see his quicksilver face, as vivid as ever it was in life. For a moment, I think I can see him among those gathered in the corner of the chamber and I wonder if I am seeing ghosts. Robert Cecil is no ghost and I can see he is still seated upon a stool, his nose buried in state papers. He has much to do, I'll warrant, as he shepherds my kingdom (is it still my kingdom?) from one monarch to the next. It hurts me that he is all business and no grief.

Perhaps it was Robert's face that reminded me of Essex, although their features could not have been more different. Despite their antipathy, wherever one of them went the other was sure to follow.

At first it was Essex who dominated their rivalry. With his feats of bravery, he left the studious Cecil in his wake.

'I leapt from the rigging, Your Grace, and ran the Spaniard through!' Essex jumped off the stool on which he was standing and mimed a vigorous sword thrust into the guts of an invisible enemy. Some of my ladies gasped at his dumb-show.

'And then I turned and struck out at all the devils around me, like this—' (and he thrust) 'and this' (he thrust again) 'and this!' This time he mimed stabbing my newly appointed secretary of state, his rival. Robert Cecil was not as amused as the rest of the court.

But I was delighted. I laughed out loud. 'What, my lord, did you kill all of Philip's men by yourself?'

'Not all. I was but one part of our triumph over the Spaniards. We singed Philip's beard, all right, with only a small party of Englishmen. Each one of them stout-hearted, brave and true!'

'I should hope so, given how generously you rewarded them – and yourself.'

It was a point of contention between us. Essex had his triumph right enough. His armada of eighty-two stout and nimble British ships (not such a small party, perhaps) had captured Cadiz and forced the Spanish to sink their fleet in the harbour for fear of it falling into English hands. We had cost Philip a pretty penny and reinforced our reputation as a formidable naval power. But I had funded the adventure and had received no return on my investment – and I had been promised a fair profit.

'You are all to be congratulated. It is amusing to singe the beard of the King of Spain, as you say, and it has enhanced our reputation. For that I am grateful. However, the victory has been gained at considerable cost to my treasury and you promised me a profit, not a loss.'

I had spoilt their fun. Essex dropped his imaginary cutlass (I almost fancied I could hear it clatter onto the floorboards). His face also fell, and my ladies sat as still and silent as statues, frozen into place. The stool that had done duty as the imaginary prow of the warship was kicked aside. Robert Cecil tactfully found business he had to attend to on the other side of the chamber. I took two steps towards the crestfallen hero. I spoke quietly so none could overhear. 'You have done well, my lord. I will not say otherwise, but let me remind you that it is not enough for you to do *your* pleasure—'

Essex made as if to dispute my words, but I held up my hand to silence him. 'Do not deny it. You enjoyed every moment of this adventure. There is nothing you derive more pleasure from than feats of glory.'

'In your service, Your Grace, always in your service.'

'Then where is my reward? Where is my share of the bounty you realised? You boast of capturing Spanish gold, but I am yet to see a single glittering coin. No, my lord, I funded this expedition and have received nothing in return.'

'I risked my life for you, Your Grace.'

'That is your job.' Essex and I were sometimes more like rivals than friends. It was a rare evening now that passed without some upset or acrimony between us. I had not entirely forgiven him for the death of Dr Lopez. I was uneasy about the possibility that an innocent man had lost his life. Essex was quick to take offence and to see a slight where none was meant. I seemed to be spending much of my time in his company smoothing down his ruffled feathers and I was growing irritated. His reckless desire for action was costing me money! When the time came to divvy out honours after the raid on Cadiz I saw my opportunity to make my displeasure felt.

'Why have you made Charles Howard the Earl of Nottingham, when I was the more deserving of your generals?' Essex had stormed into the room without waiting to be announced. As usual, I could see by his face exactly what was going on in his mind and I braced myself for the onslaught. However, I had not ruled over men for more than thirty years without learning that a monarch never explains herself to a subject.

'It is not for you, or anyone else, to question the wisdom of my decisions, my Lord Essex.'

'I want you to take the honour from him. He does not deserve it, he did not earn it and you should not give such titles away so easily. Please, Your Grace, I beseech you, do not promote on false reports.'

I was astonished at Essex, particularly as his impudent words were spoken in public, in my audience chamber, while surrounded by others. I knew that he took liberties and that I had given him more leeway than any other in my court. I had heard the grumblings of those who were not so favoured. I was treating him very much as I had treated Robin Dudley, but Essex was not Robin, who had only ever taken such liberties when we were alone, and otherwise was very careful of my status. Even when I tore up the paperwork granting him an earldom, Robin had swallowed the insult with dignity. If only his stepson had been as wise! Essex's presumption had to be rebuffed. 'You overstep yourself, my lord. I am the prince here and you are my subject. Do not presume to lecture me, or dispute with me about my decisions. I have rewarded those who I believe are most deserving and it is not for you to question. You would do well to think upon my words.'

I turned on my heel, my cheeks burning. As I stormed out, shocked courtiers bowed low. I saw from the corner of my eye that the Bacon brothers had hastened to Essex's side and were urgently whispering to him. I paused and turned. Then I spoke loudly so that everyone present could hear. 'Give him good counsel, Sir Francis, Sir Anthony. Tell him to subdue both his temper and his expectations.'

I gave Essex so many chances – mostly in memory of the stepfather who had promoted the younger man's interests so assiduously when he was still alive – but there was no sense in the earl. In an attempt to win back my favour (or to prove me wrong), he undertook another naval expedition against the Spaniards. His plan was to scatter the remaining Spanish fleet and capture the treasure ships laden with gold from the new world. He did the one, which may well have made our small island kingdom safer, but he completely failed at the other. Once again, Essex depleted my treasury and did not contribute one farthing.

'I recommend Sir William Knollys, Your Grace. He is a good man, your loyal servant and has proved himself on the battlefield.'

We were discussing who should fill the post of Lord Lieutenant of Ireland. As usual the Irish were in open rebellion and the situation required a level head. Robert Cecil was well briefed and ready with his recommendation. Indeed, as was now our habit, he had previously sounded me out about the position and we had agreed on our favoured candidate. We were both also aware that this was a post the Earl of Essex deeply desired. Neither of us believed he was the right choice. Our conversation, observed by Charles Howard (he who had been made Lord Nottingham instead of the earl), Essex himself and one or two others, was for show.

'An excellent suggestion, Master Secretary. Draw up the papers and notify Sir William of his new posting.'

'I protest, Your Majesty! Is this now all it takes for such important decisions? Your secretary of state suggests a name and you concur? Surely we are entitled to a more thorough discussion than that?' The Earl of Essex was bristling with indignation. This was not entirely a surprise. Both Cecil and I had expected a reaction. Whenever Essex felt slighted he became angry. Indeed, my secretary and I had discussed whether we should inform him of our decision in private, but I was sick of pandering to his sensibilities. I was the queen. I did not need to explain myself to him.

In the face of the earl's fury I felt an answering passion. His disrespect was becoming impossible to ignore. There were sharp words on the edge of my tongue, when Robert Cecil intervened smoothly.

'I am happy to discuss the merits of Sir William's appointment with my Lord Essex, Your Majesty, and I am happy to hear any alternative suggestions he may have for the post.' Cecil was attempting to pour oil on troubled waters. He was doing what he could to calm things down. But my blood was up, and I ignored his peacemaking. I took a step closer to Essex.

'Who would you recommend, my lord? Yourself? There seems hardly a position in my court that you do not have an opinion on. It seems you cannot imagine that anyone could have any merit compared with you. Indeed, I sometimes wonder that if I needed a new steward or serving wench you might not put up your hand. Mind you, I might see fit to give you those positions. You'd make a fine serving wench!'

Essex stood deathly still as he digested my deliberate

insult. To his credit, he managed to hold his tongue. What he could not do was control his features. He looked at me – his queen, his mistress in all things, the woman who had done her best to give him opportunities, promotion, sinecures – with contempt. Then he turned on his heel and presented his back to me. This was unforgivable. I leapt at him and before I even quite knew what I was doing, I was raising my hand. 'Go and be hanged!'

Then I boxed both his ears. He ducked under my sharp onslaught and instinctively grasped the hilt of his sword. I wondered for a ghastly second if he was about to run me through.

Charles Howard stepped between us. 'My lord, my lord, you forget yourself!'

Had Essex raised his sword against me, whether he used it or not, his life would immediately have been over. Howard put both his hands on the hilt to force the earl's sword back down into its scabbard.

Essex pulled his hand from under Howard's and shook his fist at us all. 'I would not take such a blow from the king, her father! It is an indignity that I will not endure from anyone, no matter how high or low their station, let alone from ...'

And then he hesitated, finally sensing the extreme danger that he was in, but such was the intensity of his passion, such the intemperance of his nature, all he could manage was to lower his voice. It made no difference. I heard what he muttered as clearly as if he had yelled it across the room.

'I will not endure such treatment from a king in petticoats.'

Six

The only sound in my normally raucous audience chamber was that of the earl's boots echoing along the hallway as he stormed away. Every other soul in the room stood silent.

'Are – are you all right, Your Majesty?' Cecil was the first to find his voice.

It took me a moment to gather myself before I could answer. 'I – I – am quite unhurt.'

'The earl thought better of his impulse, it seems.' Charles Howard had retained the power of speech.

'Did he, my lord? Or was it your prompt action that saved the queen's life?'

'I do not think that Essex would actually have drawn his sword.' I still could not quite believe what had just happened.

'But how can we be sure of that, Your Majesty? Every man here witnessed what he did and there was no mistaking the gesture. Even if the earl might have thought better of his action, to have contemplated such an act, to have allowed his hand to move towards his weapon – it is treachery, Your Grace. I should send soldiers to arrest him.'

'No, no, Cecil. He knows full well what he has done. Leave him to stew upon it, but do not allow him into my presence again until I bid you otherwise. He is banished from court and must keep his distance.'

'You show him more mercy than he deserves.'

'My head is cooler than his and I would like to keep it that way.'

But my head did not feel cool despite my brave words. The room was swimming slightly in front of my eyes, my skin was icy, and I had a strange black and yellow sensation. The assassin's dagger I had spent my whole life fearing had almost become a reality. Worse, the threat to my safety had come from a member of my intimate circle, a man I trusted – despite our differences. The shock was overwhelming. I knew I had to remove myself from public scrutiny as quickly as I could. 'If you will forgive me, my lords, I will retire to my privy apartments.'

Two of my ladies tried each to take an arm to help me from the room, but I waved them away. The gathered counsellors bowed as I made my way to the same door that Essex had stormed through only a few moments earlier. And then I remembered the purpose of this meeting and paused before I crossed its threshold.

I held onto the doorjamb to steady myself. 'Confirm Sir William in his position, my lord, and offer him my thanks and congratulations.'

When at last I sank onto a chair in the safety and relative privacy of my own chamber, my agitation must have been plain to see. My ladies gathered about me, their brows furrowed with concern.

'Would you care for a cool drink, Your Grace?' Philadelphia Carey, cousin to the Earl of Essex, was offering me a goblet.

'No, thank you. I am perfectly well. Stand back, stand back – I need to breathe.'

And where I had felt cold before, suddenly I felt hot, as if the very air of the chamber pressed against me.

My ladies shuffled backwards. Philadelphia handed the goblet to a waiting maidservant and replaced it with a fan, which she passed to me. This time I accepted the proffered object gratefully. I unbuttoned the ruff about my throat and fanned my face and neck. My ladies said nothing, but the rustling silk of their gowns still assaulted my ears. I needed space and clear air around me. And yet, all the while I was inwardly berating myself for my cowardly reaction. No harm had been done me. No blood had been spilt. Why was I so upset?

'Back, back!' I said again, gesturing at them with my eyes closed. I heard by the creaking of the floorboards that they had done as I commanded. The fan was doing its work and I began to feel a little better. I opened my eyes and glared at the assembled women. 'There is no need to fuss! As you can see I am entirely unharmed. It is hot in this room and you were standing too close – that is all.'

'Is it true that my Lord Essex made an attempt on your life, Your Grace?' Only Philadelphia had the courage to ask the question that hung so heavy in the room.

'No, it was nowhere near as dramatic as that. Your cousin lost his temper and put his hand on his sword hilt, that is all.'

The women gasped.

'Is he under arrest?'

'No, Philadelphia, but he is banished from court and will stay that way until further notice.'

'And you have been so good to him. And, pardon me, Your Majesty, but you have always seemed so fond of him.'

That slight nod to the gossip that had surrounded my relationship with the hotheaded earl made me think of his poor wife. 'Where is the Countess of Essex?'

'I am here, Your Grace.' Her voice came from the back of the room. At the sound of it, the ladies who were crowded in front of her parted so that I could see her. The countess stood with her head bowed, her hands rigid by her side.

I spoke to her gently. 'You must go from court too, Frances.'

'As you wish.'

'It is not as I wish; it is your husband's behaviour that compels it. I am glad your father is not here to see this.'

The Countess of Essex was Francis Walsingham's only surviving daughter. The irony of this did not escape me. It had always been his greatest care to protect my person, so the dilemma the old man would have found himself in when confronted by the behaviour of his son-in-law did not bear contemplating. He was not the only one of my dear friends who would have been similarly disturbed by the earl's behaviour. How would Robin have reacted? Or his grandmother, my dearest friend and cousin (some say half-sister) Catherine Carey – how would she have felt?

'It is a small mercy.' Frances spoke in a low and tearful voice. This event was a great blow to her.

'I do not hold you responsible for your husband's behaviour. I hope you know that.'

'Your Majesty is very kind.'

'Come closer. I do not wish to bellow at you.' I exaggerated, but it annoyed me to see her cringing away from me. At this moment I felt a great deal more affection for the countess than I did for the earl. She had done me no wrong.

The poor woman curtsied and made her way through the cluster of brightly clad ladies until she stood directly in front of me. She kept her eyes lowered, staring at the floor. I reached forward and took her gently by the chin and raised her face until I was looking directly into her eyes. She blinked, but dared not look away.

I spoke to her quietly. 'You have always shown me good and loyal service and my affection for you has not changed. I want you to be assured of that, but I cannot have you here while your husband is banished. Talk some sense into him if you can. Get him to apologise and make amends. Then, when some time has passed, and tempers have cooled, I may be able to forgive him. But, mark you this, he must fully and freely admit his fault. I will accept none of his half-apologies where he tries to blame others for his own misbehaviour.'

'He is a proud man, Your Grace, but I will do all I can.'

Poor Frances, I could see she very much doubted her ability to persuade her husband to do anything. Their marriage had not been a love-match. Frances had previously been married to Sir Philip Sidney and – as he lay dying on the battlefield – Sidney had bequeathed his wife to the earl, as if she were livestock, or household goods. She, like most women, had little say in the matter. Whether she loved Essex or not, I do not know. She did not speak ill of him in my hearing, but then she did not speak well of him either.

I watched her back slowly out of the room. She was not a pretty young woman, having inherited her father's long nose and narrow-set eyes, but her marriageability was never in doubt, especially when her powerful father was alive. Her best asset – as far as the men in my court were concerned – was her large annuity and her ability to bear healthy children. She had borne the Earl of Essex three already. But I found her good company. She had inherited her father's penetrating intelligence. She did not chatter, but held herself aloof from the other women at court and I valued her quiet good sense. When she did speak, I found her remarks worth listening to. I imagine she bored her impetuous husband. More to the point, although I doubt he ever considered this, I suspect he also bored her.

As I think back over the people I have known, I find my heart swells with pity for so many of them, but particularly for the women. It is a sympathy I did not feel often while they were alive. I am glad I was kind to Frances of Essex.

Few if any of my female friends had either long or happy lives. There were some – Mildred Cecil comes to mind. My aunt Mary Boleyn was the most blessed of her siblings, dying (when I was ten) in her own bed, surrounded by her loving husband and children. I have only hazy memories of her. I think I only saw her once or twice after my mother's execution. She wisely kept clear of the court. But it has been my pleasure to promote her children, and her children's children where I can. The earl is her great-grandson. Philadelphia Carey her granddaughter and all the Knollys clan are related to Mary Boleyn in one way or another. It is ironic,

I think, that the Boleyn blood flows thick and fast into the future, while the Tudor strain is rapidly drying up. Unless, of course, Catherine Carey really was my father's daughter and not a Carey at all.

Women, even aristocratic women, have so little power over their own lives. A woman's happiness or otherwise depends so much on the nature of her husband. Seeing the misery that is so often the result of marriage and the mortal danger that stalks the birthing stool, I cannot regret my spinster status. Yes, I missed what Mildred and my Aunt Mary may have had, but they were the exceptions. Mostly, when I think of the married women I have known, I have missed nothing but unhappiness and the threat of agonising death.

Mary Boleyn's eldest child, my cousin Catherine Carey, was one of the more fortunate and yet even she suffered for love in the end. She married Francis Knollys when she was but sixteen. I remember very well her excitement when he proposed. They were two young people in the rarest of situations: they approved of one another as much as their parents approved of their choice. Catherine could not wait to be wed. Her romantic fantasies about love and children and domestic bliss were all she talked of throughout her betrothal. I listened grudgingly. I was a child of seven, a neglected princess. All I knew was that this marriage would take my dear friend, playmate and cousin away from me. I was jealous of the young man she loved and pulled scornful faces whenever his name was mentioned.

Of all my many relatives she – and she alone – never caused me any trouble but gave me only friendship, support and love. She was nine when I was born, and she had little reason to love me. My mother, Anne Boleyn, had supplanted her mother, Mary Boleyn, in the king's affections.

Catherine was born in 1524 while her mother was still my father's mistress and she had the red hair and small mouth characteristic of the Tudors. That is why so many still believe that Catherine is my half-sister as well as my cousin. Many took pleasure on remarking on her resemblance to my father and, later still, to me. I do not know if she and her brother Henry were the king's bastards and I doubt Catherine knew either. My aunt took her secret with her to the grave – that is, of course, assuming that she herself knew whose child she had conceived. All I know is that from my earliest memory, Catherine was kind to me, even when I was not quite three years old and my mother was executed, and I became – like my sister Mary Tudor – a bastard princess.

I was too young to understand what had happened, but it did not escape my notice that everyone who once had been so loving was now indifferent. Everyone, that is, but for three young women. Kat Ashley was newly promoted to be my governess and her love and care for me never wavered for a moment, not until the day she died. Another who remained loyal was twelve-year-old Catherine Carey. Perhaps because she was also a Boleyn the cold wind of indifference blew just as icily on her as it did on me. The third person who became much kinder towards me in the face of my misfortune was the most surprising one of all. It was my sister Mary Tudor.

I suffered much when Mary became queen (as indeed did Catherine Carey), but I remember our early years together with great affection. Perhaps my sister warmed to me because she saw that my fate in many ways mirrored her own. No doubt she was lonely and friendless, and I was but a small child and therefore easy to love. In giving me comfort perhaps she comforted herself. In mothering me perhaps she also mothered herself. Whatever the reason, she turned quickly from my enemy into my friend.

It takes very little for me to imagine myself back in our cramped apartments at Hatfield or Hunsdon. There is Mary, her dark head bowed over her embroidery as she peers at her stitches. Despite the short sight that forces her to hold the cloth just beneath her nose, her stitches are always the smallest and the neatest. Kat is gossiping with a servant at the rear of the room, her arms full of linen she is supposed to be repairing. She is paying very little attention to us. Catherine is by the window, fully aware that our guardian's attention is elsewhere. Surreptitiously glancing upwards at Kat, she is playing with a pack of cards, turning them over and forecasting our futures just as an old woman at a recent fair has taught her. Catherine has the great good fortune of not being royal, or acknowledged as such, anyway. This means that she has more freedom than either Mary or me. If the fair or a circus comes to town, Catherine can go. Mary and I are forced to remain behind. I watched my cousin and many of our attendants skipping down the avenue with delighted anticipation on their way to one such excursion recently. With my face pressed up against the window, I watched them until they were out of sight.

When they return, I insist on hearing every detail from Catherine. The world that seems ordinary to others seems very exotic to me. She enjoys telling me of the fun she has had and promises she will show me some of the skills she has learnt from the Gypsies who run the fair.

As we sit together on that long-ago afternoon, Catherine has just persuaded me to shuffle the pack and is arranging the cards according to the Gypsy woman's instructions.

'You will marry a great prince, Elizabeth, and bear him many children.'

'No, I will not. I am going to run away to sea and become a great explorer.'

'Girls can't run away to sea.'

'Well, I will. You just watch me.'

*

In fact, it was Catherine who would run away to sea, many years later with her husband and her five youngest children. They slipped away from England in the dead of night to escape the wrath of the near-sighted young woman who now sat next to her, laughing at her nonsense. But on that autumn afternoon, more than half a century ago, we had no idea of what was to come. Indeed, that is precisely why Catherine had decided to play the Gypsy and attempt to foretell our future.

'Don't be so foolish, Elizabeth. Girls can't do things like that. We get married and we have babies. You will see I am right when you are not such a baby yourself.'

'I am not a baby!' My voice rises in volume. I hate it when the older girls use their superiority in years to put me in my place.

It seems remarkable now to remember a time when I was almost always the youngest in any group, given that for so many years I have been the oldest. All the women in that room on that afternoon are dead now and have been for decades.

At the sound of discord, Mary raises her head from her embroidery. She speaks soothingly, as adults do to calm a child. I can hear her curious deep voice now, as if she is speaking close to my ears. Is my sister calling to me, though she has been dead two score years and more? It will not be long before I join her. For the moment, however, I am four years old, sitting cross-legged on the floor at Hampton Court, chewing on the end of my quill, listening impatiently to her dulcet tones.

'Maybe you will marry a prince from a foreign land and cross the seas to become his bride? Maybe you can explore new lands *and* marry a great prince.'

Mary is always sensible. I suppose it is because she is so much older. Already, she has an air of isolation about her. She trusts very few.

But none of those thoughts cross my infant mind that afternoon. I am too full of my own feelings to worry about anyone else. 'I don't want to marry anybody. I think boys are horrid.'

I am meant to be copying some Biblical verses for Kat Ashley, but I fling the quill aside, spattering ink on the rug. Mary's brow furrows. Mess and disorder always disquiet her.

'And you will be rich! Elizabeth – here – see? I have turned up the jack of spades – Black Jack as many call him. The Gypsy woman told me his bad reputation is undeserved and to turn up such a card denotes great good fortune, but in worldly matters – not romance. His brother the jack of hearts is the card indicating love.'

'Then you must be going to marry a great prince, because you are not rich now and it is not possible for a woman to earn her own fortune.' Mary has put aside her stitching and is leaning forward. She is interested in this game, despite her good sense.

'It is silly superstition!' I snort.

'You are right. Our destinies are in the hands of God, not a hand of cards.'

'Oh, Mary, we all know how pious you are,' says Catherine, 'but I'll warrant you are as curious to hear what the cards foretell for you as any of the rest of us. Here, shuffle them for me.'

And Catherine hands her pack to Mary, who rolls her eyes but shuffles the cards as she is bid. Catherine takes the first card from the pack and immediately her eyes widen with delight. Both Mary and I lean forward, unable to restrain our curiosity.

'What do the cards tell you? Don't keep us in suspense!'

I leap up from my copying, narrowly avoid upending the inkpot, and am standing by my cousin, trying to see the card she is hiding in her hands. She ignores me but holds it under my sister's nose. Mary narrows her eyes so she can bring it into focus.

'You will marry an emperor. Look!' And Catherine holds up the king of hearts and flourishes it for all of us to see. 'It was the very first card in your pack, Mary! And it's the luckiest card of them all.'

Catherine is a faulty fortune-teller. Of the three of us gathered together on that rainy afternoon, she is the only one who is to be lucky in love.

Seven

'You are not with child again?'

My cousin Catherine Knollys (Carey as she used to be) had just dashed from the room, white as a sheet, hand clapped across her mouth. Now that she had re-entered my chamber she was dabbing at her lips with a damp cloth. A sweat shone on her forehead, testament to the nausea she was battling. She nodded, smiling ruefully. 'It would seem so, Your Majesty.'

'Oh, Catherine! How many is it now?'

'This will be the tenth, I think, Your Grace.'

'And the last, I hope.'

'It shall be as God wills it.'

'And as your husband demands!'

'It is a wife's duty to submit.'

'Ten children are above and beyond the call of duty, surely?'

Catherine's eyes filled with tears. I saw her distress and so did some of the other ladies in attendance.

I clapped my hands. 'Be gone, the lot of you. I want to talk to my cousin alone.'

When they had left, Catherine gave full rein to her feelings and wept openly. I sat beside her and took both her hands in mine. 'Oh, Catherine. I understand your distress.'

'I am just so tired. I cannot recall when last I felt myself. And the nausea seems to grow worse with each new—'

'I will reduce your duties and get some of my other women to take on more of your tasks.'

'No, no, I enjoy serving you. To be at court and have a role and responsibilities takes my mind off my state. Sometimes I think it is all that keeps me sane.'

'But you are always so ill in the beginning. It breaks my heart to watch you suffer.'

'It passes. In only a few weeks I will feel more like myself again.'

'Does Francis – can he – does he treat you with the respect you deserve when you are carrying his child?'

'Francis is a good husband and a considerate one. We love each other and the consequences of that are … well … as you see before you.'

'I worry for your health and your strength. I could not bear to lose you.'

'I haven't died of it, yet, Your Grace.'

'You are built to endure, that is true. But after each confinement you return to me a little thinner and a little darker under the eyes. I do not like to watch you grow frail. Can your husband not see what I see and leave you alone?'

'A man has needs.'

'That's as may be, but surely there are plenty of women at court who could take care of them?'

At this suggestion Catherine bridled. 'What you suggest is a sin, and Francis is a loyal husband.'

'Yet I cannot see the virtue in wearing out a good wife in child-bearing. Surely ten children, with almost as many lads as lasses, is enough for any man?'

'We love our children, Your Majesty. They bring us great joy.'

'I am not suggesting you get rid of any you have got. I am just wondering at the cost of adding to their number. You must care for yourself too, as well as care for them.'

It strikes me again, at the end of my life, that the dreams young girls have for the future are terribly sad. Perhaps that is why I have always been irritated when the young women around me – so full of promise and potential – fall in love. I fear for them. I'd rather they married for more prosaic reasons – such as money and a title. There is much comfort to be found in those.

Even Catherine quickly discovered the real consequences of the romantic nonsense we stuff into girls' heads. The popular ballads of love and tales of chivalry and white knights have a lot to answer for. Slender, nimble little Catherine, who married for love at sixteen was rewarded with decades of discomfort, pain, exhaustion and – in the end – an untimely death. Happily-ever-after is a false promise for everyone, but especially for girls.

My cousin (or half-sister) was cursed with fecundity. She eventually birthed sixteen children – eight boys and eight girls. Most of them lived. Her third child was Lettice Knollys. I showed the young Lettice great favour because of my love for her mother and, when she grew old enough, I did not hesitate to make her one of my ladies of the bedchamber alongside Catherine. She performed her duties well enough, at first, and it was clear Catherine was proud of her. I indulged that pride and it was a mistake.

In the end, the mother was loyal, but the daughter was not. Lettice betrayed my trust and married Robin – *my* Robin – behind my back. I banished her from the court and I have not seen her since.

Lettice was a beauty when she was young. I have no idea how she looks now but she lives on quietly (I sincerely hope not contentedly) with her third husband – or is it her fourth? I have lost count. I was fond of her once – she was a fetching enough child – but never as fond as I was of her mother.

I am kind to all Catherine's children and give them preferences and sinecures, as she would have wanted, but in my heart I keep each one at arm's length. They did not mean to kill the woman who gave them life – children never do – but I cannot help feeling that their vigour slowly drained hers.

Catherine was only forty-four when she died and I was but three and thirty. Although I was a seasoned monarch by then, I needed her to live longer. The men who surrounded me were both loyal and able, but Catherine was my closest female peer and friend. I loved Kat and Blanche and the others of my attendants who had served me loyally through fair times and foul, but Catherine was my cousin and not my subordinate. I needed her love and wise counsel as much as any of her children did – maybe more. After all, did any of them rule a kingdom? I remember the dread I felt as I watched her fade with each subsequent pregnancy. As they grew in number, I gave up any pretence of being happy for her.

There were not many people I could talk to as frankly as I could to Catherine. It is lonely being a queen. I lived in fear that each new confinement would kill my friend.

Her husband, knowing my concern, always sent me news as soon as the child was born. Within weeks of the birth, she was back at court, my friend and companion once more. Each time she returned I pleaded with her to make this child the last. Each time she nodded, smiled and ignored me entirely. It was only with her sixteenth child that I was able to wring a promise from her. 'This one will be the last, surely? You must see how thin you have become, despite your enormous belly.'

'Yes. Francis and I have agreed that we will have no more children after this.'

'I wish you had made that decision some time ago. You have worn yourself to a shred.'

'I will be pleased not to have to undergo the rigours of the childbed, Your Grace, that is certain. But I will miss the lovely, wriggling little creatures that are God's reward for such travails.'

'Babies are appealing. Yours especially. They are always so chubby and vigorous.'

'Yes, we have been blessed with sturdy children.'

'Which is why you do not need to have any more. Give your poor body a rest and a chance to recover its own health and vigour. You will be no help to this child if you are left an invalid – or worse.'

'I intend to take my pleasures as a grandmother now and leave the child-bearing to my daughters.'

Robert Devereux, who later became the Earl of Essex, was one of the grandchildren my dear friend hoped to take delight in. If only she had lived long enough. After Catherine was delivered of her sixteenth child, her body could stand no more. Like so many brought to childbed, she took a fever and died. I mourned her as I did few others.

'I will pay for a monument to your wife, my lord.'

'That is gracious of you, Your Majesty. I know she loved you very well.'

'As I did her. I will miss her very much.'

'Yes, many will miss her.' As he spoke, despite the formality of his language, the great courtier's voice broke and Francis Knollys could not contain his grief. I was glad he wept for her, but I was also angry with him and resentful that his pleasure had so destroyed my friend.

'Could you not have let her alone, my lord? Could you not see she was worn out from child-bearing?'

'It is what women are created to do, she more than most.'

'Perhaps so, but why must it kill so many of us, I wonder?'

'It is not for us to question God's will, Your Majesty.'

'You sound like a priest, my lord.'

'She never complained, you see. She never said that she minded so many pregnancies, so many children.'

'She dreaded the childbed. She told me so often, particularly as her time grew near. She told me that the pain of bringing a new life into the world was like no other. Her face would go white when she told me this and she would grip my hand so tightly it hurt.'

'She never said as much to me.'

'Did you ever ask her?'

'When I asked her how she did, after each churching, she always smiled and told me she did very well. I believed her and enquired no further. And she loved our children – all our pretty ones. They gave her great joy.'

'I do not doubt that, and now you have them all to remember her by.'

'Yes, the children are a comfort to me as they were to her.'

'I tell you frankly, I would rather have Catherine back among us, as she was when she was young and full of the vitality of youth, than any number of her progeny.'

'We must trust that we will all be reunited in heaven.'

'You are sounding like a priest again, Francis. It does not become you.'

We were silent for a moment or two, both consumed by memories of the woman we had loved, perhaps. Then Francis broke the silence by telling me again what I already knew.

'She loved you, Your Grace, above all other women.'

'And, I say it again, I loved her.'

'May I have your permission to withdraw? My heart is sore, and I cannot trust myself to remain composed.'

I did not answer as I also felt very close to shedding tears; instead I merely gestured my assent. Then, as Catherine's bereaved husband bowed his way out of the room, I said one last phrase to him that caused him to lose control entirely. '*Cor rotto*, my lord.'

Or, in English, 'my heart is broken'.

I had used that phrase to his wife once before, a

long time ago, when I was a mere princess and my sister Mary was queen.

Francis and Catherine Knollys were devout Protestants and had therefore prospered under the rule of my similarly pious brother, King Edward. When my Catholic sister Mary inherited the throne, all of us who were of the Protestant faith felt the ground shift. Catherine and I hoped that the early companionship among the three of us when we were young and unimportant might give us some protection. But we felt the cold wind that was blowing. My troubles are well known. I spent the years of Mary's rule under suspicion and, not infrequently, under arrest.

Nevertheless, Francis and Catherine were much more vulnerable. Being the heir to the throne gave me some protection. My fate was being watched by the whole world. Outside of England, Francis and Catherine were unknown and therefore invisible. Mary could have rid herself of them without consequence.

As the persecutions of Protestants increased, like many others who shared the new faith, Francis, Catherine and some of their children took flight and sought sanctuary in Frankfurt. Before they left, they confided in me. I was devastated when I heard of their plans. As a young woman, precariously placed in line to the English throne, I never felt I had many friends. Under Mary, I felt particularly alone. Even those who had sworn their love for me now turned their backs.

The loss of my childhood companion and playmate therefore was doubly hard, but I did not try to dissuade them. I would rather Catherine alive and at a distance than dead and buried nearby, and I knew exactly how much danger she was in. However, I could not let her leave without saying some kind of goodbye. I did not know then if we would ever see each other again, if either of us would survive.

There was little time between news of the Knollys' imminent departure and the night of their sailing and I knew it was folly to even consider trying to see Catherine face to face. My every move was watched and monitored. Instead, I was forced to dash off a note at the full pitch of my fear and loneliness. 'The length of time and distance of place does not separate love of friends, nor stop the show of goodwill.'

It is always dangerous to cross the seas and travel to foreign places. It showed just how threatened they were that Catherine and Francis felt it safer to place their lives and those of their children at the whim of the capricious Channel than to stay in Mary's England.

'... when your need shall be most you shall find my friendship greatest. Let others promise, and I will do, in deeds rather than words. My power is but small ...' (Small? It was almost non-existent at that time.) '... my love as great as them who give you lavish gifts to tell their friendship's tale ...'

How I wished I could have done something –

anything – to prevent the necessity of their flight, but I could not even guarantee my own survival, let alone theirs. I continued to pour out my distress upon the page.

'And to conclude, a word that I can hardly say, I must write "farewell", it is in one way what I wish, yet in another way what I grieve.'

And then, as the messenger charged with delivering my hastily scribbled epistle shifted urgently behind my chair, I signed the letter.

'Your loving cousin and ready friend, *Cor rotto*.'

I wept as I watched the messenger ride helter-skelter down the avenue bound for the London docks.

But God answered our prayers all those years ago. Catherine and her family returned when I gained the throne and my heart mended. When she died so worn out, it broke again.

'*Cor rotto*,' I said to her equally heartbroken husband.

She is buried in Westminster Abbey, I made sure of that, with a fine memorial plaque extolling her virtues as a woman, a wife and a mother. After the death of her husband – another old friend over whom I wept bitter tears – they tell me the Knollys children are building an elaborate memorial to both their parents in their parish church at Rotherfield Grey. It will contain effigies of each of the children my dear friend laboured so hard to bring into the world. I weep for her still.

*

'*Cor rotto.*' I mutter the phrase to myself now that I have reached the end of my life. I too am worn out, but not with childbearing; with ruling a kingdom. Given that I lived to be nine and sixty and poor Catherine died a quarter century sooner, it seems that one task is much harder than the other. How fortunate I am to have avoided the fate that is so common to women. I thank God for the unusual life I was lucky enough to live. I thank Him for the power and control I have had not just over my kingdom, but over my own fate. It is a fine thing to shape your own destiny and one that few women ever experience.

Once more I leave the past and open my eyes and look again at those about me in the present. Few of my attendants remain. Those that do are dozing on their stools. Most have left my chamber, sensibly seeking their beds. A few candles still flicker in the room. One on the mantelpiece shrinks and shudders as if a wind sweeps over it and I look at it in hope. It would be an answer to my prayers if a kindly spirit – Catherine, or Kat, Blanche or even Robin – if a familiar spirit came to escort me from this world to the next. But I search the dark in vain. The candle has merely responded to the opening of the door as another of my attendants takes his leave – worn out with waiting for the old woman to die.

Eight

A pale dawn is visible around the heavy curtains over the window. Perhaps I dozed for a while for it seems only moments ago that I searched the darkness for long-lost faces and yet some considerable time seems to have passed. The attendants in my room have changed. Some have returned after having snatched a few hours' sleep. They settle themselves as comfortably as they can to continue their vigil.

I had many kindred spirits about me while I lived and ruled. They were the companions who helped me face what had to be faced in this world. Perhaps it is childish of me, but I can only hope they will discharge the same duty in the next. I long to die, yet I am afraid of what may await me when I do. A friendly face or two would ease the ordeal.

My eyes once again search the dark corners of my chamber. I peer at the shadows cast by the candles and into all the nooks and crannies, half longing, half terrified that I will see something or someone from the netherworld hovering there. Perhaps – because spirits have no corporeal form – they can shrink and hide at will, in places they could never occupy when alive. But my darting eyes uncover nothing. I search again, craning my neck and flicking my eyes from corner to crevice and back again.

'The queen seems to be searching for something.' Philadelphia is by my side, crouching by my cushion and grasping my hand tenderly. 'Yes, Your Majesty, what is it? What can I get for you? What will soothe you?'

But hers is not the face I wish to see, no, nor any in that room.

'Can we persuade you to go to your bed, good madam? And raise yourself from the cushions?' The Archbishop of Canterbury, John Whitgift, has come up beside Philadelphia and is once again exhorting me to take to my bed. But the mere thought of raising myself up, or of being lifted up (as is more likely) makes me feel vertiginous. I shake my head and stick my finger in my mouth. I feel safer on the ground. There is nowhere to fall from here.

'But you must be so uncomfortable, Your Majesty, and your bed is so warm and so soft.' Bishop Whitgift is persistent.

'Attendants wait outside at this very moment with a litter to carry you gently to your chamber. You have only to give the word, Your Grace.' Robert Cecil is now standing by the archbishop's side, and the two of them nod encouragingly at me, as they might at a demented child.

I groan and close my eyes against them all; their warm blood, beating hearts and moist breath that smells so pungently of life. Their vigour exhausts me and I let my mind float freely again to drift once more from the present to the past.

Frances of Essex was absent from my court for some time and so was her recalcitrant spouse, but I thought little about either of them for months. It was not a case of out of sight, out of mind, although that did no harm. It was simply because all my attention was focused on something that mattered far more: the precarious health of my oldest friend and wisest counsellor, the man who guided me from precocious schoolgirl to wise queen, had suddenly taken a turn for the worse.

'I have brought you the finest roses from my garden, my lord, and I cut them with my own hands. I chose the ones with the sweetest scents. Here, breathe in the perfume. Perhaps the fragrance will help drive out the foul humours that beset you.'

I knew William Cecil was fond of flowers. It was not something he ever boasted of, but I saw the pleasure the blooms in my gardens gave him and the knowledge he had of them. Typically, he knew their common names and their Latin ones as well. As always, no knowledge was too low to be of value. However, I did not give him sweet-smelling flowers merely for his pleasure. I hoped that they would do him good by chasing away the noxious odours that infest those who are ailing. The apothecaries tell us that bad smells both cause and exacerbate illness. I have always avoided them.

I bent over Cecil's sickbed and held the bouquet under his nose. He did as he was bid and took a deep breath, drawing in the sweet fragrance. Unfortunately, this brought on a bout of coughing that turned his gentle old face puce and left him gasping for breath. Mildred, who was seated beside him, leapt up from her sewing and took the flowers from my hand.

'I will put them in water, Your Grace.'

She left the room and I turned apologetically to my old friend. 'I am sorry, I did not mean to make you more uncomfortable.'

'It is of no moment. I know you meant only kindness. I well remember how much you hate foul odours.'

And then my old friend chuckled, bringing up yet more noxious phlegm. A maid held a bowl up to him and he rid himself of the sputum. I looked away. The business of dying is rotten. I waited until the maid had resettled him on his pillows before I turned my face towards him once more. I wanted to do what little I could to maintain his dignity, so I pretended I had not noticed his misery and took up the conversation where it had left off.

'Aye, and I also well remember how you would use

my dislike of nasty smells to keep me away from things you did not wish me to see. Wasn't there a letter from Scottish James that you pretended was infected with noxious odours from the urine-tanned pouch in which it was carried?'

Cecil chuckled a second time. Indeed, despite his obvious sickness, he seemed oddly calm and relaxed. As if his spirit and his marvellous mind floated above his frail and suffering body.

'Indeed, there was and there were many more besides. I hope you will forgive me for the liberties I occasionally took on your behalf.'

I was seated on a stool by his bedside and I leant in closely and spoke low. 'Forgive? Forgive, my lord? There is nothing for me to forgive. Of all who have laboured beside me, it is you who have done me the most good and the least harm.'

The old man's eyes filled with tears at my words and yet, even as I spoke them, the ghost of Mary, Queen of Scots flitted through my mind. For a moment it seemed she stood between us, but I brushed her aside.

'It is I who should ask for your forgiveness, for all the long hours I made you labour, for the times I swore at you and ignored your wise counsel. I led you a merry dance, I fear.'

'It has been my pleasure to serve the wisest and most gracious lady in all Christendom. I would not have missed a moment of it.'

Now it was my turn to feel tearful. 'But you speak as if our work together has ended! You will recover from your illness – you have done so many times before – and will soon be back at your old desk, by my side.'

'I think not. My dance is nearly done.' His voice was weak and his old eyes were bleary. I knew that he spoke only the truth, but I did not wish to face the burdens of my office without him. The tears began to spill from my eyes and over my cheeks. I was glad that Cecil had closed his in weariness, so he would not see them.

Behind me I heard the door open and turned to see Mildred, Lady Burleigh, enter the room. She carried a tray on which sat the roses I had brought and a large and steaming bowl of broth. She placed the roses on a chest under the open window so that the summer air that entered the chamber would be sweetened by their perfume. Then she and the maid lifted Cecil up on his pillows and placed the tray on the counterpane.

'My love,' she said in a voice so gentle my tears would not stop. 'Will you try to take a little broth? Cook has laboured all morning to make the clearest, most healthful and delicious beef broth – from the very finest cuts – to try and tempt your appetite. Will you not see if you can stomach a little?'

Cecil was like a small child, eager to please. He took the spoon in his stiff fingers and attempted to guide a little liquid from the bowl to his mouth. So unsteady was his grip that most of it fell upon the counterpane.

But Mildred did not notice. A manservant had taken her attention.

'My lady, the apothecary is below. He wishes to have a quick word.'

'You go, Mildred. I will be here with William.'

Mildred nodded gratefully. 'Thank you, Your Grace. He comes with a new physic and instructions on how it must be administered for best effect. I like to hear the details myself.'

Cecil pulled a face at the mention of the medicine. 'Disgusting muck, all of it. It does no good. It makes me cough.'

'The apothecary says it's good to cough. You must rid yourself of the ill humours in the phlegm.'

'Hush, William. You must comply with everything the doctors tell you to do. Both Mildred and I want you well again soon.'

Mildred curtsied briefly and left the room. I could see that she was worn out with nursing her husband, not to mention worrying about him. Once she had left, I turned back to my ailing friend. He had slipped further down the pillows and had deposited another spoonful of broth on his bedclothes. I could see the liquid glistening in his whiskers, and the little he had consumed – like the dreaded physic – made him cough. He put the spoon back on the tray in defeat and his head sank back into his pillows. But I was having none of it. If the man was to live, he had to eat.

I bent towards him and lifted his head from the pillows. A servant leapt forward to take up the burden, but I waved him away. My intervention even startled Cecil. 'Oh no, Your Majesty, it is … too much. It is not—'

'Do not fuss, Cecil. It is the least I can do.'

Using my left arm as a bolster, I took up the spoon in my right and gently fed him small sips of the gruel as a fond mother might her child. All the while, unseen by my old friend, tears fell from my eyes, and rolled down my cheeks to mingle with the beef broth on the counterpane. Cecil was too exhausted to fight me. He opened his mouth to accept the nourishment like a wizened old bird.

'There now, my Spirit, we will have you back in the saddle in no time.' I used my old nickname for him.

'I was never very happy in the saddle, Your Majesty.' His voice was barely a whisper, but his wry comment cheered me.

I laughed. 'Aye, but you could master a ledger like no other, and use that to hunt down the wiliest of foxes—' I stopped speaking, suddenly conscious that I was already referring to the old man in the past tense. Not that it mattered. He had fallen asleep with his mouth open and was snoring gently in my arms. I lowered his head back onto the pillows, settled the bowl of broth and the tray onto the table beside his bed and then I gave vent to my grief. I lay my head on the damp, soup-stained counterpane and sobbed.

William Cecil, first Baron Burleigh and Lord High Treasurer of England, died a few days later. It was a grief-stricken Robert who gave me the news. 'My mother has sent me to tell you, Your Grace, that Lord Burleigh – my father …'

Robert Cecil, my secretary of state, normally so cool and emotionless under pressure, could not continue speaking. I also stayed silent, watching his jaw and his cheeks working as he struggled to regain his composure.

'Your father has died, my lord? Is that what your mother sent you to say?' I spoke gently to him. For the moment his grief seemed more intense than mine. Indeed, it was so great, he still could not trust himself to speak and he merely nodded his head.

'How does your mother?'

My question brought the man completely undone and he sobbed uncontrollably.

'Fetch Master Cecil some wine, sirrah.'

And wine was brought, and Robert Cecil gulped it down.

At last he could speak. 'My mother is a remarkable woman, Your Grace. She has cared for my father day and night these past few months. She is exhausted and the doctor has given her something to help her sleep.'

'I am glad. She needs to keep up her strength. You have been very fortunate in both your parents.'

'As my father was fortunate in his mistress, Your Grace.'

'I worked him long and hard, as I now do his son.'

'He loved you for it, as does his son.'

I patted the curve of his cheek as a mother might, and he blushed at my gesture, but he was still struggling with his tears and so kept his head down to hide his distress. We both stood in silence for a moment or two.

'Did he say anything at the end? Did he leave any message for me?' As I said the words, they seemed to catch in my throat. At the break in my voice Robert Cecil looked up.

'He told me you fed him his soup, with your own hands.'

'Aye. I did.'

'He said that although you would not be a mother you showed yourself to be a most careful nurse.'

This made me guffaw through my tears. William Cecil died as he had lived – he was always like a dog with a bone. No one had wanted me to marry and have children more than he. Partly for good and solid reasons of state, but, I think, especially as time went by, mostly because he had gained such peace and happiness from his own family and wanted me to have the same.

'He was ever a tenacious old man. Even at the end he could not let himself go without one last admonition of what he saw as my great and abiding failure.'

'Oh! I am sure he did not see it as a fail—'

'Yes, he did, and it is no use pretending otherwise. And from his perspective I can see that it was a lack.

Think how much easier his task would have been if I had provided what he felt it was my duty to provide – an heir to my throne. Think how much easier your task would be, my lord, if I had a son to inherit.'

'He did not say so.'

'Yes, he did, often to me. But what he did not grasp and maybe you do not either, is that from my perspective the birth of a son would have represented a very great threat.'

'Children are a blessing from God, and a great comfort to their parents.'

'I do not doubt they are to many parents, nor that you have been a very great blessing to yours – particularly now, as I am sure you will be a great comfort to your mother in her time of trouble. But, my lord, think of the Queen of Scots and tell me how much of a blessing the birth of her son turned out to be for her.'

Robert Cecil looked at me as if I were speaking in a language unknown to him.

'I see my words confuse you, but think on it. If the Queen of Scots had never been delivered of a fair son would her people have been so quick to be rid of her? Particularly if they could not guarantee who else might seize the day and take her throne?'

'The King of Scots was but a babbling infant when his mother lost her throne. He had nothing to do with her demise. That was of her own doing.'

'I do not deny that the Queen of Scots was no

friend to her own cause, nor that the infant son had no deliberate hand in the fall of the mother. It was rather just the fact of his existence that made her more vulnerable. The Scots had an alternative, you see, and it was an alternative that I refused to provide to the English.'

'None could ever desire an alternative to the greatest queen in all Christendom.' Robert Cecil was as brilliant in his own way as his father had been, but – just like his father – he could not see the point I was trying to make. I never met a man who could. It was beyond their gender's ken, it seemed, to imagine that the birth of a child, especially a son, could be anything but a blessing. I let the conversation move to more conventional topics.

We gave William Cecil, my Spirit, a state funeral. It seemed only fitting that such a faithful servant should have his passing so marked. It was a solemn and suitably magnificent occasion, but there was one sight that seared itself into my brain. As I scanned the ranks of the mourners in the great cathedral, one man sat head and shoulders above the rest. It was the Earl of Essex. Such was his height he could never hide in any crowd. I had not seen the young man for many months. What caught my eye was that his face was white and stained with grief. I recalled that Essex had been brought up in Cecil's household and that Cecil had always been fond of him.

Essex's obvious misery for the good old man softened my heart and within weeks he was back in my court and my favour.

It is a pity that the young man had not learnt more from the older one.

Nine

'God's death, my lord, it seems I am paying the Earl of Essex a thousand pounds a day to go on progress!'

I threw the latest letter from my erstwhile general in Ireland as hard as I could towards the blazing fire. As I had failed to screw it tightly enough into a ball, the air caught it and it floated gently to the floor unscathed. Still as angry as I can ever remember being, I stamped my foot upon the loathsome thing and ground it as hard as I could with my boot so that it was muddied and filthy.

'Indeed, it has been fully three months since the earl departed.'

'And he has still not engaged with the enemy! I did not send him to Ireland for his health! I sent him to teach that scoundrel Tyrone what fate awaits those who would rebel against the Queen of England. Instead, all they have learnt is that my army will leave them alone to do as they wish, while my general rides about the countryside hunting deer with his new master of horse!'

I had stepped off the Earl of Essex's latest report in my agitation and was now pacing up and down the chamber. Robert Cecil took the opportunity to kneel and pick up the dirty parchment. He began to try and smooth it out so that it would once again be readable. I was pleased to see the heels of my boots had ripped a number of holes in it.

'May I read the report, Your Grace?'

'Read it at your leisure. You will find that it says nothing to give you any satisfaction. I want him recalled, and a more reliable man sent in his place.'

'Of course, but that will take some time. Perhaps we should give the earl one last chance to tackle the Irish rebels. He has the loyalty of his men and they will not take kindly to his replacement.'

'He must ride towards the enemy today – this instant, this second! I cannot allow my treasury to bleed money for no result. I cannot allow the Earl of Tyrone to get away with treason and insurrection any longer. Essex wrote and said he could not proceed until he had two thousand more men, and we sent them and more besides, but still he does nothing. Instead he whines that he now does not have enough food to feed the extra soldiers. God's death, did he not anticipate that two thousand more mouths to feed would require extra victuals! Is he a fool as well as a knave?'

'I will write him to that effect.'

'No, my lord, I will write to him myself.' I picked up my pen and snapped my fingers. Paper was brought.

'Let him tremble at my words. He presumes too much on my good opinion. He will find out soon enough that my continued favour depends on actions, not on honeyed words!'

I poured my fury and my scorn onto the paper, writing out my frustration at the Earl of Essex's insurrection, his incompetence and his arrogance. I listed all his equivocations. In the end, I could not resist a final blast from my pen about the myriad of excuses he had used to explain his complete lack of action, most of which had involved the weather. It seemed it was always either too hot, too cold, too wet or too dry to make war in Ireland.

'Surely we must conclude that none of the four quarters of the year will be in season for you.'

Perhaps this last finally convinced Essex that I meant what I said, because after receiving my letter, he finally set out to tackle the man I had sent him to fight. Or so I thought.

What compounded my fury was that the Earl of Essex had persuaded me to make him my general in Ireland against my better judgment. I had excluded him from my court for months following his public fit of temper. While I did not really believe that he had seriously meant to do me physical harm when he put his hand on his scabbard in my presence, I had not forgotten his lapse. No, nor his insult. I was aware that it was my sex that made it easier for him to disregard his sovereign's commands and that he grew braver the further away from my – what did he call them, petticoats? – he became. He was adept at flattering me, but he did not respect me.

Once, his spontaneity had been endearing. In his swagger he was like a small boy, charming in his transparency. For someone who was surrounded by the mask of diplomacy, such unguardedness was like a cold drink of water after a lifetime of hot milk. It cleared my head and refreshed me.

Now I was becoming wary of the very thing that had originally attracted me. I dreaded where his impetuous nature might lead.

Nevertheless, seeing Essex so grief-stricken at Cecil's funeral had softened my heart towards him. When next he attempted to gain my favour I allowed my guard to drop. God forgive me, I allowed myself to be amused, even flattered, by his persistence. As he tried to minimise his sin, he swivelled from charm to petulance, from argument to flattery. The dizzying array of his mercurial feelings was disarming. And he reminded me so much of my beloved cousin. His blue eyes were like hers and the auburn tinge to his hair. His cheek and his charm reminded me of Catherine, when she was young and full of life. He made me laugh as she had done.

*

'Why so gloomy, Elizabeth?' Catherine and I were together at Hatfield. It was during the reign of my brother, when we were both young and carefree. She was engaged to Francis Knollys, but not yet married to him. I was third in line to the throne and of little importance to anyone, so we were mostly left to our own devices.

'I am sick of the rain. I am bored with being trapped inside.'

'What?' She spoke with exaggerated surprise, delighted to have the opportunity to tease me. 'You have become tired of reading great tomes in Latin? Or of translating from the Spanish into Greek or the Greek into Hottentot?'

'I don't speak Hottentot, silly.'

'There remains a language you do not speak or read? We must correct this oversight immediately. Quick, sirrah …' And she clapped her hands imperiously for an attendant. 'Fetch the best teacher of Hottentot in the kingdom and send him to the Lady Elizabeth!'

The man's face as he looked at my cousin was so comically bemused we both burst out laughing, which only made his confusion worse.

'It is all right, my good fellow,' I said soothingly, taking pity upon him. 'Mistress Carey is teasing me. We do not need any teacher. You may go about your usual business.' The relief on his face was also comical and again we found ourselves in gales of laughter, fortunately after the poor man had left the room.

'Hottentot! You are ridiculous, Catherine.'

But her silliness had done its work and my melancholy had passed.

Her grandson was not much disposed to be silly, he was far too careful of his dignity for that, but he was theatrical, as she had been, and broke through the stuffiness of being with a queen, just as she had done. And I so longed to drop the mantle of monarchy sometimes ...

The earl's determination to return to my favour flattered me and I gave in. Despite my misgivings and those of many around me, I let him return.

No sooner did he feel himself once again safe in my estimation than he began pressing me to let him command the army I was planning to send to fight the rebel Tyrone in Ireland. I was reluctant, very reluctant, to give him the position. I had wanted to send William Knollys or Baron Mountjoy to fight the Irish, but Essex was determined to have the appointment and went into a terrific sulk. He believed I owed it to him as a reward for his remorse. After all, our quarrel had been over the appointment of Knollys as Lord Lieutenant in the first place. Perhaps his unpredictable flashes of temper had fulfilled their purpose. I did not want to face another tantrum. Worse, when the earl's mood darkened, all his charm disappeared. I reassured myself that he had proven himself as a soldier many times over in my service and that he was a man of action and so the decision was a good one. Moreover, he would be in Ireland and could pose no threat to me from there.

'They have done what, my lord?' I was standing with my back towards Cecil, leaning forward, resting my weight on my hands, which, in their turn, rested heavily on my writing table. I looked down at the coronation ring I always wore on my finger, the one that contained the picture of my mother. I looked up at the tapestry in front of me. It was my old favourite of the women engineers, architects and joiners building the stout wall around the City of the Ladies. Would that I could have found a woman general to lead my troops! Not even the most hysterical female could have led me on as much of a dance as my Lord Essex.

In contrast to the last time Cecil and I had spoken about the debacle in Ireland, my voice was low and steady. I had passed from a hot fury into a cold and deadly contempt.

'The Earl of Essex and the Earl of Tyrone have made parly on the banks of the River Lagan, Your Grace, and have come to terms.'

'Have they indeed?' And with this I turned to face my advisor. He was, as always, in the enveloping black robes of the puritan, his small face made even smaller by the volume of the white starched ruff that surrounded it. Now my back leant against the desk, my fingers behind me on its edge. I could feel a small nick in the wood and rubbed my thumb against it as we spoke.

'Aye, madam, they have arranged a truce.'

'So, Robert Devereux and Hugh O'Neill have decided what the fate of their two kingdoms shall be. How noble of them. And tell me, my Pygmy' – (I am afraid once again I gave undue emphasis to the nickname he so disliked the better to make my point) – 'what terms have they come to?'

'It is a truce very favourable to the Earl of Tyrone.'

'I see. Please, my lord, perhaps you can answer this question for me?' Poor Cecil, he had done nothing wrong, but such was the venom in my voice he could not help shrinking away from me just a little. I stuck my fingernail into the groove in the wood and dug at it.

'I will do my best.'

'If I had simply intended to give Ireland to the Earl of Tyrone, what need did I have to send the Earl of Essex there? Not to mention an army? What need did I have to lavish funds from my treasury upon an expedition that would do no more than leave things as they are?'

By this time, I was speaking to Cecil through gritted teeth, spitting each word out as if I was just resisting the temptation to sink my teeth into something or someone and draw blood.

Cecil, understandably, took another small step backwards. 'You make a very reasonable point.'

'They have not shot a bullet in anger?'

'No, Your Grace.'

'Nor fired an arrow – except at deer?'

'No, Your Grace.'

'Nor raised a sword, pike or hatchet?'

Cecil took another small step away from me. I stood silently, no longer leaning my weight against the table. It came to me suddenly that I hated the Earl of Essex. The strength of my feeling frightened me.

'The Earl of Essex asks to return to court, now that his mission is accomplished.'

'His mission is accomplished? It has not even begun! Command the earl to remain at his post and continue to prosecute his commission, which is to defeat and destroy Tyrone and his rebels, not come to terms with them.'

'He will object to breaking the truce.'

'And what is that to me? He had no right to make any truce and I am under no obligation to abide by it. He is my general. I am his queen – petticoats or no!' I turned my back on Cecil. I looked down at the desk. I had dug a great splinter of wood from its carved edge with my fingernail.

This time I would not be placated. This time there would be no return to my favour. The scales had finally fallen from my foolish, sentimental eyes. The earl was not his grandmother. He was not his stepfather. He had not one whit of their intelligence, maturity, humility or – and this was the greatest deficiency of all – loyalty.

'Tell the earl to fight, my lord, or else he must answer to me.'

The earl did not listen. When did he ever listen?

It was scarce ten o'clock in the morning and I was seated at my dressing table, my wig rested on its stand in front of me and my cropped grey hair, unbrushed and unkempt, was in disarray. Suddenly I heard scuffling outside my door. My attendants and I turned as one to the source of this sound. Then, before we had a chance to register what was happening, the door burst open and a filthy, sweating Earl of Essex flung himself into the room. My hairdresser just had time to step out of the way before the man launched himself at me. I recoiled, terrified, but the earl merely fell to his knees and grasped my hands, covering them with kisses.

His face and clothes were marked with splashes of Thames mud. Such was his haste that he had not even attempted to wipe the muck from his person before he hurried to the Presence Chamber, and, when I was not there, on to the Privy Chamber and from thence, without permission and despite the efforts of my guards, into my bedchamber.

Breathing heavily, he remained at my feet with his head bowed. This gave me a moment to compose myself. When he hurled himself into my presence my first response was blind panic. The earl headed my army, and people never ceased to tell me how beloved he was by his men. My first terrified thought was about who would follow the earl into my most private chamber. Did he bring with him armed men who meant to have my throne out from under me? Or, did he mean to keep me on my throne, but as a figurehead only, forced to do his bidding at gunpoint? I knew better than anyone how impetuous and arrogant he was.

I was profoundly afraid, but I knew this was not the time to try to impose my authority. Instead, I put my hand on his auburn curls and stroked them, with every appearance of affection. The pungent odour of the Thames assailed my nostrils, but I did not recoil again. I knew I needed to buy time. My ladies had stepped back from us in horror. But, as the seconds passed, it became clear that there was no army outside my door and I relaxed slightly. The earl was here at Nonesuch instead of there in Ireland, that was clear enough, but it seemed he was in my palace with only a few lieutenants at his back. This was not, it seemed, a full-scale rebellion. I saw my own guards appear at the door and their presence calmed me, but the earl was armed, and he had already shown how little control he had when he was in the grip of fierce emotion. I had to tread carefully. 'My Lord Essex, how is it that you are here and not in Ireland?'

'I knew that I had to come and put my case to you in person.'

'Yet I did order you to stay?' This I said gently, tentatively. Not for a moment did I want to upset this man. He lifted his face and I could see tears glistening in his eyes. His face (it still hurts me to remember this) was shining with hope.

'Aye, you did, and I apologise for my disobedience, but when you hear why I have come, you will understand. I knew from your letters that my enemies were filling your ears with lies and I knew that I had to come and put my case in person.'

'Indeed, I would like nothing better than to hear your explanation. You and I have always been good friends, have we not? It seems a shame to let misunderstanding come between us.'

I could see the relief on his face. I almost felt sorry for him despite my fright. He was so easy to read and so fatally easy to convince. I have observed this in many men with a high regard for themselves – what they wish to be true they easily believe.

'You see, my lords ...' He had turned towards the equally travel-stained men who accompanied him. I recognised Sir Christopher St Lawrence. 'I told you that once I talked to the queen in person' – still holding my hands, he turned back to me – 'this great queen, this Gloriana' – he kissed my hands again – 'would understand everything and, as you see, she does!'

I listened to the earl with a smile upon my lips, but I grasped the opportunity to get him out of my chamber.

'But, my lord, as you may also see, I am in no fit state to receive you or to hear your news. You must withdraw now and leave me to my toilette. Indeed, good gentlemen' – I turned now to his attendants, who were also on their knees – 'allow me to have hot water brought and clean linens so that you can wash the dust of your journey from your persons, and then we can meet and talk at our leisure. You can tell me your story, then, my Lord Essex.' Gently, I extricated my hands from his grip. 'Without assaulting my nostrils.'

They laughed, and the tension was broken. As they left the chamber I heard Essex speak to his companions. 'I thank God that although I have suffered many storms and much trouble abroad, I have found sweet calm at home.'

Foolish, heedless little man. He was not at home, not in my presence, not ever again.

'You have disobeyed my command.'

'Yes, Your Majesty, I know, but I had no—'

I held up my hand to silence him, but it was with great difficulty that the Earl of Essex held his tongue. Many hours had passed since he burst into my bedchamber. He and his companions had washed and changed their clothes as I instructed them, then I made them cool their heels. I worked at my desk with Robert Cecil as I did every day. I had dined with selected members of my court as was also my habit. We had not hurried our meal or curtailed our pleasure at the amusements provided by my fool and my musicians. Food had been provided to the earl and his friends, but they had not been invited to join me at my table.

I was quite calm as I went about my day. Previously when the earl disobeyed me or behaved badly, I had felt torn between fury and pity. Now I felt neither – just a clarity that I had not experienced before.

This friendship was destructive. It was at an end.

I performed my duties with particular care. I pointedly did not make mention of the unusual start to my day. If any of my attendants attempted to do so, I silenced them and, recognising my seriousness, they obeyed. My tactics and my silence were deliberate. I wanted the earl to come into my presence unsettled and uneasy. I was determined to control this interview. I was sick of him appearing unannounced and uninvited. He took advantage by being unpredictable; I would counter it by being slow and deliberate.

After we had eaten every course of my leisurely meal, including the fruit and sweetmeats, I finally allowed the earl to enter my presence. The remains of our repast were scattered across the table. The message about whose side I was on could not have been any clearer.

The earl opened his mouth as if to speak, but I held up my hand. Somewhat to my surprise, it worked. It seemed that for once I had him on the back foot. 'Now is not the time to explain yourself to me.' With a sweep of my hand, I took in the members of my council with whom I had just shared a meal. To a man they were leaning back in their chairs, looking not only sated, but as if they were enjoying the spectacle unfolding before them.

'Given the nature of your offence, we have decided it is only reasonable that you must explain your actions to the Lords of the Council.'

'But – they are my enemies, Your Grace! The very men who have caused all these misunderstandings between us.'

'I didn't see any of us force your hand onto your scabbard.' Charles Howard muttered the words *sotto voce*, but he meant them to be heard and they were.

The earl flushed, but I ignored the remark entirely. 'They are *my* council, my lord. They do *my* bidding.'

Now, the earl went white. 'But, if you will just allow me to explain—'

'There is little to explain, my lord. You insisted on the commission, I gave it to you and – despite everything – you have failed to carry it out. You had men, supplies, money, everything you asked for, but you failed. Without my say-so, you made parley with the enemy and I am still unclear about the terms of the pact you made in my name. All these require detailed explanations, my lord, and many witnesses.'

'There were problems with the terrain, Your Grace, with the people, with the weather – oh!' Now, as the shock wore off, he began – fatally – to lose his temper. 'You cannot be expected to understand. You have never been to war.'

'Nor have you, sir – in Ireland, at least.' I could not resist flashing back at him, but then I regained my cold, detached demeanour. I did not wish to trade words with him. Indeed, his disrespect had provided an opportunity. 'But perhaps you are right. What would I, a woman, know about leading an army? No doubt that is why you will be better served explaining yourself to the Lords of the Council, who have more experience in these things than a king – how did you put it? – "in petticoats". The Privy Council is meeting at this moment and has already officially opened its preliminary investigation. You will be heard by them, my lord, and not by me.'

With that I nodded to my factotum, who politely but firmly ushered the earl out of the room. He went without protest. The wind seemed to have gone out of him. It was the last time I ever saw him.

The lords confined him to his chambers that evening and the next day he was placed under house arrest at his London residence. He was to remain within the confines of York House until I decided what was to be done with him. Daily he beseeched me to allow him to come into my presence and explain himself. Daily I refused his requests. This continued for weeks. Lord Egerton – the man charged with keeping the earl within – told me that in his frustration and the agony of inactivity and uncertainty, Essex had made himself quite ill. He tried to use his sickness to appeal to my sympathy, but I would not be moved.

The only person who was able to win a little clemency was his wife, Frances. She came to me (or was sent by her desperate husband) almost straight from childbed, dressed all in black. She looked pale and tired and I could not help but notice that, despite her relative youth, her hair was going quite grey.

'Are you well enough to be out and about, dear Frances?' I stepped forward and kissed her on the cheek. I even tucked her arm into mine and led her to two chairs by the fire. I did not blame the wife for the husband's folly, and I wanted her to tell him of my kind treatment. I wanted him to know that my displeasure was personal as well as politic. The countess and I were to converse together comfortably, without the barrier of pomp and circumstance. I gestured for her to sit. 'You must not stand for too long and wear yourself out.'

'I am quite well, Your Majesty, and I am the lighter of a fair girl. We are calling her Frances.'

'Congratulations. I am glad that her name honours your dear father as well as yourself, but I am also sorry that the child has been born into such difficult circumstances.'

'Will you not take pity upon her father for the love you once bore him? Or, if not that, the love you bear me or, perhaps, for love of my father?'

'Oh, Frances, I do not think Walsingham would ever have counselled me to do as you have just asked. Your father was a stickler for the rules. It is both noble and right of you to come and plead on your husband's behalf – but be specific. In what way should I take pity?

I will not free him from house arrest or allow him to return to my court, if that is what you are asking.'

'It is certainly what he is hoping for but I would not be so bold as to meddle in such affairs of state.'

'That in itself is a rarity. There are many who feel no such reluctance. What can I do for you then? And, remember, it is to you that I am happy to grant favours, not your husband.'

'May I visit him? I have been forbidden access to York House and I would see him if I could and present to him his new daughter.'

'I am glad you have had a daughter. Sons seem to cause no end of trouble – particularly to their mothers.'

When Essex was riding high in my favour, when his mercurial energy enlivened my dreary, duty-bound days and I made no secret of the pleasure his company gave me, I knew what the court said of my attachment. They believed me to be in love with the earl and laughed behind their hands at the spectacle of the old queen making a fool of herself over the young man. But they were mistaken. I was not in love with the Earl of Essex. My flesh did not burn with desire when he touched me. I did not imagine his arms about me, or his lips upon mine as I had once imagined those of his stepfather, Robin Dudley. No, I felt about the Earl of Essex the way a mother might about an impetuous and energetic son. I say again, I loved the young earl more for his stepfather and for his grandmother than for himself.

I indulged him in their memory. I enjoyed spoiling him. It gave me pleasure. That was why I did it, but I was wrong. It ruined him, and I must bear the guilt for that.

Perhaps it would have been better if I had loved him the way a woman loves a man. Husbands of queens are trouble enough, but sons of queens cause their mothers nothing but heartache and, too often, deadly danger.

'I hope the earl has the wit to delight in his daughter. I have never understood the desire for sons over daughters. As I say, the one causes so much more trouble than the other.'

My preference for daughters was not a common one and I could see Frances was puzzled by the turn our conversation had taken.

'Daughters are lovely, but my sons are also a great joy to me. They yearn to see their father as well. May we visit him? You know my loyalty to you and need have no fears on that account.'

I smiled and shook my head. 'No, I have no fears. Loyalty to your father's memory will keep you loyal to me – not to mention your own good sense. Of course, you may visit your husband. Every day, if you are so minded, but you may not reside at York House with him.'

'You are very good, Your Majesty, and I am grateful.'

'I do this for you, Frances, and not for him. Make sure you tell him that.'

*

They tell me that when I banish a person from my presence it is as if the world has turned into night. I remember that feeling from my childhood when I was in disfavour with my own father, and later when I trembled beneath the ire of my sister. Essex had grown accustomed to basking in the full warmth of royal good opinion, albeit intermittently, and he did not know what to do with himself now that a chill had descended. Despite the comfort of his wife's presence (and, after our interview, she visited him daily, from dawn to dusk), he sickened further and took to his bed, declaring himself to be at death's door. The people of London heard of his plight and, because they loved him, they became restive. They loved him for the same reasons I had. They believed his publicity. They liked how handsome and vigorous he was, and they revered his few, but very skilfully publicised, triumphs over the Spaniards. He was young, he was handsome, he made a change from the old queen who had been around so long that they took her for granted. This was, no doubt, another reason why I now regarded the earl with such suspicion. No monarch can ever take kindly to a member of their court, whether actual or surrogate son, who threatens to transcend their own popularity.

'There are slogans supporting the Earl of Essex and decrying his enemies daubed on walls throughout the city, Your Grace. Indeed, there is one insulting me on the very walls of Whitehall.' Robert Cecil was not his usual calm self. Two spots of colour rode high on his cheeks.

'I hope you have ordered the offending words removed.'

'I have indeed, and they are being scrubbed off as we speak.'

'I am pleased to hear it. Issue a proclamation that those who insult my ministers also insult me.'

'It is not the rude words about my own person that I find upsetting.'

'No?'

'No. It is what they indicate about the mood in the city and the risk that entails.'

'You smell rebellion? Is it as bad as that?'

'My Lord Essex is popular, and the people do not like to see him in disgrace. Now that word is out that he is dying, what was once muttered behind closed doors may soon be shouted in the streets.'

'And Essex will know this, of course.'

'Aye and will be emboldened by it. He has always revelled in his popularity with the people.'

'I know how heady that can be. It is one of the great joys of my reign that I have held the people's loyalty. Does my popularity fall as his rises?'

'Your name is not daubed on any walls, Your Majesty.'

'I should hope not!'

'But there is much talk about a particular book.'

'A book, Cecil? What book?'

'A history of Henry VI, which links the Devereuxs with the Plantaganets.'

Ice crawled through my veins. This was real danger. It was the old curse that had haunted all the Tudors. Everyone knew that our connection to the blood of kings was tenuous and weak, though few dared speak of it.

My claim to the throne of England is still seen by some, particularly zealous Catholics and my foes abroad, as the weakest of all. If you did not accept my father's repudiation of his first wife and so the legality of his marriage to his second, then I was a bastard, born while his first wife was still alive. That is why, whenever anyone spoke of ancient blood lines, of claims to the throne that were at least as good as mine, it touched my deepest ancestral fear. Only now, as I lie upon my deathbed (or recline upon cushions) can I let that old anxiety go. It seems I will die as I lived – as God's anointed queen.

The Earl of Essex was not my son, but it seemed some may still have seen him as my successor or, worse, replacement. I stood up from my chair and walked towards Cecil, lowering my voice so no one else in the room could hear what we said.

'When Essex talked terms with Tyrone do we know everything that was said? Did we have someone present whose loyalty to me was beyond question?'

'No. The earl was careful to take to the parley only those men loyal to him.'

'Damn that man! He was supposed to do my bidding. This is what comes of going against my better judgment. I wonder what else the Irish traitor and my supposed general talked about on the banks of that accursed river?'

'There have been rumours.'

'Rumours of what?'

'That they agreed to make the Earl of Tyrone King of Ireland and in return the Irish would help make the Earl of Essex King of England.'

I clenched my fists but held my nerve. 'As you say, Cecil, these are but rumours. Despite his hot-headedness, I do not believe Essex plans actual treason.'

'Do not forget his vaunting ambition and his vanity.'

'I forget nothing, Cecil. I never have.'

She never told her love, but let concealment, like a worm i' th' bud, feed on her damask cheek. She pined in thought; and, with a green and yellow melancholy, she sat like Patience on a monument, smiling at grief. Was not this love indeed? We men may say more, swear more; but indeed our shows are more than will; for we still prove much in our vows but little in our love.
Cesario (Viola in disguise)

My court sat transfixed as we watched Master Shakespeare's latest play on St Stephen's Day. Suitably enough it was called *Twelfth Night.* All the usual *sotto voce* jokes and witticisms that often interrupted court amusements – setting off gales of inappropriate laughter – were forgotten. At these words, spoken by a character pretending to be a boy who is really a girl in disguise but is, of course, played by a boy actor, the silence was eloquent. I wondered how a man with the *braggadocio* and swagger of Shakespeare could find within him the sympathy and understanding of my poor sex to read us so accurately. We too easily believe the promises made to us by men because we have no other choice.

Beside me the Count Palatine – in whose honour the play was produced – looked nonplussed. Lord Grey, who sat on his other side, and I had been translating Shakespeare's words in whispers, so our foreign guest could better follow the action. Now I stayed silent, my chin resting on my hand, leaving Grey to do the honours.

The scene in front of me had moved on and now the audience were in gales of laughter at some tomfoolery on the stage. Master Shakespeare had an uncanny talent for changing moods quickly and smoothly, but it seemed I was not so skilled. I was caught by the image of Patience on a monument, smiling at grief and unable to speak her heart. Was this not my predicament exactly? Viola claimed it as the state of all women, condemned to feel more than we are able to express, while men expressed more than they actually felt. This summed up my dance with the Earl of Essex entirely. He protested his adoration at every opportunity, he flattered me outrageously and gave me constant and gratifying attention. And yet, as it now seemed utterly clear to me, he meant not one word of it. He loved me when it suited his purposes. It was a love of convenience and could be switched off as easily as it was switched on. He used the same strategy on me as he did when attempting to part one of my ladies from her maidenhead, and I had fallen for it just as foolishly. The shock of the realisation made me draw a sharp breath.

I looked up from the orange I had been slicing into segments and surveyed the court surrounding me. I knew every man and woman. I knew their parents, their children, their allegiances and their religion. I knew their strengths and their weaknesses. I knew who was clever and who was stupid. They all professed their love for me – and their undying loyalty – but I knew that should I be whisked from that room in an instant – by apoplexy, perhaps, or by men with swords – they would make haste to curry favour with whoever it was who replaced me. Then they would swear the same oaths and compose the same compliments. They would express what they did not really feel. I was Patience on a monument. I had been always.

I looked down again at the hand that still held a segment of orange. I had removed my gloves (I wore them almost permanently now) so that they would not be stained by the juice. My hand was old. The flesh between the thumb and forefinger was eaten away by age and arthritis. The fingers themselves, that once I had been so proud of, were bent with rheumatics, the joints swollen and stiff. I had spots on the back of my hand, and my fingernails, buffed and filed to perfection as they were daily by my ladies, looked like the talons of an old buzzard. I would die soon, of that I was certain, maybe not this year or the next, but soon and when I did, these same laughing men and women would turn their backs on the setting sun and swear undying love to the rising one.

Eleven

January passed, then February, March and April and still I did not send for Essex. Such was his desperation, he began to get others to argue his case. His sister, Lady Rich, sent me a foolish appeal begging me to think better of my behaviour. She insulted me by trying to flatter me into changing my mind. My reply was to confine her to her house until further notice. I was not some giddy girl or (worse) some delusional old woman, whose head could be turned by a surfeit of false praise. Not any longer. Essex and his party still had not realised how deadly serious this business had become.

In May I moved him to his own house, but he remained confined within its perimeters. Those whose job it was to tell me such things (indeed, until recently, they had worked for the very man they now reported on) kept me intimately acquainted with the earl and his moods. His physical health had improved, and he had risen from his bed, but his anguish increased with every passing day. I knew this and yet I felt no pity. My anger at this arrogant young man had become immovable.

I might have forgiven him for his military failure. Perhaps I could have softened in the face of his petulance and immaturity. What I could not forgive, however, was my sense that he had contemplated betraying me with Tyrone. Worse, I was suddenly aware that, despite his protestations, he did not feel loyalty to his queen and never had. He thought he could rule me through flattery and I had an uncomfortable sense that he had joked about his power over me with his cronies. I had seen the way he turned in triumph to the men who followed him from Ireland all the way to my bedchamber. I had seen how he boasted to them when I appeared to listen to his appeals. I had seen his certainty and I did not like it. I could forgive weakness, foolishness and vanity. I could not forgive contempt.

Maybe I could even have tolerated his disloyalty if it were not for his popularity with the common people of England and, chillingly, with my soldiers. Now that Essex could no longer control me through flattery he might seek to take power by other means.

The events I am relating happened only a few years ago, yet at that time I still felt as if the future stretched out before me. I knew I was ageing, but I still felt vigorous and in control. I was not ready to give my throne to anyone. I still refused to name an official heir.

Now, it feels as if the events I am relating happened to someone else.

As my mind wanders through the corridors of my past, a movement in the corner of the room brings me back once again to the present. I open my eyes. A messenger has entered, and the noise he makes shatters the hush that now surrounds me. I know what news he brings. As the old queen is dying, preparations must be made for the new regime. The messenger is a harbinger of a future that does not include me. Despite all its difficulties, betrayals and danger, I find I prefer the past, both because I was very much a part of it and because it is over. Whether for good or ill, I know how it turned out. What lies ahead of me is utterly unknown.

I close my eyes in hope of returning to the safety of what has gone before, but my moment of consciousness has alerted me to the sufferings of my mortal body. My back aches on this cushion and I must adjust my weight to relieve it. As I shift, I again open my eyes and my attendants look at me in their turn. I do not acknowledge them, and the moment passes. I find a more comfortable position and close my eyes once more. I shift the finger that has been in my mouth all this time and drool escapes from my lips. I care not, because what happens now matters not at all.

Essex wrote me a letter, a sulky, self-pitying letter which showed that his long exile had taught him nothing.

'Your Majesty that hath mercy for all the world but me ...' I could hear his voice and see his pout as I read the words. 'Your Majesty! I say that in the eighth month of my close confinement ...'

Eight months! Had it really been as long as that? I felt a small thrill of satisfaction. The balance of our relationship had so altered that I now held all the cards and he none. It was his undoing that, for all his fine words, he saw me as a silly old woman who had succumbed to his charms and had forgotten I was his queen. Not just any queen, either, but a monarch of more than four decades of experience who, like Patience on her monument, was well practised at keeping her emotions in check and knew when to be indulgent and when to strike. He had not realised that he had a tiger by the tail. By the tone of his letter, he still did not.

'... the eighth month of my close confinement as if you thought mine infirmities, beggary and infamy too little punishment. You have rejected my letters and refused to hear of me, which to traitors you never did.'

Where once he had the unique ability to say exactly what I wanted to hear, now he did the opposite. I looked up from his angry and petulant scrawl and saw that Robert Cecil was watching me anxiously from the other side of the room.

'He has learnt no humility. He still thinks he can bludgeon me into submission.'

'He is a man of very particular character, Your Grace. He has been so since he was a child.'

'I do not forget that you grew up together. Indeed, it was his grief at your father's funeral that softened my heart towards him the last time he indulged in treasonous behaviour.'

'He was very fond of my father.'

'Was your father equally fond of him?'

'The young Robert Devereux amused him and infuriated him. He was a very appealing child, until he was thwarted.'

'And you are of a similar age, but that is the only similarity between you, I think.'

'I am glad of that, at least.'

'There is no love lost between you, is there, my lord? It is you he mostly refers to when he talks of "traitors", I suspect.'

'The Earl of Essex and I have very little in common, that is true, but I bear him no ill will.'

'It must have been hard for you growing up alongside the athletic and vigorous young earl.'

'He could certainly outdo me in every physical endeavour, but not in any scholastic pursuit.'

'Indeed. And here you are, enjoying my favour and my every confidence and there he is, locked inside his own four walls. We venerate physical prowess in boys and are not so impressed by scholastic achievement. I have often thought our priorities topsy-turvy.'

I did not answer the letter and left its author where he was. Then I turned the screw. I compelled him to submit to further interrogations from the very men he saw as traitors. I wanted to wash my hands of the business, and let others decide his fate, but try as I might, I could not let the problem go.

'To the bride and groom and the queen's great majesty, long may she reign!'

I was seated at the top table beside one of my ladies, Anne Russell, and her new husband, Lord Somerset. All the great and the good (saving any member of the Essex party) were in attendance at the wedding feast. A boar's head with a baked apple crammed into its mouth was set down in front of us, along with trenchers of meat, platters of game and dishes of vegetables. Wine was poured into every glass and copious toasts were drunk. We ate, we drank, and we celebrated.

I tried to take pleasure in the feast, but the problem of the Earl of Essex weighed heavily. I spoke the necessary pleasantries to the newlyweds, but my mind was elsewhere. Trailed by my attendants, I had begun taking great walks about the park. Despite my increasing age and the creaking of my joints, I walked quickly, driven on by the problem I was turning over and over in my mind. What was I to do with the reckless earl? I could not return him to my favour; nor could I keep him under house arrest indefinitely. I searched in my mind for a posting to a distant court where he could do little harm, but it did not matter which realm I thought of, the idea of the earl free to do what he pleased while full of hate towards me sent shivers down my spine. Wherever he went he would want to be the most important person in the kingdom. It was not in his nature to submit or take second place. He would foment problems everywhere. He could not help it.

Suddenly my attention was drawn away from the problem of what to do with my Lord Essex, and back to the wedding celebrations. An attendant clapped his hands and the musicians in the gallery above us began to play a great fanfare. The wedding guests turned towards the double doors at the end of the room. Two dwarves pushed the doors open, making exaggerated show of how heavy they were. Once the doors were wide a company of tumblers somersaulted into the room, calling to one another as they leapt about the place. They moved so fast and with such agility their feet appeared never to touch the ground.

After a few minutes of this, culminating in the young men forming a pyramid with the biggest and strongest tumblers at the bottom and the smallest and lightest at the top, they leapt nimbly back to the ground and flipped legs over arms in perfect formation until they stood – chests puffed out and arms extended – in two lines fanning out down the room. As one they turned and gestured towards the open doors. The musicians began to play an introduction and eight masked maids of honour, dressed in glittering silver and crimson, entered. They curtsied to the company and began to dance. When they had finished their figure, a maid I recognised as Mary Fitton – despite her face-covering – formally entreated me to join them on the floor.

'Thank you for your kind invitation, pretty maid, but I cannot accept. You do not want an old woman joining your elegant company.'

'Oh no, Your Majesty! Your grace and athleticism are praised throughout the world. We are but poor imitations of your great glory.'

I smiled and shook my head. I took Mary's hand and patted it kindly. 'You are beautiful, and you are young. My pleasure now is to watch the eight Virtues charm us all with their dance.'

'Please dance with us, Your Grace. It would be such a compliment to those who have been joined in matrimony today.'

It was expected that I would resist for a while and she would entreat, until I acquiesced. So, I still had not let go of her hand.

'What quality do you represent, my dear?'

'I represent "affection", Your Grace.'

The smile disappeared from my face and I dropped her hand. The word had pierced me to the heart.

'Affection?' I turned my face away from Mary and scanned the room. 'Affection's false.'

A silence fell. Mary was undaunted, however, and continued her entreaties.

'Please, Your Grace, will you join us in our dance? All here long to see you perform the steps. Your prowess and elegance are world-renowned. Our performance will be a poor show without you.'

The fun of the ritual had gone for me, but custom and courtesy required that I – like Mary – follow the script. I knew that my age would stand in contrast to the youth and vigour of the girls who surrounded me, but I was also proud of my ability to move to the music and leap and prance almost as high as I had done in my youth. I still loved to dance just as I still loved to hunt. Indeed, only a few days previously we had brought down the boar whose head now graced the table.

'You are persuasive, dear …' Custom demanded I address her by the virtue she represented, but I could not do so. '… lady, so yes, I will join you in your pavane.'

The pavane was a slow and courtly dance unlike the more energetic and showy galliard. I did not have the energy that evening for the latter. So, I danced and the court exclaimed and clapped and I knew they did so because of who I was, rather than how well I performed.

I wonder, do they dance in heaven? The Catholics would say yay, the high Anglicans would dispute over it and the Puritans would say flatly nay. I do not know whether the Allah of the Musselmen approves of the dance or not, but I hope they dance in heaven. I found little joy in this dance, however, which is perhaps why I recall it so vividly. (Was it the last time I danced? I cannot quite remember.) Even as I performed the steps, my mind continued to ruminate over the problem of Essex.

Eventually, against my better judgment, I agreed to release the earl from his detention. After all, he had been charged with no actual crime. But I still would not allow him into my presence or to attend my court. I did not need any legal reason to keep him away from me. Attendance at court lay entirely within the monarch's discretion.

Essex chafed under the continued humiliation. He felt excluded from everything that mattered. But there was worse humiliation to come.

When the earl had ridden high in my favour I had rewarded him with profitable sinecures. But he was as heedless about his income as he was in everything else. He spent his own money as freely as he had often spent mine. His debts were high and now that his disgrace was common knowledge, his creditors were no longer prepared to offer him unlimited grace. They were clamouring for payment.

'The awarding of the monopoly-tax on the import of sweet wines is due for renewal, Your Grace.'

I was seated at my desk only half listening to the catalogue of administrative items that were falling due, but my ears pricked when Cecil got to this item. It was via this rich sinecure that Essex earned the bulk of his income.

'Is it indeed?'

'The rights are currently held by the Earl of Essex.' Cecil was trying to sound as bland and disinterested as he had when he listed the other rights and rewards, but the tension in his voice betrayed him.

'Well, my Lord Secretary, what is your advice? Should I renew the earl's rights or not?'

'The decision is entirely yours, but it is one of the richest sources of income in your purview and there are many bills levied on your own household and on the treasury that will be coming due ere soon.'

I cocked an eyebrow at Cecil. 'Your father trained you well. You are skilled at the art of giving advice without appearing to.'

Robert Cecil ventured a small smile. He was still not as relaxed with me as his father had been, but it was not really fair of me to expect him to be. His father had known me and worked with me when I was a neglected and despised nobody. The son had only ever known me as a great and powerful queen. It was at such moments that I missed my peers.

'And how has the earl been behaving of late? Has he been brought to heel? Has there been any note of contrition or apology for his behaviour?'

'He has written many letters, Your Grace, but I have not found an apology in any of them. I am unaware of any change in the Earl of Essex's behaviour or his view of his grievances.'

The mention of his grievances annoyed me. *He* had no grievances! The grief was all mine. It was I who had given him every preference, showered him with gifts – aye, like the monopoly on the importation of sweet wines – and been persuaded to let him do what he thought he should do. He had touched his sword in my presence. He had insulted me within my hearing. He had made parley with my enemy without my permission. He had failed to carry out my explicit orders. It was he who had spent much of my gold for no return. Worse, he had brought armed men into my bedchamber. It was the earl who owed me, not I who owed him. I got up with so much force that I upset my chair. It clattered noisily onto the floorboards and I saw Cecil jump.

'An unruly beast must be stopped of his provender!'

It is one thing to humiliate a man, to restrict his freedom, to exclude him from everything that he values; it is quite another to take from him his source of income.

Twelve

'The earl's mood has moved from self-pity to fury, Your Grace.'

'So, he has understood nothing, Sir Henry?'

Sir Henry Lee was my contemporary; we had known each other since we were little more than children and he was attendant on my father. Since then, such was his skill at navigating changeable political climates, he had successfully served my sister, my brother and me. Such was his athleticism, he had served as my champion and head of my armoury until quite recently. Now, as almost the last of my peers, he had become a confidant.

'I don't think he has ever understood very much, but I think events are gathering a dangerous momentum and – although I know I am no longer Your Majesty's champion – I still feel a responsibility to warn you when I can.'

'I am not afraid of the Earl of Essex.'

'But perhaps you should be. He feels himself to

be cornered, and such animals are always the most dangerous.'

'The means of getting out of his corner, as you put it, are entirely within his own grasp. If he could admit his fault, ask for my forgiveness – and really mean it – I could find it in my heart to be magnanimous.'

'But he will never regain his old position. That is lost to him forever and he is not such a fool that he does not know it.'

'What you say is true, but, even so, he has created his own dilemma. In honour of his grandmother and his stepfather, I have given him more leeway than I can remember ever giving anyone else.'

'He has not the grace nor the wit to see it and I fear for the balance of his mind.'

'The earl is going mad?'

'Not as such, but he is losing perspective and saying things he should not. I fear his sense of grievance will lead him to do foolish things. There are many about him now who encourage his feeling of resentment.'

'What has he said, my lord?'

'He rails from morning until night against the injustices you have done him and sometimes speaks of you with much disrespect.'

'What has he said, Sir Henry? Fear not to repeat the words to me, however treasonous they may be.'

'He speaks often with scorn and fury of your desire for an unqualified apology. He has said that your conditions are – forgive me, Your Grace, I repeat his words exactly – as crooked as your carcass.'

I fell silent.

'It is a foul insult, Your Grace, and as inaccurate as it is traitorous.'

I could see that my old friend Henry Lee was looking anxious. I knew he feared I might blame him for the words he repeated. I put my hand on his arm. I had asked him to tell me because, as my old friend, I hoped he would tell me the unvarnished truth. 'So, where once there was nothing but honeyed words, now there is nothing but the darkest insults.'

'He may not be fully responsible for what he says. The earl has come to believe many strange things of late.'

'What things?'

'He believes that Cecil and Raleigh are in league with Spain to have him murdered.'

Sir Walter Raleigh, another up-and-coming young man, who had been regarded by Essex as a great rival, had returned from one of his long voyages of exploration and was listening to our conversation with interest. At the mention of his own name, he stepped forward. 'He *has* gone mad, then, Your Majesty.'

'Not quite mad, Raleigh. Do not deny that you are pleased to see Essex fall.'

'I do not like the man and never have liked him, that is true, but I take no pleasure in anyone's suffering. I know what it is to fall from your favour …' Raleigh had spent some time in the Tower for marrying without my permission. Unlike the earl, however, he had returned to my service a wiser and more thoughtful young man. '... and to accuse me, and my Lord Secretary' – Raleigh nodded respectfully at Cecil – 'of conspiring with the Spaniards for any reason is a foul calumny!'

'There is worse, Your Grace.' Now Cecil stepped forward, his hands folded across his chest. There was something monk-like to his aspect, particularly given his serious expression. I signalled for him to continue. 'The earl and his friends are planning to "surprise" the court and your royal person. The earl intends to tell you to dismiss all his enemies from your service. He would then put these so-called traitors on trial for their lives. I presume by "traitors" he is referring to me, Sir Walter, Sir Henry and many others here present. He then intends to summon parliament and – pardon me, Your Grace, but these are his exact words – "alter the government".'

'Alter it how?'

'He has not made that quite clear.'

'But it is not hard to imagine!' In my alarm I had interrupted Cecil. 'He means to rule England himself with me as his puppet and his captive.'

'To be fair, he has not said so.'

'A pox on your lawyerly caution! If he means to dismiss the men I have appointed and replace them with his own familiars, where exactly would that leave me?'

I turned to my old friend and champion. 'Send an armed guard to Essex House, Sir Henry, and arrest the earl and his fellow conspirators.'

As I gave the order, a messenger stepped into the room and whispered something in Cecil's ear.

He looked up. 'It seems it may be too late for that.'

The capital of my kingdom is a small place. Rumours fly through the streets and alleyways faster than even the fleetest of my messengers could possibly carry them. All my people, from the greatest to the most humble, were gripped by the unfolding drama between Essex and me. All knew it must come to a head. All knew that it was Essex who would act first. Once he knew that we were aware of his plans, he had no choice.

Despite it being the Lord's Day – not that such a consideration would likely have given the earl pause – at eleven in the morning, Essex marched through London. Behind him in lock-step were more than two hundred armed men. They walked with their swords drawn. As Cecil had said, his original plan was to surprise the court, but my spies (the very same who once took orders from the earl) had put paid to that. Instead, thinking on the fly, he had turned his men towards Ludgate Hill in the hope of commanding the city from its heights. As he made his way through the streets, he called out to the watching Londoners, exhorting them to take up arms and join him.

'For the queen!' he cried, explaining to passers-by,

many of whom were returning from church, that my kingdom had been sold to the Infanta of Spain and that his life was in peril.

But, as the earl's erstwhile friend Sir Francis Bacon explained to me afterwards, my faithful people just watched the traitor in silence. 'In so populous a city where he thought himself held so dear, there was not, Your Majesty, one man from the chiefest citizen to the meanest artificer or prentice that armed with him.'

Despite my fright – and I could not contemplate an armed band in my own capital without feeling fear – I almost found it in my heart to feel sorry for the foolish, half-mad earl.

'The people stood silently as Essex and his men marched by. All that disturbed the peace of this Sunday morning was his hollering traitorous lies at the top of his voice and the crunching of the rebels' boots on the cobblestones. Not one man or woman cried back to him. They did not call out in encouragement; nor did they hurl insults.'

'It is a foolhardy man who insults an armed horde.'

'There is that, but their mulish silence was almost worse than the foulest language. It emphasised how mightily the earl had miscalculated, how delusional he had become. He seemed pathetic in the face of their indifference, rather than frightening. I did wonder whether some who came out to see him might not begin to laugh.'

'He could not have abided that.'

'As the terrible realisation that no one else was joining him began to dawn on the earl, he went quite white, and became drenched in sweat. Not from exertion, you understand, but from humiliation and fear. Eventually he stopped at a sheriff's house and went inside to change his shirt—'

I laughed out loud at this detail, interrupting Bacon's tale. 'He was always vain about his appearance, no matter what the circumstances. Go on, Bacon, go on!'

'Thank you, Your Grace. No sooner had he entered the premises than the sheriff smartly exited from the rear. I am afraid that the sight of the earl going in the front door, shortly followed by the sheriff coming out the back, did cause some hilarity among those who watched.'

I snorted again, but as much in sympathy as derision. 'Poor, foolish man.'

I could not help remembering – as Sir Francis told me of the earl's utter humiliation at the hands of my loyal people – another similar incident, many years in the past, when John Dudley, Earl of Northumberland and coincidentally Essex's step-grandfather, tried to whip the English people into armed resistance against the accession of my sister Mary. Just as they did now, the people stood by then, silent and unmoving as armed men marched past them. I gave thanks for the good sense and loyalty of the ordinary men and women of

England. Without their refusal to rebel, I would not be on my throne.

Bacon had not finished regaling us with the details. All the men and women in the room were hanging on his every word. 'When the futility of his enterprise became obvious even to him, Essex decided to turn back towards his own house. Your watchmen had already dispatched heralds into the streets to proclaim the earl a traitor and their voices could be heard ringing through boulevards and alleyways. In response to their cries, the mood of the people began to change. Their anger was not, as the earl had hoped, turned against you. It was focused on him. Someone bent down and picked up a mess of horse dung. They threw it. It landed harmlessly enough at the earl's feet, but the shock of it made him flinch. He was losing his nerve, Your Grace. In response the people closest to him began to mutter ominously and jostle him. It was then, I think, that he realised the full extent of his folly.'

'He has always believed only what he wanted to believe. It is a fatal flaw.' I spoke softly, almost to myself. The emotions I was experiencing were complicated. I felt relief and gratitude to the people of London. I felt fear and anger at the audacity of Essex and his men taking up arms against me, but I also felt pity for the man I had once regarded with such affection.

'Such was his terror, Essex fled down a side street to the river, commandeered a boat and made his way up the Thames to the water-gate at Essex House. And that is where he is now, barricaded behind locked doors.'

'Where he cannot remain, my lord.' I had taken a step towards Sir Francis in my alarm.

Cecil had been listening to Bacon's report as intently as I had been, and he also now stepped forward to reassure me. 'I have already dispatched Charles Howard and Sir Robert Sidney to Essex House with orders to arrest the earl and take him to the Tower.'

But I was not so easily soothed. 'I doubt he will leave his own home meekly, my lord, just because we ask him to. Sir Henry warned me he was a cornered animal, and he is now a mortally wounded one. I hope you gave Howard and Sidney the men they will require to get the job done.'

I was right. Essex refused to leave his house. He conveyed his intentions to the two men sent to arrest him from the roof of that establishment. My emissaries were forced to shout up at him from the garden. Despite everything, the earl was still attempting to dictate terms. He was adamant that he would surrender only as long as he was promised an audience with me.

What delusions was he still labouring under? Did he really think that I knew nothing of what was occurring? Had he convinced himself that I did my council's bidding rather than the other way around? If so, he did not know me at all and never had. I could not help wondering if he would ever have thought so little of the authority of a king. It was my sex that enabled him to think that I did not know what was done in my name.

Yet there was even greater insult. Did Essex really believe such was his personal charm that I had only to see him face to face and I would be putty in his hands? It pains me to admit it now, but I was hurt by the realisation that all of Essex's attention to me was due to my office. He had seen nothing of the flesh-and-blood woman beneath the crown. And he had not seen me because he was not interested in me. To him my all-too-human carcass had always been crooked. It was my crown that dazzled his eyes.

I had cause to be grateful that the redoubtable Charles Howard was sent to detain the rebellious earl. In reply to Essex's demands, Howard sent some men to fetch gunpowder from the Tower. He then delivered his own ultimatum to the Essex household. He would give the earl an hour so that his sister, wife and their children and gentlewomen could leave and get to safety and then, said Charles Howard, matter-of-factly (if at the top of his voice), he would blow the house up. Some of the ladies set to shrieking as they listened to the admiral, and who could blame them?

As I think back on the fall of Essex, memories of Henry, Lord Darnley, rise up. It is impossible not to see the parallels between the situation at Essex House and the peculiar episode of the explosion at Kirk O'Field that was meant to kill the estranged husband of the Queen of Scots – but didn't. Who had blown up the house and strangled Darnley and his servant in the garden as they tried to flee? The world points its finger at Mary's lover, the Earl of Bothwell, and some at Mary herself. But I shall die not knowing for certain.

It was not until the kegs of gunpowder were being unloaded from the boat onto the earl's lawn that the earl and his confederate Southampton accepted reality and came down from the roof. At the point of muskets, they knelt on the lawn and presented their swords.

Both were charged with high treason.

I reprieved Southampton, he was Essex's follower, not his leader, but there could be no reprieve for Essex himself.

I was playing the virginals when a messenger arrived with news from Tower Green. He fell to one knee and I paused at the keyboard.

'Your Majesty, my lords, ladies and gentlemen, I am sent to inform you that on this day of our Lord, the twenty-fifth of February, 1601, the sentence of death has been carried out and the Earl of Essex has paid the ultimate price for his crime of high treason. May God have mercy upon his soul.'

No one in that room said a word: not Raleigh, nor yet Francis Bacon or Robert Cecil. We all stood (or sat, in my case) as still and silent as if we had been cast in stone. Then I returned to my instrument and played the song through to the end.

'I am Richard the second! Know ye not that?'

The man opposite me took a step backwards, frightened by the ferocity of my tone. I was also surprised at the power of the emotion that suddenly had me in its grip. My eyes filled with tears and I had to fight to retain my composure. I had not expected that this simple audience would excite such feelings. I was speaking with Mr Lambarde, an antiquarian who had collected and transcribed all the records at the Tower of London and gathered them into a book. He had come to present me with a copy. I had looked forward to this interlude. I have always been interested in history and in my ancestors. Lambarde's book encompassed both. At first, the interview proceeded as I had expected. I asked him some questions about his research and how he had arranged his narrative, and he answered eagerly and enthusiastically. Then he began to take me through various sections and it was when he opened the pages devoted to the betrayed and murdered Richard that the wave of – of I knew not what – overwhelmed me. Richard II, of course, had lost his throne to the rebel Henry Bolingbroke, who became Henry IV. The betrayed king had then been murdered in his cell.

I had grieved a little over the death of Essex. Indeed, once he was no longer a threat to me or to my authority, my memory turned towards our earlier, happier experiences. I remembered his sense of fun and, yes, his handsome, mercurial face. He had added youth and energy to my court, elements that now were sadly lacking. I regretted that I had been forced to execute a man with so much vigour, of course I did. I am not a monster and I always hate to shed blood. But I did not fret as I had over the execution of the Queen of Scots or the Duke of Norfolk or even Dr Lopez. Had I become hardened? Were my softer emotions worn thin? Or was my lack of grief or any guilt really because Essex had been so utterly the author of his own fate?

It was not until I was reminded of my tragic ancestor that the full import of what had occurred became clear to me. But it was not just Richard losing the throne and his terrible death that brought me undone. The ghost of Richard had been haunting me for some time.

The night before Essex's attempt at rebellion, his supporters paid the Earl of Southampton's players forty shillings to give a special performance. The Earl of Southampton's players included Master Shakespeare and it was his play *Richard II* that they were specifically asked to perform. Their intent in having this text produced was obvious. It is a play about the betrayal of a foolish king by a good man forced against his will into rebellion. Subtlety had never been Essex's strong point. In the end the king is foully murdered. I have no doubts that the aim of the special performance was to stir up those who saw it and persuade them that Essex was like the rebellious Bolingbroke. In which case, I was Richard.

I did not hear about this special performance until Essex had been arrested and was awaiting his fate behind the thick walls of the Tower. Once I knew, I insisted on hearing about every detail.

My informants told me that the atmosphere in the playhouse was febrile and excitable. Many in the audience, including the two earls, must have known they were on the brink of rebellion. They must have known they were preparing to act out in real life many of the themes presented in the play. I had seen the play when Shakespeare first presented it a few years earlier. I had obtained a copy of the manuscript from the playwright and had often read one speech in particular. I returned to it so frequently I had committed it to my memory.

For God's sake, let us sit upon the ground
And tell sad stories of the death of kings;
How some have been deposed; some slain in war,
Some haunted by the ghosts they have deposed;
Some poison'd by their wives: some sleeping kill'd;
All murder'd: for within the hollow crown
That rounds the mortal temples of a king
Keeps Death his court and there the antic sits,
Scoffing his state and grinning at his pomp,

Allowing him a breath, a little scene,
To monarchise, be fear'd and kill with looks,
Infusing him with self and vain conceit,
As if this flesh which walls about our life,
Were brass impregnable, and humour'd thus
Comes at the last and with a little pin
Bores through his castle wall, and farewell king!

Poor, foolish Essex. If only he could have kept his powder dry and stilled his impatience but a little while, God would have done his work for him, and with his little pin, bored through my castle wall. I can feel its sharp point now, penetrating my flesh and sucking out my life's blood. Had Essex but found it within himself to come to me cap in hand and beg my forgiveness, he could have been here now, standing there, in that corner, clustered about with lords and ladies waiting for the new king to take my place. Instead, if he is here at all, he joins the ranks of those ghostly phantoms who stand about me, waiting impatiently for me to join their throng.

Thirteen

... let us sit upon the ground
And tell sad stories of the death of kings.

The phrase had lodged itself in my brain. Whenever I was alone and unoccupied, it repeated itself inside my skull. A feeling settled upon me – a heavy feeling, as if everything I did was a great effort. I felt as if I were dragging a heavy chain. It weighed me down. I often caught myself staring into space, my mind wandering. I had begun the habit of stalking about the grounds while I wrestled with what to do about Essex. I continued this practice after the earl's execution, heaving great sighs, walking at a fast pace, despite the great phantom chain I now dragged behind me. I was determined not to allow its weight to restrain me.

It was not only by walking that I fought the invisible shackles as stubbornly as I could. I still rode to the hunt whenever the weather permitted. I returned to my court aching and exhausted, my legs, as I complained loudly and often, benumbed by their time in the saddle, but I refused to stop. It was hard that the pastimes that had given me pleasure now exacted a price, but it was the nature of my work that gave me the greatest difficulty. Despite my bone-deep weariness, the business of governing my kingdom went on, without ceasing. It ground me down. I greeted each day, each new missive, each arriving messenger with more great sighs. There was no rest from this, no rest except the grave.

For God's sake, let us sit upon the ground
And tell sad stories of the death of kings.

Lying upon these cushions, I suppose I am as close to the ground as I am able to get. Cecil and the Archbishop of Canterbury keep exhorting me to go to my bed. I ignore them. I wish to sit upon the ground and tell myself my own story. I am not quite ready to loosen my grip on these last few hours of my life. There are things about my sixty-nine years that are not completed and I feel I must try to understand them – at last.

Maybe that is why, only a few scant years ago, I still saw some kind of earthly future for myself. Perhaps it was this sense of events, relationships and experiences left unfinished that kept me struggling to go on despite everything, despite my sense of a heavy chain. I feared that each phantom link was a sin. One was the Queen of Scots; another Thomas Howard, Duke of Norfolk; another Edmund Campion; the Earl of Essex; poor Dr Lopez and many, many more, both great and small. I remembered some whose death I caused, but there were many I did not. And there were many other sins too, both big and small. It is not possible to rule over others and commit no sins. I had no one I could talk to about these feelings, no one to whom I could unburden myself. I sighed because I could not speak. I was lonely after Essex was gone. I had always been lonely but now my isolation felt profound.

Nonetheless, chained by my multitude of unspoken sins or not, I fought to carry on. Perhaps it was the thought of my many sins that made me determined to keep living. I cringed at the idea of God's judgment.

After Essex's execution (he required three strokes of the axe before the bloody business was done) there arose mutterings among my people. If there is one thing I have learnt in my long years of rule it is that nothing is as changeable as the common folk. One day, they throw dung at a would-be rebel; the next they weep over his fate and grumble against her whose hand was forced.

Essex was only dead to himself. He was still very much alive to my people. I began to worry that he would be more successful at undermining my kingdom from the grave than he had ever been in life. It was Robert Cecil, growing in skill daily, particularly as I left more and more of the business of ruling in his hands, who found the answer to the growing discontent.

'The Commons are debating the taxation monopolies, Your Grace.'

'It is always a contentious matter.'

I had been staring bleakly out of my casement window. It was, as I knew all too well, the same window through which my mother had pleaded with my father for her life. It was not a view to cheer me, yet I sought it out deliberately. I was sitting in the window-seat, so I could turn my face away from those around me and yet seem as if I was occupied in examining the flower gardens outside. One of my ladies was playing the lute. Had you asked me, however, I could not have named what tune she played or what flowers had bloomed in the garden. Nor could I have told you the thoughts that occupied my mind. I was sitting in a great blank.

Cecil approached me, bearing in one arm, just as his father always used to do, a great sheaf of papers. 'Forgive me, Your Grace, but there is unrest in the Commons.'

'There is unrest everywhere these days.' And I fetched another of my great sighs.

I still had not turned to look at my secretary of state. I wanted him to go away and handle this difficulty without me. Cecil stood his ground. 'The Commons feel you are now taxing staples to reward your courtiers. They complain that this largesse comes at the expense of the ordinary folk while costing you nothing.'

I turned to face him now. There was some truth in what he was telling me.

'Members are listing the items that are so constrained, including currants, vinegar, lead, pilchards, various types of cloth and even ashes. One had the audacity to ask whether bread was not included and, when told it was not, remarked that given the rest of the list, it soon would be. His comments are being reported far and wide and discussed in every market square and public house.'

'And discontent is growing about this?'

'It is, and fast on the heels of the death of Essex …'

'That traitor!'

'Indeed, Your Grace, but the people loved him.'

'Not enough to rise up in rebellion on his behalf!'

'Indeed not. They loved you better.'

'Do they not still?'

'The danger has passed, and it is the way of the world that we forget how frightened we were when once again we feel safe. And so it is with the people who called for his death and then greeted the event with much weeping. Their tears have emboldened those who were already discontented, and they are taking every opportunity to add fuel to the fire.'

'It is an old, old story.' And I sighed again.

'The discontented are always with us, no matter how judicious the government.'

'What is your advice, wise Master Secretary?'

'This is something that would be easy to fix and would earn you much good will.'

'It will cost me money and you know how little I like to deplete my treasury.'

'Aye, and a wise policy it is to spend only what you must. However, your care for the Crown's resources has put you in a strong position and you can well afford to make these concessions. Surely the point of having a well-managed treasury is that you can spend money when it is right and necessary.'

Cecil was adept at lifting me out of my melancholy. He well knew that my thrift was something I was proud of. I sat up a little straighter before I replied.

'And what could be more right and necessary for a queen who loves her people than to spend money removing unfair burdens from them?'

'You put the case exactly, Your Grace.'

'Fetch me the Speaker, my lord. This, at least, I can put to rights.'

And I did feel a burst of my old energy at the thought of tackling something that could and should be corrected. Most of the problems I had to deal with were much less easily solved. I also recalled the monopolies I had given to Essex and how little gratitude he had shown in return. I now felt less inclined to reward the great and the self-obsessed with sinecures.

Cecil and I had calculated correctly. Parliament was

so pleased at the cancellation of the monopolies that they sent a deputation to thank me.

November 30, 1601 was a good day, although the weather had turned bleak. The skies had already drawn in, and the cold got into my bones in a way that it had not when I was younger. I made sure the fires in my palace all blazed accordingly. My loyal members of parliament arrived at Whitehall at about three in the afternoon and, no doubt, were pleased to stand in the warmth of the great fire crackling in my audience chamber. I saw a couple of them flip up their surcoats the better to feel the warmth of the fire on their silken-clad behinds. I could not help thinking to myself that while sometimes my MPs were hot-heads – I much preferred them as hot-bottoms. It is a remark that in the past I might have made to the courtiers standing nearest to me but now I held my tongue. Since most of my contemporaries have died, since the death of Essex, I had few close to me who I felt I could trust with my humour. Moreover, I did not want any note of cynicism to mar this day. I had made these tax concessions to increase my popularity and now I wished to reap the rewards. After all, I had paid for them.

The Speaker's vote of thanks was as fulsome as I could wish and the acclamations from the members of parliament gathered in my presence were heart-warming. I looked down upon the MPs from my seat on the dais with real affection. Perhaps I was softening in my old age. I had previously regarded parliament as an annoyance; now I felt a kinship with these men. When the Speaker had finished giving his thanks we of the court applauded. Then, it was my turn to speak. I did not stand, pleading my advanced years as an excuse, but I leant forward on my throne and scanned the room slowly. It was gratifying to see the men's response. My gaze made them bashful. I waited until I had met the eyes of every man there before I began my reply.

'Mr Speaker, we have heard your declaration and perceive your care of our estate. I do assure you there is no prince that loves his subjects better, or whose love can countervail our love. There is no jewel, be it of ever so rich a price, which I set before this jewel: I mean your love. For I do esteem it more than any treasure or riches; for that we know how to prize, but love and thanks I count invaluable. And, though God hath raised me high, yet this I count the glory of my crown, that I have reigned with your loves.'

As I spoke, I felt my heart swell with affection for all in that room – yes, even those I knew were quick to see fault in their queen. I had composed this speech for political reasons, but as I came to say the words, I found that I meant them.

'Of myself, I must say this: I never was any greedy, scraping grasper, nor a strait fast-holding prince, nor yet a waster. My heart was never set on any worldly goods. What you bestow on me, I will not hoard it up, but receive it to bestow on you again.'

It was as if I knew that this would be the last great speech I would make to the men of my parliament. We had experienced many ups and downs in forty-three years, even though none of the men now before me had been in their seats when I first spoke to their company. We had been through much together, not all of it easy or pleasant. But we were colleagues, we were comrades and we had prevailed.

I thought of our past disagreements. I remembered well how one member called me 'tyrant' and 'a great Turk'. I remembered my fury at their impertinence when parliament after parliament urged me to marry and give the kingdom an heir, as if I were some kind of brood mare. Yet, all of this was now past. The shape of my reign, whether it went on for many more years or ended on the morrow, was set. *Semper eadem*, it would not now change.

My thoughts affected the words that I uttered. I suddenly felt strongly that I wished to speak to these men, not as queen to subjects, but as equal to equal. As I say, I did not know that this was to be my last speech to them, but if I had thought about it, I might have suspected as much. Nevertheless, I knew the effect I wanted this speech to have on those who listened.

'And I am not so simple to suppose that there are some of the Lower House whom these grievances never touched. I think they spake out of zeal to their counties and not out of spleen or malevolent affection as parties grieved. That my grants should be grievous to my people and oppressions privileged under the colour of our patents, our kingly dignity shall not suffer it. Yea, when I heard it, I could give no rest unto my thoughts until I had reformed it.'

I even began to confide in these men – these good and honest Englishmen. I shared with them some of the ideas I had formed during my long and wearisome rule. And I suppose although they stood about me on Turkish carpets and I sat upon my throne on a dais, beneath my cloth of state, I felt, at last, that I could sit upon the ground and talk of the death of kings.

'We know the title of a king is a glorious title, but be assured that the shining glory of princely authority hath not so dazzled our eyes, that we do not know and remember that we also must give an account of our actions before the Great Judge. To be a king and wear a crown is a thing more glorious to them that see it than it is pleasant to them that bear it.'

And, at the end, with my eyes swimming with tears and my heart as full as ever I can remember it, I departed from the politically acceptable words I had written and spoke directly from my heart.

'There will never be a queen with more zeal to her country, care to her subjects or with a willingness to give her life for your protection. For it is our desire to neither live nor reign any longer than shall be for your good. And though you have had, and may have, many princes more mighty and wise sitting in this seat than we are, you never have had nor shall have, any that will be more careful and loving.'

When, at last, I stopped speaking and sat back in my chair, the room was still and silent. All that could be heard was the crackling of the logs in the great fire. Then, as one, all the people in that room broke into thunderous applause and I saw that tears were streaming down many of the faces turned towards me. I put up my own hand to dash away a tear as, like them, I was quite overcome.

Some of the men began to call out in response to my words. 'Long live the queen.' 'God bless Queen Elizabeth!' and such-like. In fact, the wave of love and approval almost became too much for me. I held up my hand.

'Mr Speaker?'

Sir John Croke turned towards me and I could see that he was also crying.

'I pray to you, Mr Comptroller, Mr Secretary and you of my council, that before these gentlemen go back into their counties, you bring them all to kiss my hand.'

They came meekly, almost shyly, one after another. Some muttered blessings, some spoke of their loyalty and their love, some were silent, some sobbed, some crushed my hand in their enthusiasm, some treated it as if it were made of delicate glass. Some dropped tears upon it, some more noisome stuff, but I did not flinch, nor did I lower my arm, although my shoulder soon ached. As each paid his respects, so he made his way out of the room.

I was told later that one member of parliament spoke these words to general agreement as all of the Commons made their way out of my palace.

'We love her for she said she did love us.'

Other kings may have said as much, nay, may even have felt as much, but I think that my sex has had some advantage – although there were many burdens peculiar to me due to my gender. My advantage as a woman was that I could speak of my love for my people in a way that a man could not. I think also that it became easier for me to speak of this love as I grew older and as they all slowly (albeit reluctantly) accepted that I meant what I had always said and that I would not marry or bear children. Over time, I became their loving mother and in return for my care of them, just as an infant does to their parent – despite Essex, despite religious differences, despite my lack of an heir – they loved me unreservedly in their turn.

And yet … and yet … the love of multitudes is all very well, and I do not belittle its importance or the comfort and sense of security it gave me. But I am alone, and I have always been alone. Those few who sincerely loved me for the flesh-and-blood woman I am are gone. Now the only love left to me is impersonal. There is no one left who loves Elizabeth. Those who remain love a queen.

Fourteen

Because the love of multitudes is only a thin comforter, my good mood lasted only a day or two. Quickly I returned to my sense of melancholy and isolation, to my compulsive walking and the sense of the heavy phantom chain weighing me down. Its heaviness seemed always with me, from the moment I woke until the next time I slept. It bent my back, slowed my steps and exhausted me. Its weight forced me to think of every link and every sin. The people I had hurt, the misery I had caused by exercising my power and keeping my throne safe and my country stable and prosperous.

Maybe this is why they say ruling is not the business of women. Maybe it is true that we are made for love and kindness more than for domination and ruthlessness. I do not know if any kings ruminated over their mistakes in the way that I did. As my health and vigour began to fail, I began to go back over my sins, so I could make my peace with God.

It was not just the great and the ambitious who suffered at my hands. Any poor soul who was close to me by blood was also a victim. It is no use me trying to pretend otherwise. I could not behave to them as I might an ordinary mortal. I could not allow them to live an ordinary life. The only comfort I could find for the destruction I had wrought on my royal cousins was that their fate could so easily have been mine if circumstances had been just a little different.

I had not thought about my Grey cousins for years, but now that I knew there were links in my phantom chain with their names upon them I was forced to revisit cruelties I had long managed to forget.

This business of dying is inexorable. It forces me to face things I would rather not see. At least the fate of all three of the Grey girls was not down to me. I had nothing to do with the demise of the first. It was my sister Mary Tudor who had to answer for that.

The only sensible member of the Grey family – the ill-fated Lady Jane – was brought low by the ambition and folly of others. Her execution at the tender age of seventeen is an event, even after all these decades have passed, that I can only recall with pain. I did not like her when we were young. I competed with her and my envy of her intellect led me to delight in teasing and bullying her. I regret my foolish, mean-spirited behaviour now, but I never did her any real harm. It is not on her account that I could face hellfire. Indeed, even if it was my sister queen who was forced by circumstance to have the poor girl executed – an action I know she regretted bitterly – it was the little nun's father, mother and father-in-law's religious fanaticism and vaunting ambition that were the real culprits. When she died, England lost one of the great minds of our era, a fact few were ever aware of. Because her razor-sharp brain was carried in the vessel of a mere girl, no one but her teachers (and her nearest scholastic rival) ever valued her abilities. Her broad, deep and serious mind was not missed by anyone. I wonder sometimes at the waste.

Now, as I sit waiting my turn to die I cannot help but wonder what she might have achieved had she been allowed to live. I do not believe for a moment that the foolishness that tripped up her less gifted younger sisters would ever have snared Jane. I hope that in only a little while (a few more hours only, please God) I can apologise for my childish cruelty to her. For if there is one soul I am certain stands on the right hand of God, it is Lady Jane Grey. Of the fate of her sister Katherine's soul I am not nearly so sure.

'She loves him, Your Majesty.'

I was seated at my mirror while my ladies combed and arranged my hair. They had only permitted Robin Dudley to enter my chamber at such an early hour because many of them already knew what he came to tell me. He had come to tell me about my cousin, the granddaughter of my father's younger sister Mary – my erstwhile lady-in-waiting Lady Katherine Grey.

In the small hours of the night, as Robin had just finished telling me, Lady Katherine had appeared at his door and the story she had told him, in floods of tears, was astonishing in the extreme.

'Love, Robin? Love? She has no right to love or to marry where I have not given her permission. She is of blood and a lady of my privy chamber – some even tout her as a possible heir to my throne. Love is not for her.'

'She carries Edward Seymour's child.'

'Aye, or else she would have kept this marriage a secret much longer.'

I turned and commanded my nearest lady-in-waiting. 'Fetch Lady Katherine and bid her to attend me immediately, and, once you have done that, fetch the guard.' Then I turned back to my master of horse. 'She has used you, Robin. She has sought to soften the impact of this news by having you do her pleading for her.'

'She came to me in distress and asked for my advice, that is true, but all I agreed to do was tell you everything as soon as it was light and this I have done.'

'The girl is a fool.'

'In that she is not unusual.'

I will say it again; I find it hard to have much sympathy with those who are lovesick; so many people – particularly of my own sex – are undone more by love than by hate. They follow their desires with little thought of tomorrow and then sob and plead when the consequences become all too apparent.

I heard my cousin approach before I saw her – so loud and uncontrolled were her lamentations. When she came into my presence and saw Robin standing beside me, she threw herself onto the floor and hid her face in her skirts – her arms thrown out towards me. Her swelling belly was obvious to me now that I knew of its existence and I wondered at my own blindness in not having noticed her condition earlier.

For a few moments, the only sound in the room was my cousin Katherine's desperate tears.

'Sir Robin tells me you have married Edward Seymour with no permission. Is this true?'

'Forgive me, Your Majesty, forgive me, we meant no harm. We love each other.'

'Love? What care I for that? I can see the fruits of your love, right enough. But you claim to be married?'

Robin had told me that her difficulty was compounded because she had no actual proof of the legality of her union.

'Oh, yes, Your Grace, we are legally wed. I would not – we would not …'

'Do you have proof of this marriage? Where is the prelate who performed the ceremony? Where is your witness? Where the certificate of marriage?'

'Jane Seymour – our only witness – has died. I have searched and searched, and I cannot find the paper, and the minister's name I have forgot.' She dissolved into desperate tears as she spoke these last words and snot coursed from her nose. In her extremity she did not look as comely as usual.

'You are either remarkably foolish and careless, or a whore and a liar. Which is it to be, madam?'

'I am a fool. A fool!' She said this thickly and her sobs came so fast they threatened to overwhelm her. She had crumpled into a puddle of heaving silk on the floor.

'You are a fool, no doubt, but an even bigger fool than you have any inkling. Do you not know why you must ask my permission to marry? Because – according to my father's will – you are my heir, madam, and any child you carry could one day sit upon the throne. You are not a free person, able to choose your own fate, any more than I am. And to choose a Seymour, of all people! How many times has that ambitious family attempted to control the throne of England? Are you so foolish to think that this boy loves you for your pert charms, rather than your proximity to my crown?'

'Forgive us, Your Grace. We will retire quietly to the country and make no trouble, I swear.'

'It is not within your power to so swear. You forget, I have been a second person and I know how disgruntled men will scheme and plot, whether you would have them do so or nay. You cannot choose *not* to be who you are.'

'But I will not be your heir for long. You will marry soon and have your own children.' (I was still young enough for that to remain a real possibility.)

'Maybe so. But until that time you, your husband or paramour and your bastard, once born, will sojourn in the Tower.'

'No! No! No! Please not the Tower. I am afraid of that place. They killed my sister there and my father. Forgive me, Majesty, please, please!'

Try as I might to hide it, I have a heart and I could feel her terror. Once it had been mine. I reached down from the chair on which I sat and lifted her face up from the folds of her skirts where she had hidden it in her despair. I knew what it was to be sent to the Tower. I spoke to her quietly and in a softer tone. 'I can do nothing else. But you will be well housed and treated gently and when your time comes I will send a good midwife to help ease your child's passage into the world. You think I have some choice over your fate and could pardon you if I would, but I do not. I may look like the mistress here, but my choices are curtailed by circumstance just as surely as your own.'

I stood and turned to walk from the room. I had seen the armed men approaching to take my cousin to her prison and my mouth had gone dry. I remembered witnessing the horrible scene of another Katherine, condemned for love, pleading hopelessly for her life. Now it was I who wished only to flee, but I was prevented. I felt a hand around my ankle and looked down. Katherine Grey had grasped it.

I bent over and whispered to her so that only we two could hear. 'Let my foot go and get up onto your own. There is no avoiding this fate: you can either face it with dignity or be dragged from here in an unseemly fashion. You will be treated kindly, I will make sure of that.'

She looked at me with tearful eyes and made a desperate mewing noise. Then she let go of my ankle. I turned and hurried from the room. I had no desire to see whether she had taken my advice or not.

It is perhaps the curse of the Tudors that we birth more female children than male. My father certainly thought so. Such is the different value that God and the world place on the two genders that to be born a girl is always a misfortune, but to be born a girl in a royal family is a tragedy. As events have turned out, it was the making of my triumph that all my close relatives were female. It was the making of their disaster. The only reason I gained the throne at all was because every one of my male relatives, by which I mean my frail brother, were dead. All the other possible heirs to my crown during the early years of my reign were female and they caused me no end of trouble.

The devil is a woman, the poets like to say, and so it sometimes seems to me.

My cousin Mary of Scotland is the she-devil over whom I have cried more tears and pulled out more of my thinning hair than any other person alive. But Katherine Grey was almost as bad. As with the Queen of Scots, I wished Katherine no harm, yet I destroyed her.

The last time I lay close to death, forty years ago now, it was with the pox. While I writhed in my delirium my council, particularly my Protestant councillors, cast about for a successor, and it was Lady Katherine Grey they turned to. (It is as well that God saw fit to spare me, for I shudder when I think of the fate of my poor country if such a witless and idle jade should ever have taken control of its destiny.)

Before her fall from grace, Katherine made little impression on me except for the marked contrast between her behaviour and that of her sister, Jane. She was pretty enough and vain about it, while Jane, whose magnificent mind was deceptively housed in a mousy, freckled and under-sized frame, had cared nothing about outward appearance or finery. Had Jane lived she would have made a fine abbess. Her sister Katherine had no more inclination to dedicate her life to God than a tabby cat. Her one devotion was to her own appearance and pleasure. Nevertheless, it gave me no joy to imprison such a silly young woman. I did it because I had no choice.

'Ahem.'

I looked up. It was some months later. I had been so absorbed by my papers that I had not noticed William

Cecil enter the room. Whatever it was he had to tell me was obviously making him feel very uncomfortable. I gestured for him to speak.

'The Lady Katherine Grey, your cousin …'

'I know who she is, Cecil, get on with it.'

'She is with child for a second time.'

It took me a moment to absorb the news. At first, I did not believe my ears. 'How so, my lord? She is behind lock and key in the most formidable prison in my kingdom.'

'It has occurred in the usual fashion, I believe.'

'Is this a miracle? Or treachery?'

'Misguided mercy, I suspect. If Your Grace will forgive me, there has been some corridor creeping between Lady Katherine and her husband, Edward Seymour, and the gaolers have turned a blind eye to it.'

'God's death! Perhaps they'd like an actual blind eye for their trouble!'

'They are very sorry for their failure. The warden trembled as he told me the news.'

'Trembled! I'll make him tremble! What incompetence is this? I try to be merciful to the foolish pair and they – and everyone else, it seems – take this as a sign of weakness! Do they think to make a fool of me? Nay. Nay, do not answer that. They *have* made a fool of me and I will no longer allow them such leeway. Take Lady Katherine and her bastards from the Tower and place them under house arrest. I don't care where – just somewhere as far away from here and her husband as possible. Send her to Wales, to Cornwall, to Cumberland, to hell for all I care, just rid of me of this foolish girl.'

This time, my orders were obeyed. After she gave birth, Lady Katherine and her younger son, Thomas, were separated from her eldest son and her erstwhile husband. The next time I heard of her, the poor witless woman had died, of a broken heart, or so they told me. I was sorry, but I did not grieve for her – not then. I had too much else to worry about. Now, as an old woman, I feel differently. Poor Katherine, she only wanted what most women want: a husband and children. What she did not realise was that because I did not have them, her closeness to my throne meant that neither would she.

At the time, and this is another of my sins, I was probably relieved. With Katherine's death – and I had not executed her: it was God, not I, who took her – I had one less Grey to worry about. To my astonishment, no sooner was Katherine dead than her last surviving sister began to cause me trouble.

Mary Grey was the youngest of the three sisters and while not as gifted as Jane, she was not as foolish as Katherine. Nature had blessed her with good sense but not much else. She was dwarf-like in stature and crook-backed, with one shoulder much higher than the other. She did not seem to be of an amorous disposition and her great ugliness lulled me into a false sense of security.

I found her a pleasant and commonsense companion and felt grateful that at least one of my relatives on my father's side was someone I could rely on. I should have known better.

One evening I saw Robin Dudley and a group of his cronies laughing together over a game of cards. I was bored with the company of my ladies, so I made my way across the banqueting hall. Robin was the one person I could always rely upon to amuse me.

'Share the joke, my lords!'

I could see immediately by their expressions that whatever had caused their amusement was not something they wished to share with me. Nothing could have piqued my curiosity more.

'It is a trifle, Your Grace. A bawdy joke that is not fit for your ears.'

'You are not usually so careful of my ears, and I am of a mind to be amused.'

'I would rather tell you tomorrow. I have no wish to spoil the party.' As Robin said this I became aware of whispering around me. It seemed that many of my courtiers knew what had caused the laughter. I frowned. I have never liked to be ignorant of what others know.

'What is it that causes such amusement, and now such unease? It seems many of you know why these fine gentlemen laugh so loudly.'

'It is but gossip, Your Majesty, foolish gossip.'

'Gossip? About whom? It must be someone

important for you all to turn so pale and evasive when I ask about it.' An unpleasant thought struck me. 'Are you gossiping about me?'

'No, no, Your Majesty. We are all your loyal and loving servants. I, and every man here, would kill anyone who dared to bandy your name around in our hearing.'

'Then who is the subject of this amusing tittle tattle?'

'Lady Mary Grey.'

I could not have been more astonished if they had said William Cecil, a man known for his absolute rectitude. 'And what are they saying of my poor cousin?'

'She is in love.'

'That is cruel, to tease the poor little lady so.'

'It is not a tease, it is true, but it is who she loves that causes the most amusement.'

'Who does she love?'

'Thomas Keyes.'

'Thomas Keyes?' I had been astonished before; now I was incredulous. Thomas Keyes was my sergeant porter, a commoner in charge of the security of my court. This was unsuitable enough. Lady Mary was of royal blood and far above him in rank, but that was the only way in which she was above him. As befitted his office, Thomas Keyes was a giant of a man – the tallest man in my court, if not in my kingdom. Mary Grey had not attained the height of a nine-year-old child.

*

'It is not a flirtation, Your Majesty. We are legally wed.' Lady Mary stood before me and, to her credit, she did not sob or beg as her sister had done, but drew herself up as straight as she could, given her infirmity. Also, unlike her sister, she carried her marriage papers in her hands.

'You are *what*? Have you learnt nothing from your sister's sad example? You have no right to wed without my permission.'

'But we knew you would not give it.'

'You are not a fool, are you, Mary? You are right, I would not have given you permission to marry so far beneath your dignity.'

'But surely that is why my marriage is no threat to you. By marrying so humble a man, I have ruled myself out of any consideration of the succession and so may attain my only desire, to live quietly and unobtrusively with my husband as an ordinary wife.'

Had her precipitate actions not reminded me so forcibly of her foolish sister's irresponsible behaviour perhaps I might have been more merciful, but I was the queen. I could not allow my rules to be broken with no consequence and I also remembered what occurred when I showed mercy to her sister. Regardless of my liking for Mary or even, perhaps, my admiration for her dignity and courage, I was a queen and was obliged to act like one. 'Madam, to marry without the queen's permission is high treason. You will be placed under house arrest for the foreseeable future. Your so-called husband will be thrown into the Fleet.'

Now Mary flung herself onto her knees and began to beseech me. 'Not the Fleet, merciful queen, please do not send Thomas there. My husband is ailing, and he will not survive such conditions.'

'He is a commoner who has presumed above his station. He should have thought of the consequences when he first set eyes on you, as should you, Lady Mary. I thought God had blessed you with a modicum of good sense. It seems I was wrong. Foolishness and giving in to intemperate impulse appear to run in your family. All three sisters ruined by their marriages. I thought you had learnt from their example. It seems I was mistaken. I do not understand you, for all the blood we share. People never cease pressuring me to think of marriage. When I protest, they tell me it is desirable. Desirable? Unlike you, foolish cousin, I would rather be a beggar woman and single, than married and a queen.'

Poor Mary is dead now too, but of natural causes, I am relieved to say. She died in her own bed a free woman, proud to the last of her status as a married one. Her husband was not so fortunate. He died only a year after being released from the Fleet. I did not allow them to meet again and I am sorry for that. Thomas Keyes is another link on my phantom chain. If he had lived longer, perhaps I would have relented and let them enjoy a little happiness together. I like to think I would have done so, but I cannot be sure.

Fifteen

'The queen wishes to stay where she is, my lords.'

Yet again, Cecil and Archbishop Whitgift exhorted me to allow orderlies to carry me to my chamber, but I was not yet ready to go. I knew that as soon as I took to my bed, I would never rise from it again. I wanted to die. I was impatient to leave a world that no longer had a place for me, but I was also afraid. As the litany of my past sins and errors unfolded itself before my mind's eye, I became more afraid of the divine judgment that awaited me. Like a child anticipating a beating, I wanted to delay the inevitable for as long as I could. Somehow, sitting on cushions on the floor soothed me. Perhaps it was my earthly version of limbo – I was neither quite alive nor quite dead. And I have never liked to be rushed into anything.

This time, Cecil and Whitgift had been more insistent about my need to retire and I had shown my displeasure by grunting and feebly waving my hands at them in a gesture of dismissal. Their forceful tone had made me afraid that they would disregard my wishes and drag me away against my will. I began to whimper in my distress.

Philadelphia Carey, who had attended me so carefully, came to my rescue. 'The queen wishes to stay where she is, my lords.'

And the two great men backed away.

I have always relied on my ladies in waiting. With them and with them alone, I could relax and throw off my masculine guise of sovereign. Each of my ladies, with their different duties and responsibilities, resembled a wife. (I have never quite realised until now how much I had in common with a Turkish sultan and his harem.) My ladies variously soothed my brow, gave me rest, entertained me and protected me from care and woe. Perhaps I was as harsh a husband as any Great Turk in that I expected them to give to me and never the other way around. Yet parents queued to have their daughters enter my service, so I cannot have been such a harsh mistress. Of course, I also knew those same parents wanted a good husband for their daughters and that there was no finer place to hunt one down than in my court. Particularly if I had become fond of the young woman in question, it irritated me that her parents merely regarded me as a way station on the journey to marriage and motherhood. I was a queen, not an interlude!

Indeed, it was not simply my relatives who caused me

trouble by falling in love indiscriminately. My ladies-in-waiting did so with monotonous regularity. It became so commonplace for some young lady to approach me and confide tearfully that she was with child and needed permission to marry her swain (usually also a member of my court) that I began to wonder if any marriages ever took place in my kingdom without a baby already resident in the incontinent bride's belly.

I did not like all this marrying and fornication! If I could control my basest urges and live a life of discipline and virtue, then I found it hard to understand why it proved so difficult for others. I was not sympathetic – particularly as each tearful girl pleaded that she had been swept away by love. As if such self-indulgence excused anything! Even women I had respect for, who had some brains in their heads and a modicum of commonsense, used the same absurd arguments to justify their foolish behaviour. I expected my ladies to love me, not some sweet-smelling popinjay. As I grew older and saw more of the consequences of love I reasoned that the same maidens who had begged and pleaded to be allowed to marry their paramour (or, alternatively, be forgiven for having done so already), would have fared much better if they had remained faithful to me and lived out their days in my service, rather than in their husbands'.

In my forty-five years on the throne, I have had many gentlewomen attend me. Some I felt little for, many I liked and a few I loved. Now, after so many long and weary years, all but a handful of my dearest attendants have died. There was none that I loved as I loved Kat Ashley, who cared for me when I was a babe in arms and stood beside me through my darkest and most dangerous days. She was my chief gentlewoman until she died. I miss her gruff voice and bawdy commonsense as much now as I did the day she left me. Of all those I hope to see in heaven, it is Kat's plain face that will give me the greatest comfort when I stand before God on my day of judgment. I know that she will nod and smile at me just as she did when I was an infant, and that her approval will give me the strength to answer the questions that are put to me.

'*Unus, duo, tres, quattuor, quinque, sex, septem, octo … octo …*'

I do not know how old I was as I stood in the centre of my father's great audience chamber repeating my numbers in Latin, but I could not have been much more than four years old. My new stepmother, who turned out to be kind enough, was all but unknown to me then. She sat beside my father on the royal dais, but she was not looking at me. Her eyes never left the king. She gazed at his face, the quicker to anticipate his mercurial changes of mood, perhaps, but also because it flattered him. I suppose my mother's terrible fate must never have been far from her mind.

My father's new queen was fair and round faced, with pale hair scraped back tightly under an elaborate headdress. I knew her name was Queen Jane but I only recall addressing her as 'Your Majesty'.

I hesitated in my recitation because I sensed my father was bored. He sat slumped on his throne. His hands were fiddling with a tassel on his shirt and I could see he was only listening to me on sufferance. Despite my infancy, I was aware he did not like to see me anymore – not since my mother had been replaced by the lady who now sat next to him. I don't know if I understood Queen Anne was dead at that time, or if I knew of the manner in which she met her end, but I knew she had vanished and that with her disappearance, my status and importance had also collapsed. I felt the change as a chill, as if a cloud had covered the sun. As my father glared at me resentfully, the chill became an icy blast.

I knew my numbers well enough, but I began to feel afraid and my voice began to falter. Then I heard a cough and saw that just to the left of the royal dais my governess Kat had managed to work her way to the front of the gathered throng. She smiled at me and nodded. I could see her mouthing the words I was to say, the words she had taught me. She was willing me to succeed. Her love radiating across the room chased away my father's displeasure. I stopped looking at him and concentrated on Kat's face until I felt safe again.

'... *octo, novem, decem.*' I took a breath and, encouraged by Kat, I began to count in Greek. '*Ena, dio, tria, tessera, pente, eksi, efta, okto, enia, deka.*' This time I did not hesitate. By the time I had counted to ten in French, Spanish and Italian, my father's face had changed from thunderously bored to pleased and proud.

'Well done! I see you have inherited your father's skill with languages.'

'I have excellent teachers, my lord.'

'And modest withal! I know not from where you received that trait, my girl.'

The court laughed and applauded my father's witticism and – although I did not understand its full meaning – I felt a thrill at having been the trigger for such a response. Such a pleasant feeling, but it lasted only a moment before my father was turning away from me and towards something else.

That is the most common memory I have of my father. I was always just catching his attention, for a brief but intense moment or two, as he made his way towards something or someone else that mattered so much more.

Kat scurried to my side and led me away.

'Was my father pleased with me, Kat?'

'Indeed he was, my lady. Pleased and proud.'

'Were you pleased with me?'

'Nothing you could ever do or not do would displease me. I love you no matter what.'

'But were you pleased with me?' I did not want to be fobbed off with generalities. I was hungry for praise.

'Of course! You are the cleverest child I have ever seen.' She picked me up and hugged me hard and I buried my face in her velvet gown. I put my thumb in my mouth and sighed happily. As long as Kat was with me, I was safe.

This is a feeling that followed me into adulthood and onto the throne. Kat Ashley was my nurse, my governess, and, eventually, my chief gentlewoman of the bedchamber. After she died, I never felt quite as safe again. Indeed, if I think of heaven now, I see Kat's face smiling and nodding at me, just as it did all those years ago in my father's audience chamber. Except this time the throne she stands behind is God's.

If your father is a king it is hard to separate him from God when you are a child, perhaps even when you are a grown woman. When I pray to God, I must confess – and this is blasphemy – that it is often the image of my father that I see. Is this how each of us must stand before our Holy Father when the time comes (a time which is now so very near to me)? Must we stand as naked and defenceless as an infant, with all our excuses and disguises stripped from us? Must we recite the story of our lives before the great judge, cringing in shame, desperate for his love and mercy? I did all that I could to win my father's love and mercy but to no avail. I hope I will be more fortunate with God. I hope that Kat is there to plead for me in heaven, as she did so often on earth.

I loved Blanche Parry almost as much as I loved Kat Ashley. When Kat died, Blanche took her place as my chief gentlewoman. She served me loyally and well. Unlike Kat, and almost alone among my ladies, Blanche never married; she saved her devotion entirely for me. She served me until she died despite threatening frequently to leave. When she felt hurt or tired or slighted she would sulk and tell me how much she looked forward to the day she could retire to her family estate. But that day never came. Despite the occasional flash of temper and cross word, she never left my side.

As I near the end of my life, despite the flibbertigibbets who annoyed me by marrying, it is the love and loyalty of women I value. The friendship and support they gave me was quieter than that of men. Their love asked for little in return. There is a myth among men that women cannot be real friends; that we spend our days in bitter competition to win one of them. And so it is with some women. Indeed, it is possible that my mother was one such – not that it did her much good. However, among the women I loved and who loved me in return, I never found other friendships that endured so long or gave me so much. There were men whose loyalty came close to theirs: Robin, of course, William Cecil, and a few others, but they expected favours in return and public acknowledgement – which I gave them freely and with gratitude. It was the women closest to me who were content to serve me entirely for my own sake. And, yes, there were rivalries and jealousies and squabbles but so there was among the men of my court too, much as they liked to think themselves above such trivialities. Blanche, the longest serving of any, was prone to jealousy particularly as she grew older, but it was her love of me that made her so, not her love of preferments.

A few years before she died, Blanche began to lose her sight. She did not go blind completely, but could only see that which was directly in front of her. (I am glad that despite my frequent headaches and all the long hours I spent peering over official papers, I have kept my ability to see. I can still read with the help of my pince nez. My ability to hear is a different matter – or so I am told by some of my courtiers.)

'Dearest Blanche, take my arm and let me lead you to the window.'

'Oh no, Your Grace, it is not seemly for you to give me aid.'

But I was frightened for my friend. I had seen how often a tumble and a broken bone could lead to permanent disability and even death in the old, and Blanche suffered with the humped back and frail bones so common to old women. I leapt to her side and took her arm despite her protests. 'There is no one here but you and me, and I fear that you may stumble and hurt yourself.'

'I get about very well with the aid of my stick.' With that she tapped the floorboards sharply.

'You do indeed, but it gives me pleasure to have you lean on my arm. Will you not allow me that small service at least?'

'If Your Grace commands I must, of course, obey.'

She did not like to accept help – something I understand much better now than I did then. Blanche Parry valued her independence. She was proud that she was able to support herself without the help of any man. She had thriftily amassed a tidy sum, thanks to the financial rewards I gave her in recognition of her long, loyal and loving service.

Grudgingly she took my proffered arm and walked to the open window. An intoxicating scent perfumed the air. Sweet briar bloomed in profusion on the trellis outside.

'Can you smell the sweet briar? It is gorgeous this year.'

'Aye, and see them too. I am not so blind as to have to rely on my sense of smell to know there are flowers nearby.' She spoke crossly and I knew that her dignity was still injured.

'I did not mean to offend you. It is simply that the fragrance is so heady.'

She allowed herself to be mollified. 'They smell sweet enough, I grant you.'

I plucked a pink flower stem and gave it to her. She took it and curtsied.

'At least I have never had to rely on any man to help me.' She held the bloom up to her nose.

'A proud boast for us both. Take a deep breath, Blanche, as you say, your eyes may not be as sharp as once they were, but your nose is as acute as ever.'

'Aye, and with some of the young people who now surround you, I have often had cause to regret that. They do not seem to bathe as frequently as they should.'

As Blanche grew older she became more critical of the young. It is a common failing, I think, among those of us who live long enough to get old. We envy those in their prime and yet pity them at the same time. Their heedlessness annoys us and we recognise the folly of their assumption that the youth they possess now will remain theirs forever. We recognise it because it was our belief once. I remember thinking when I was but a girl that the old had always been old. I was therefore somewhat bewildered when one of their number reminisced about their youth and childhood. If anyone started a sentence to me with 'When I was a girl (or boy)', I listened politely as I had been taught to do, but never really heard a word they said. I suspect many of the young in this chamber regard me the same way now.

Blanche took much pride in her financial independence. She used some of her wealth to build a tomb for herself in the church of her girlhood in Bacton on the Norfolk coast. She told me proudly that the sculpture she had commissioned for her monument depicted her kneeling at my feet. 'My epitaph is a simple one, Your Grace.'

'This is a morbid conversation! I command you to live many years yet.'

'I intend to live for as long as God allows and not a day longer, but it does no harm to prepare for the inevitable in advance.'

'What is your epitaph, Blanche? It seems you are determined to tell me.'

She smiled triumphantly. She stood as if she were about to recite before some long forgotten teacher, clasping her hands in front of her and looking up to the heavens. She spoke in a booming, formal voice. 'With maiden queen a maid did end my life.'

I was deeply touched. She was wedded to her queen.

But not all my female attendants pleased me as much as Kat Ashley and Blanche Parry. One who led me a merry dance was the daughter of my first ambassador to France, Nicholas Throckmorton. I had known the girl since she was in swaddling and she had always been a vivacious little thing. She was also my namesake. Bess Throckmorton came into my service in her twenties and I found her sense of fun invigorating. I indulged her rather more than I should have, even tolerating a little impudence now and then. I like women and men with some spirit. It wearies me to be surrounded constantly by those who only ever say 'yes, Your Grace' or 'if it pleases Your Majesty'. I am suspicious of such courtiers. I do not know what their motives are. I prefer those who allow me glimpses of the real person underneath and so I encourage their sense of independence. Sometimes I have lived to regret it, as I did with Essex.

'You are pulling a strange face, Mistress Throckmorton, as if something displeases you.'

'It is nothing, Your Grace.'

'If it is nothing, Bess, why pull such a face?'

'I have never been a good mistress of my face. You must forgive it. It has a mind of its own, despite my best intentions.'

'I like your face and I also like to know the thoughts that are behind its expressions.'

'As I say, it is nothing.'

'Fie, girl, it cannot be nothing! Perhaps your belly pains you – I have told you that you are altogether too greedy at table. You eat your food too quickly and failing to chew properly gives you wind. It is either that, or you do not approve of the cap Mistress Parry has just put upon my head.'

Mistress Throckmorton had very decided opinions about clothes and I saw immediately from her guilty expression that I had guessed right. She did not like my new cap.

'Ah hah! It is my cap that gives you pain, not the contents of your belly!'

'Oh, Your Grace, I am sorry. I tell myself a thousand times to keep my opinions to myself, but I fail more often than I succeed.'

But I could see that she was not sorry, because she smiled at me in such a way that said as clearly as any words that while she knew she was not technically entitled to have opinions about anything I did, she remained convinced her response to my new cap was the correct one.

I reached up and removed the offending object from my head. 'What is it about the poor thing that offends you so much?'

'It is the colour. I do not think it is the most flattering for your eyes.'

I looked closely at the confection. It was in a bright shade of green with feathers dyed purple. I had thought it rather fetching when my milliner first brought it to me.

'Do you think it an unsuitable colour for a woman of my advanced years, perhaps?' I felt rather offended by her poor opinion of my choice of headdress.

'Not at all. I just think this one would show your features to better advantage.' With that she produced a headdress of tawny brown with trimmings in a bright shade of russet. Without asking, she placed it where the offending item had sat only moments before.

My irritation died when I saw the effect of this cap on my pale skin and dark eyes in the mirror. Suddenly, I looked brighter and younger. 'Hmmm!'

I was not about to give her the satisfaction of telling her she was right, but I was also pleased that she had not allowed me to go out into the court in a cap that did not suit me. 'I will wear what you recommend, Mistress Throckmorton. It doesn't matter to me what fripperies I wear. I have more important things to think about.'

From that time on I allowed Bess Throckmorton to choose my ensembles. Indeed, I allowed her to advise me about which of my gowns I should keep and which should be discarded. Blanche, who had helped me select my clothes previously, felt slighted and began once more to threaten retirement in Bacton.

'You must not leave me just yet, Blanche, for I do not know how I would manage without you.'

'That Bess Throckmorton can look after you well enough.'

'Not at all. She can only help me with my outward coverings. It is only you who can soothe my heart and soul.'

This pleased her but, just to be sure, I gave her first pick of the gowns that were being discarded and this pleased her most of all.

I wonder, when I get to heaven, if virtuous Blanche will be wearing one of the gowns I gave her. I know that she, like Jane Grey, will have gone straight to God's side. She never sinned in her life.

But, and this is a recurring thought, I find I am wondering what people wear in heaven. The smartest gown they wore in life? Or the clothes they died in? What will my spirit be clothed in? Will it be what I am wearing now?

I looked down at my soiled and crumpled gown. Such a prospect did not fill me with delight. But if they eventually put me in my bed in my nightclothes, is that what I will be wearing to ascend to heaven (or, God forbid, descend to hell)? Or do you stand before God in the clothes you were buried in? And then I wished heartily that I had not become so estranged from Bess Throckmorton. She would have made sure I was seen in what suited me wherever I was going.

Sixteen

Once again, I was staring at a weeping girl who had flung herself at my feet in a puddle of silk brocade – and, once again, I remained unmoved. I tapped my fingers on the arm of my chair, drumming along with the rhythm of her sobs. I wanted this unpleasant interview to be over. We had already said too many harsh things to one another. The weeping girl had just told me that I did not understand what it was to be young and in love, and I had told her to hold her impudent tongue.

'Do you think I have never been in love? Do you think you are the only girl who has ever wept over a man? You know nothing of me and my life.'

It was then that she prostrated herself across the floor.

Who did she think she was talking to? I suppose she thought she was talking to that strange, inhuman creature – an anointed queen – rather than a real flesh-and-blood woman who happened to wear a crown. Of course I understood what it was to be in love. I also understood how hard it is to resist being carried away by your emotions. I had seen more misery than this silly girl had any conception of. I also understood – better than anyone – that however desperate you might feel at the time, life goes on and it is possible to live and be happy without the man you desire. When this young woman declared so dramatically that she could not live without the man she loved and had secretly married, I snorted. Unfortunately for her, I was now impervious to such theatrics. Indeed, they were having exactly the opposite effect to the one she intended.

'And you have had his child?'

The girl nodded mutely between sobs, without lifting her head.

'But the child died – as so many do – and that is why you returned to my service, claiming you had recovered from your "illness", as you called it, and acted like nothing had occurred?'

Now the girl moaned in misery and I did feel a glimmer of pity for her. I often find I feel more sympathy when people admit to their failings, rather than deny any wrongdoing. Notwithstanding, I was determined that I would not soften.

'You thought you could keep a clandestine marriage to one of the most famous men in my kingdom a secret, and that I would never be any the wiser. You have no conception of how many times I have heard this story before.'

I waited for an answer but the girl said nothing, just wept pitifully at my feet.

'What sort of a fool do you take me for? You, Bess Throckmorton, of all people, should know that I have eyes and ears in every corner of the kingdom and nothing Sir Walter Raleigh does can be kept secret from me for long.'

Now she spoke. 'It is not his fault, Your Majesty. If you wish to punish someone, let your wrath fall on me. It is I who persuaded him to marry me, not the other way around.'

'You must really have no respect for my intelligence if you think I would believe that! As if anyone – even you, Mistress Throckmorton, despite your high opinion of your charms – could persuade that man to do anything he did not want to do.'

Sir Walter Raleigh was a force of nature. Like the Earl of Essex he was young, handsome and full of energy. Unlike Essex he was also a man of intellect and substance. When Raleigh took on a project, he not only finished it, he succeeded. He was an adventurer, a poet, a scientist, a soldier and an explorer. He was always asking permission to make sail for some exotic location in the New World. His enthusiasm for the promise of these heathen lands – laden as they were with precious metals, strange fruits, spices and condiments – persuaded me to grant him a special charter to explore and colonise the Americas. I set one condition: that he gave me a fifth of everything of value he found. He made me much profit and he added to my prestige. He named his new colony Virginia in my honour. He was a man of action, but he also had a subtle and nuanced understanding of human nature, something his contemporary the Earl of Essex never had. Raleigh knew that this tribute to my chastity would please me more than any number of new places named Elizabeth.

I valued and admired Raleigh, but perhaps my positive feelings towards him were also helped by the fact that he was so often absent from my court. Our relationship was largely epistolary. He wrote me letters, very good letters, letters filled with descriptions of strange places and people that I would never see. Unlike most of my correspondents, whose missives I approached in the spirit of duty, I looked forward to reading letters from Raleigh. They gave me windows into worlds that made my heart leap with excitement and my mind's eye struggle to imagine the strange scenes he described. I had wanted to be a great explorer when I was a girl. The closest I could come to realising this ambition as queen was to finance and encourage Raleigh.

Perhaps this is why I responded with such fury when I discovered that this uncommon man had done such a common thing as marry in secret. Of course, it was imperative for my continued authority that I did not soften my stance on the need for royal approval before any aristocratic marriage, but sometimes I raged and punished and separated more for the sake of appearance than anything else. My fury was not feigned, however, with my close relatives like the Grey sisters because there were political imperatives. Nor was it feigned with those of whom I was truly fond – like Raleigh and, yes, Bess.

Since she had taken charge of my wardrobe I found I trusted her taste more than that of any of my other ladies. I would miss her fine eye. 'You will go to the Tower, Lady Raleigh, as will your husband.'

I said the words wearily and signalled for the guards to come forward and take her hence. My actions sobered the young woman and she stopped weeping at last. She waved away the hands of the guards and stood up of her own accord, brushing down the crumpled silk of her blue gown. She curtsied with her head held high, but rather spoiled the effect by wiping her nose with the back of her hand.

'I will go to the Tower happily, as Your Majesty commands. It is a fit punishment for my sin, but may I beg you one last time not to so confine my husband? He is a wild bird, who must take regular flight and he will not take kindly to having his wings clipped.'

'It does you credit to plead so, Bess, but it is not possible for me to imprison one and not the other. You must both be caged for a time, as all who disobey their prince must, but you will not be treated cruelly.'

*

'I need your services, Raleigh. That is the only reason I am temporarily releasing you from the Tower.'

Bess Throckmorton's husband doffed his cap and swept me a fine bow.

'I am fully aware of the limits of Your Grace's mercy.'

I raised a warning eyebrow. 'Do not presume too much, my lord. I can as easily change my mind as not.'

'Your Majesty is as quick in comprehension as always, I see.'

'And you still have a predilection for sailing very close to the wind.'

Raleigh smiled and once again doffed his cap but, wisely, remained silent.

'I suppose that is why I need your skills as a sailor and a warrior now. You are not a man who is easily daunted.'

'I am delighted to be once again at your service. What task do you have in mind for me?'

'There is an expedition returning from the New World and I want you to meet it off the coast of Spain. Your charge is to protect my ships, at any cost.'

I saw his eyes light up as he listened. Nothing could delight a sailor more than to find that he was to set sail after almost a year behind stone walls.

We discussed the details and I gave him permission to take whatever action was necessary. 'You are likely to attract more than the usual interest from the Spaniards.'

'How so, Your Grace?'

We were standing over a navigation map by this time,

which was laid out upon a table. Raleigh was absorbed in plotting the course of the ships that had already set sail from the New World, calculating their likely speed given the prevailing winds, the better to plan when and where he could intercept them. He looked up from the document as I spoke, but did not lift his finger from the point in the ocean where he felt the expedition must at this moment be.

'They have captured a Spanish merchant ship, the *Madre de Deus.* She is loaded with gold, silver and spices and Philip wants it back.'

'A carrack!' Raleigh literally rubbed his hands with glee.

'Your orders are to protect the ship and the expedition, then to organise and divide the treasure that it carries, ensuring that my part is allocated fairly.'

'I am at your service, Your Grace.'

Since the defeat of the Armada, my small but nimble fleet had become ever more confident of its ability to go wherever I sent them. I often quietly sent them to intercept the Spanish treasure ships as they attempted to haul great loads of gold and other precious cargo home from their colonies. Such was their success, I was rapidly building my treasury at the expense of Imperial Spain and nothing gave me greater pleasure. I could see it gave Raleigh great pleasure as well.

I could also see that he could hardly wait to begin his commission. Laughing at his impatience, I gave him permission to withdraw and he almost bounded for the door before I stopped him.

'Not a word, my lord, about the imprisonment of your wife? Do you not wish to plead for her release also?'

He turned and smiled at me. 'I am not such a fool as to presume on good fortune. I intend to so undertake this task that my pleas for my beloved wife will be very hard for you to ignore on my return.'

'You may be absent for a year or more.'

'That is so, Your Grace.'

'Time that will go very hard on your wife, languishing in prison.'

'I will bring her back something to make up for her solitude – with your permission, of course.'

'You think to mollify her with a trinket, sir? And men wonder why I never wished to marry!'

Raleigh gave a great bark of laughter and hurried on his way, shouting for his horse while still within earshot. I called after him.

'Do not forget, your freedom is temporary, my lord. Temporary!' But he had gone.

I liked Walter Raleigh. He was clever and he was honest. He did not try to fool me with honeyed words the way so many others did. Yet I also felt great pity for his wife. How easily men turn their backs on the women they claim to love. Worse, it did not escape me that perhaps he was not all that sorry to leave his wife under lock and key. He need have no fears for her behaviour or her loyalty while she was literally a prisoner.

Raleigh performed his task with great success, but it took him more than a year as I had warned it might. And I remained true to my word. Notwithstanding the great boost to my coffers from the *Madre de Deus*, on his return to England I had Sir Walter immediately re-arrested and escorted back to the Tower. No doubt his reunion with his wife was touching and I hope the trinket he gave her was pretty enough to compensate.

I let them cool their heels under the weight of my displeasure for a few more months, but in 1593 I relented and released both Sir Walter and his wife. Perhaps the sad fates of Katherine and Mary Grey weighed on my mind. Perhaps I was becoming softer in my old age. I wanted no more deaths on my conscience. No more links on my phantom chain. And Raleigh was too valuable a man to be wasted in prison for long. I gave him many more commissions in the years that followed and he sailed to the New World seeking gold and other precious commodities on more voyages than I could count. As far as I know he and Bess remained devoted to one another. They had two more sons, both of whom are still alive and for that I remain sincerely thankful.

Seventeen

Perhaps I have been asleep?

It seems to me that just this moment I was talking to Sir Walter Raleigh. He was telling me of some exotic place or other, which cannot be, because I know full well that he is on the Jersey Islands – being their governor – and exotic they are not.

The phantom Sir Walter has evaporated now. Rather than his weather-beaten face, when I open my eyes I find I am looking at my hand. It must be my hand because it is in front of my face and it moves when I want it to, but it does not quite feel as if it belongs to me. Perhaps I am dying by inches, bit by bit, starting with my extremities. The hand I am staring at is that of an old, old woman, withered by age. The skin is wrinkled, the flesh hollowed out and the knuckles of the fingers are bent and swollen. Even the nails, well-cared for though they may be, are thickened and yellowed. But it is my ring finger that looks most strange to me. It is naked and strangely exposed. Something is missing, the weight of it is wrong and I notice how I hold it oddly, apart from its fellows. I hold my hand up and turn it slowly this way and that, in front of my face. It *is* mine, I am sure of that, but it doesn't look like the hand I remember.

I was proud of my hands. They were narrow, long-fingered and graceful. My skin – the skin I remember – was milky-white and velvet-soft, yet it had vigour and strength. It coated the bones and muscles of my hand snugly. I liked to attract attention to my elegant fingers by drawing my gloves on and then off.

But it is not just the fact that my hands are so old that puzzles me; there is something missing. I have lost something, but I know not what it was.

My ring! My coronation ring! The ring I have worn for forty-five years. It is not on my hand. I can see where it once sat; the skin is whiter there and worn smooth. The finger itself is narrow where the ring has left its mark, but the skin and knuckles above and below are swollen. I take the finger of my other hand from my mouth and use it to feel where the ring used to be. Did I lose it? I turn to look in the folds of my gown and between the cushions on which I sit.

There is a small healing wound above the imprint of the ring, as if the jewel had dug into my flesh. It had hurt for a long time. I used to move the ring up and down on my finger habitually to try and relieve the pain. Eventually it would not budge at all. Maybe it was as little as a week ago that my apothecary finally confronted me about the problem.

'We will have to cut it off, Your Majesty.'

I recoiled and put my hand behind my back. 'I have worn it since I was crowned queen of this kingdom. It is a sacred ring.'

'I am sorry, Your Grace, but it is either the ring, or the finger. It has grown so tight the ring is cutting off the blood, and I cannot prevent an infection setting in and that could put Your Majesty's life at risk.'

'I have not long left on this earth, anyway. What does it matter if I go a little sooner than a little later?'

'You may have many years left to you, Your Grace. You are otherwise healthy and your subjects pray daily for your continued health. You cannot betray them for the love of a ring. I have seen gangrene proceed from the smallest of wounds and it is not a pleasant way to leave this world, rotting from the finger outwards.'

The man was not a fool. I could not think how to answer him, and he took advantage of my silence.

'I can call for a surgeon now. It will be the matter of a few moments discomfort only. Once the ring is from your finger you will experience instant relief.'

And my finger was sore. Every time I moved it, the gold of the ring dug itself into my already chafed and weeping flesh. Sometimes the finger went numb because so little blood could get to it. Sometimes, the pain of it woke me in the night and I was aware that the chafing wound had become foul-smelling. Still, I hesitated. I am not brave when it comes to facing physical pain. It was another of the reasons why I was glad not to marry. I had never understood how women went into childbed with such equanimity. The whole idea of it terrified me.

I remember the last time I had a rotten tooth – my teeth have been nothing but agony to me for as long as I can recall – and the surgeon who then attended me recommended extraction. Again, I recoiled and again I delayed the operation, day after agonising day.

I remember I could not eat or sleep, nor even think due to the pain. All I wanted was to be rid of the ghastly tooth and a number of times I actually sat in the extractor's chair and opened my mouth to allow him to do his gory work. But every time, as he began to prise my jaws wider and bring the hideous clamps closer to my throbbing incisor, I called a halt, bounding from the chair, pushing the man and his hideous implements aside as hard as I could in my panic. Once, taken by surprise, the man fell backwards and landed hard upon his rear, something that might have made me laugh at any other time, but which simply made me shriek louder as I fled from the room.

I could not bear the thought of anything touching my poor tooth, let alone the iron jaws of the surgeon's instrument. I knew that once he had the offending item in its grasp, there would be no freeing myself.

Eventually it was John Aylmer, the Bishop of

London, who persuaded me to undergo the procedure. By the time he did, I was almost mad with the pain. My physicians brought him into my presence. I was seated on my dais, under my cloth of state, trying vainly to conduct the business of my office. I clutched a cold compress to my swollen cheek and my ladies had packed the tooth with soothing herbs (as I screamed and winced whenever they touched it). I could not speak except thickly, because I had to keep my tongue away from the source of the pain. No doubt I was a picture of misery.

'Your Majesty, it grieves me to see you in such discomfort.'

'Discomfort!' (It sounded more like 'Dithcomfor'.) Pah! This is agony, my lord! Agony!'

'Indeed, Your Grace, I have suffered with my teeth as well and there is little that causes us greater pain.'

'It is a curse, a curse!' (A curth, a curth!)

'I have a diseased tooth as I speak to you now, Your Grace, and have come before you to have it extracted by these skilled physicians you see here beside me.'

I looked at the men on either side of him. I had thought when he entered that they were merely his attendants and had paid them little mind. Now I saw they clasped their hands behind their backs, as if hiding something there.

'You are having your tooth removed here and now?'

He did not need to answer, as I could see that the

physicians were already bringing in the appropriate chair and the dreadful instruments to perform the operation.

'Yes, Your Grace, with your permission. I want to show you the skill and care that these men take and, by my example, give you courage to allow them to finally rid you of the source of your suffering.'

Before I had time to protest, the bishop was in the chair, the surgeon was upon his chest and his assistants were holding his arms tightly.

'My lord! My lord!'

But before I had time to say anything further the surgeon straightened up and brandished the bloodied tooth. It was now in the jaws of his extraction implement rather than the jaws of the great prince of the church. The operation had happened in the blink of an eye. The surgeon wiped the bishop's mouth and within seconds Aylmer was standing and, apart from a cloth he held to the corner of his mouth, it was as if nothing untoward had occurred.

'As you see, Your Grace, the operation is fast and clean and now I am rid of the source of my pain.'

His speech was slightly thickened, but not nearly to the same extent as mine.

'Does your mouth not hurt at all anymore?'

'It throbs a little, I will not lie, but it hurts much less than it did before.'

The surgeon handed the bishop another linen with which to stop the blood that was now filling his mouth.

He gave him a drink and instructed him to swill it around and spit it into the proffered bowl. This the bishop duly did and then he smiled, and I could see the gap where his painful tooth had so lately been.

'You may take my word for it. The operation is not as bad as you anticipate and the relief it affords is well worth it.'

I was impressed by his courage and by his devotion and, I had to admit, his example had comforted me. Moreover the pain in my tooth was becoming impossible to bear. I signalled to my ladies to help me from my throne and into the surgeon's chair.

'I will submit to your surgeon's ministrations, my lord bishop.'

Gingerly, I lowered myself into the seat, but the second I rested my weight upon it fully, the surgeon was upon me, his knee on my chest, his assistants grasping my arms firmly. My shock at this manhandling caused me to gasp and the second my jaws parted his instrument was in my mouth and grasping the tooth. There was a moment of intense pain, a sensation of great pressure, but before I even had the chance to scream, the blackened tooth was in the tight grip of the implement and no longer in my jaw.

The lords and ladies who were gathered around us broke into spontaneous applause as the surgeon brandished my rotten tooth. I was too shocked and breathless to speak.

There will be no pain in heaven, of that I am sure. I wish I could say the same of hell.

My brain is becoming addled. I am not sure anymore of what is real and what is not. Maybe I was dreaming, for it seems to me I was talking to Bishop Aylmer but moments ago and he has been dead almost ten years.

I hold my hand close to my nose and peer at it. The skin that covers the loose flesh is wrinkled and transparent. Brown spots discolour it and blue veins stand out from the flesh. Yet I am not so far gone that I do not know it as my own hand.

But something is missing. I twist and turn the hand as if by doing so I can somehow discover what it is I lack. One of those who watch from the corner of the chamber sees the gesture. 'The queen is signalling something.'

It is a woman's voice, young and clear like a bell. Suddenly she is close to me, bending down. 'What do you require, Your Majesty? What can I fetch for you?'

I cannot find any reason to answer her, so I do not. Instead I close my eyes. I do not require anything now except the one thing I cannot think of. It strikes me that she may know what it is I have lost, so I take my finger out of my mouth again and speak. My voice is dry and croaky from being so long unused, but it remains distinct. 'Something is missing.'

'What is missing, Your Grace? What is it that you lack? I will fetch it for you immediately.'

But I can tell by her answer that she does not know what I seek and I turn my face away from her. I hear her ask others in the room for help.

'The queen is missing something, but she cannot tell me what.'

'Shall we give her water? It is a long time since she took any.'

And water is fetched and they hold my head and I sip a little from the beaker. The taste and feel of the cool liquid are good, but water is not what I seek.

And then, quite suddenly, perhaps the drink has refreshed my brain, I know once more what it is that is missing and I know how it is that I came to lose it. My coronation ring is no longer upon my finger. I am missing its familiar feel and weight.

'It is either lose the ring, Your Grace, or lose the finger.'

Now as I study the naked finger, which looks so frail and unprotected without its armour, I think it might have been better to lose the flesh than the jewel. 'But how will you get it off, Master Surgeon? The skin has grown around the gold. It has become a part of me in literal truth.'

'I will be gentle and will saw it through at its thinnest part with a fine rasp, but I cannot promise that there will be no pain at all.'

And I was frightened, not so much of the pain but because it seemed to me that to lose my coronation ring was but a precursor to losing my crown and that in a year full of losses, this loss was the greatest of all.

'You will be like the dental surgeon and perform your deed quickly?'

'For in truth, my finger used to hurt quite badly but now it is worse, because I can feel little at all above the ring.'

'Aye and that is why we must have it off, for otherwise gangrene could set in and you could lose much more than your finger.'

His warning echoed that of my apothecary. Silently thanking Bishop Aylmer for his example so many years before, I closed my eyes and thrust my poor swollen hand towards the surgeon. 'Have you the implement now upon you?'

'I do indeed, Your Grace.'

'Do your worst then, but as you value your queen, do it quickly.'

And then there was a grip of iron about my wrist and a terrible thrill of pain as something sharp pierced the swollen flesh above the ring. I drew in my breath and tried to pull away, but the grip on my wrist did not move.

'Only a moment or two longer, Your Majesty, and the job will be done.'

The man's face was close to mine and I could feel his hot breath on my cheek. It smelled faintly of onions.

Then the horrible, hot rasping began and with it a

sense of damp skin tearing. I squealed a little at the shock of it and wondered how long I could bear the torture, when suddenly, as quickly as it had begun, I felt the pop of the gold as it broke away and I opened my eyes. The iron grip on my wrist relaxed and I stared at the now broken ring still embedded in my finger.

'There, Your Grace, the deed is almost done.'

Then I watched, fascinated, as the surgeon carefully and gently pulled the gold band out from my flesh. It hurt a little, but I steeled myself to bear it without complaint. When finally my finger was liberated and soothing unguents were gently rubbed upon the skin to aid in the healing, I felt nothing but relief. It was not until later when I was alone in my chamber that a great dark weight fell upon me.

I remember I put my hand up before my face, rather as I am doing now, and stared at the place where the ring had been.

'So this is how it begins.'

Eighteen

I am in my bed and I do not know how I came to be here. I can hear lamentations from my ladies who cluster about me and Archbishop Whitgift is praying for my soul. I hope he is praying hard.

It is an odd thing to die and yet it is so ordinary. Every man must die, aye, and every woman too, even every queen. I am in no pain. In fact, my body feels already lost to me although my ears and my other senses register the movements of the living around me, so I cannot yet be quite dead. The living smell, I suddenly realise. They have a meaty, oily stench that comes off them in waves. The dead smell too, of course, but only in their grave if they are buried quick enough. My father's poor corpse lay in state for so long, as his ministers squabbled about who would control the boy who was to inherit the throne, that it swelled and burst, emitting a stench so foul they buried him in a lead-lined coffin. I hope they bury me quickly enough that only the worms shall be offended.

I am in my bed and in my night clothes. I am not so removed from my disintegrating flesh that I am unaware of my corsets having gone from me. I will never wear them again. I am sure they do not insist on whalebone in heaven. I hope I spend eternity in my night shift as it is the most comfortable garment I ever wore in life and I yearn so now for comfort and for peace. Angels are always depicted in loose white gowns and maybe that is because so many of us die in our beds. They bury us in our finest garments, of course, and bind up our jaws with bandages. They will put coins on my eyes too, so I can pay the ferry man on the River Styx – even though that is a pagan superstition and one that is no longer meant to be believed.

But as they lower my corpse into its resting place, now that all my struggles are at an end, what have I achieved? How will I be remembered? Will posterity treat me kindly or …?

My father's memory has been treated kindly. He presided over great changes in England. He was a colossus, he changed the very God we worshipped, such was his power on earth. To this day he is remembered fondly by the ordinary folk of England as Bluff King Hal. There are few left who actually experienced his rule but his legacy remains a proud one. Truth be told, his legacy is probably more golden now than it ever was when he was alive.

Would he have been proud of me, I wonder? The

daughter whose birth felt like a direct slap from God? The girl he could not bear to look upon for so many of my earliest years? The child he neglected, discounted and mostly ignored? When he was alive I longed for his approval. Now that I am dying, I find I long for it still. The few times he showed his pleasure at something I had done or said I store in my memory like golden talismans. I take them out every now and again and polish them, turn them this way and that so I can glory in his momentary pride.

Madame Isabeau, he sometimes called me, a name no one else ever used. Whenever he said that name I knew I was in high favour. The first time was when my sister Mary and I gave him a book we had created together. I had written the translation inside and Mary had embroidered the cover. The second was when I presented another book to my last and most beloved stepmother, Queen Catherine Parr. This one I had worked entirely myself. I was eleven years old.

'Your Majesty.' I held the book behind my back as I curtsied to the queen. She was reading by the window, her dark auburn hair scraped back off her face. Her headdress was black, bordered by small white pearls. Her dress was black also, embroidered in silver and pearls. She almost always wore sombre colours – she was a widow as well as a wife – but with such style and grace that she made the other ladies look gaudy. I admired

Catherine Parr. It was all I wanted in the world to grow up to be just like her.

'Lady Elizabeth! How delightful. I am in need of some company and I can think of no one's I would enjoy more than yours.' She had such a talent for making people feel welcome and at ease. No doubt it is what my father liked about her also.

'I have made you something, Your Grace.' I felt almost shy about my little offering. I had laboured over my New Year's gift for months because I wanted it to be perfect. The translation was challenging enough, but the embroidery on the cover had almost defeated me. I'd had to unpick my stitches over and over to make them even and straight. It was why my sister had embroidered the cover of my father's similar gift a few years earlier. But this time, for Queen Catherine, I wanted to do it all myself.

'Have you? How lovely!'

I held it out to her. 'It is a translation of Margaret of Navarre's poem "The Mirror of the Sinful Soul".' I blurted the words out in a rush. I was so desperate for her to like my gift.

She took the book in her hands and turned it over silently. Then she opened a page at random and read the words I had written there. I stood, arms again behind my back, chewing on my lip. I was in an agony of suspense.

'Oh, Elizabeth ...'

She spoke – finally – after what seemed like an age. 'This is … this is … magnificent!'

And then she got up and hugged and kissed me most heartily. I loved it when she did so. Almost no one ever held me anymore and I was still quite a little girl.

'You translated all this by yourself? And embroidered this beautiful cover?'

I nodded, too overcome to speak.

'I am always telling your father what a remarkable girl you are and now I realise that I did not understand the half of it. Here, let us go to the king and show him what you have done. He will be so proud of you.'

As we walked along the corridor of Richmond Palace (the palace where I lie now, on my deathbed) the queen held my hand.

(It strikes me now how rarely in my life I have experienced affectionate touch. I can probably count the number of times I was hugged or held on less than ten fingers. How I wish someone would hold my hand now.)

She leant down towards me, so that no one but we two could hear. 'How did you know the poem is one of my favourites?'

'I heard you say so when you were discussing poetry with Lady Suffolk.'

'Your mother knew Margaret of Navarre well, from her days at the Royal Court in France. Did you know that, Lady Elizabeth?'

I shook my head, but I was lying, which is why I dared not speak. Blanche Parry, who had known my mother better than almost anyone, told me many tales of my mother's time in France and I knew well that she had been friendly with all the royal children of King Henri's court, including Princess Margaret. As Catherine Parr had perhaps guessed I had chosen the poem for two reasons. Because I knew my stepmother liked it, but also because I knew the author had known my mother.

'I do not know much about their relationship first-hand, but they must have known one another. The French court is not so much larger than the English one and here everyone knows everyone.'

'Aye, and their business.'

'You are sharp, little Elizabeth. Not much escapes your notice.'

I was an ignored and neglected princess. It was easy for a little girl to slip unnoticed behind a curtain or secrete herself in a window seat. If I was in a room and others of the court entered, I often tried to keep my presence unknown. I knew I made the courtiers uncomfortable. They were not sure whether to treat me as my father's daughter, or my mother's. It was better for everyone if I remained hidden. By making myself unobtrusive I heard many things. Perhaps it was in those years that I learnt what really goes on behind a monarch's back.

We had arrived at the king's apartments. The queen asked his factotum to announce our arrival and then we waited for a few moments.

I was always nervous before an audience with my father. I hoped for so much but usually received so little. I could see the queen had no such qualms. It was in the early days of their marriage and she was riding high in his favour.

We were ushered into the king's presence.

My father sat in front of a great casement window in the chair with wheels that he now favoured. There was a stench in the room, only weakly ameliorated by the incense that burned in every available vessel and the scented candles that lit the room more effectively than the wintry sun. The stench followed my father everywhere. It was the smell of the rotting flesh in the wound on his leg that would never heal. One of the reasons he was so pleased with his new queen was that she was deft and gentle at dressing the weeping sore and soothing it with herbs and unguents.

Like all who entered, I knew better than to react to the smell, but it took a few moments to grow accustomed to it. I curtsied low and let the queen approach my father while I hung back. The king acknowledged his wife, but it was as if I were made of thin air.

'What ho, my darling? What brings you to my pain-wracked rooms?' The king was pleased to see the queen, but he was also pouting like a sullen schoolboy.

He needed her to know how sore his leg was. It rested on a footstool in front of him.

'Is your poor leg troubling you very much today, Your Majesty? I am so sorry. Here let me change the dressing.' And she took a few steps forward, but he stopped her.

'There is no need. The surgeon has just this moment left, having performed the task and – while he does not do it nearly so gently and deftly as you do, sweeting – I could not bear to go through it again so soon.'

'Of course not, my dearest lord. It is foolish to submit to unnecessary pain. But I have brought you something that might distract you from your leg a little.'

'Good. All distractions are welcome.'

Now I felt deeply frightened. What if the king did not like my little book? What if it failed to distract him? I would rather the queen had played down my offering.

'It is a book, an ingenious little book, a gift to me from your remarkable daughter the Lady Elizabeth.' She was holding it out to him, but he did not take it. Instead he looked around her as if he had only just noticed my presence.

'The Lady Elizabeth? Yes, I wondered what she was doing here. Come here, child! I will not bite you!'

He might not bite, but he certainly barked. The loudness of his voice made me jump.

'What are you squirming for? I cannot abide a child who will not keep still.'

'She is nervous, Your Majesty, because she so much wants you to like her book.'

Queen Catherine held out both arms to me, encouraging me to walk forward, which I did, my heart hammering in my chest so hard I felt sure all in the room could hear it.

Now my father took the book in his hands. He was enormously overweight by this time, his facial features shrunken in a face and neck of quite extraordinary proportions. It took two strong men to push him about the palace in his chair.

The king's fingers were plump and each one carried a large and priceless ring. This made him clumsy and awkward. He turned the book over the better to examine its cover. 'Did you embroider this, Elizabeth? Or did you get one of your attendants to do it for you?'

'I did it myself, Your Majesty.'

'Hmmm. It is nicely done. It is good to see you pursuing more female accomplishments, my girl, at long last.'

It was often this way when he spoke to me (a rare enough occurrence on its own). Even when he praised me, there was always a sting in the tail.

'The cover is marvellous, but wait until you see what she has done inside.' And my stepmother stood beside my father and gently helped him turn the vellum pages, reading snippets of my translation to him in her beautiful, soothing voice.

'The child did this all by herself?' he asked after a time.

'Indeed. Without help of any kind.'

'How old are you now, Elizabeth?'

'I was eleven in September, Your Grace.'

'Eleven? As old as that? We will need to be looking for eligible husbands for you soon.'

My heart went from hammering to standing still. It was my greatest fear – that they would marry me off to some unknown prince and ship me off to God knows where. I planned to get very, very ill if such a thing was ever threatened.

'This is a remarkable achievement for a child of eleven. I have been telling you that your youngest daughter is a prodigy. She has inherited your talent and your character.'

'Just as well, given who her mother was.'

Again, the slap in the midst of praise. I ignored it. I had become practised at ignoring snide references to my parentage.

'You should be very proud of her, my darling, and of yourself. She is a living tribute to her father and the Tudor House. Here, let me read you some more.'

Which she did.

'Ha!' My father gave a great bark of appreciation at one deft translation. I flushed with delight.

'You are right, Catherine. This is a work of exceptional erudition. Why, I doubt even Master More's daughters could produce something as fine.'

Thomas More, who had been dead for many a year, was famous for his brilliant daughters, educated to as high a standard as any man. I think my father had always felt a rivalry with More, and that I could match the man's daughters was important to him.

'Come here, Madame Isabeau.'

I came closer, suffused with silent pleasure that he had used my nickname. Even more thrillingly, my father then chucked me affectionately under the chin.

'It is such a pity you were not a boy.'

My father terrified me and yet I hope to be reunited with him in the afterlife. My father made me feel bad more often than good, but I also knew that in his own way he loved me and that no actual bodily harm would come to me while he was alive. But, if I do see him in heaven (or, God forbid, the other place), will he praise me and tell me that I have made him proud? I have created a peaceful and prosperous England. More than that, I have made our little island formidable to its enemies and important to its friends. If we meet, will he call me Madame Isabeau and stroke my hair as he sometimes did when I was very small? Or will he berate me because I did not become some man's wife? My failure to marry and bear children means that the Tudor dynasty he was so desperate to secure dies with me.

Would his spirit be right to be angry? Did I refuse to even try to produce further generations of Tudors out of spite? Was I unconsciously determined to thwart my father's greatest desire? It sometimes seems to me that we do not understand all the reasons we do what we do, and that is why our actions surprise us as often as they surprise others.

I give another of my great sighs. No matter how I regard what I have done with the life he gave me, I suspect that my father is much more likely to berate me for my failings than praise me for my successes.

'The queen is stirring.' Archbishop Whitgift has stood up from his prayers to lean right over me. 'Is there something you wish to say, Your Majesty? I am right beside you. It is I, John Whitgift, your Archbishop of Canterbury, here to take your final confession.'

I open one eye and glare at him. Confession! As if I would bare my soul to a fool like him! The only man I will confess to is my God.

'Do not be afraid, Your Grace. It is a glorious thing to ascend to heaven, as a virtuous queen is sure to do. You will be greeted by all you loved best, made young again – and whole – when you arrive at St Peter's gates. Your ears will be soothed by heavenly choirs, the weight of the world will lift from your shoulders and you will float like a dandelion from place to place. No rough roads any longer, no mountains to climb, no difficulties or hardships of any kind. Just eternal bliss and peace from now until Judgment Day.'

Unfortunately for the archbishop my imagination has been rather captured by the picture of me floating on air, so I do not listen very closely to the rest of his well-meant words. Instead I close my eyes again and my mind drifts away just like the dandelion he has imagined.

Nineteen

I am alive. My heart beats, my skin is warm, I breathe, my limbs still move. I am alive, but I am dying. I am dying in my own bed with my head still attached to my neck, my skin unpierced by any blade, my stomach untainted by any poison. I am dying at the time of God's choosing and not of any man's. Such a fate has not always been as certain as it is now.

I am alive and I am awake. I do not know the o'clock. I do not know what day of the week it is or even what month of the year. I am alive, but whatever this day may be, it is certainly the day on which I will die.

I am alive and I am afraid. I do not know what awaits me only a few minutes from now, or in an hour or so (surely no longer than that). My world has shrunk to this darkened room, this soft and warm bed. The only sounds that now assail my ears are the faint murmur of prayers. I cannot make out the words of those who pray. I cannot muster the energy required to understand.

Is this what it feels like when you are about to be born? In our end is our beginning, or so they always told me. A new baby is squeezed and pummelled by titanic forces beyond their control, propelled from the warmth and darkness of the only world they have ever known into the wide, cold brightness of earth. Like a baby being born, I only know the world I am leaving; I have no knowledge of the world I am about to enter.

I hear my heart beat; thump, thump, thump. It is the noise that has accompanied me for every moment of my existence. It will cease soon.

I do not know why my thoughts return to the very beginning of my life just when my weary journey is so near its end. I seem to have no control of my wayward brain. It has a mind of its own – if a mind can be said to have a mind.

I have but a few early memories and I was so hungry for them all the way through my life that I often begged those who witnessed my infancy to tell me what they knew. I persuaded them to repeat their words so often that I can no longer separate genuine memory from a story I have absorbed so thoroughly I merely think I remember it.

I think I remember the rustle of skirts and the bright flash of dangling jewellery. I think I remember my infant hands reaching for the glittering objects that hovered so enticingly before my eyes. I think I remember soft skin, a sense of warmth and safety and a low, lilting voice, speaking to me in French. But do I remember this? Or do I simply wish that I did?

I do remember receiving a letter from the Scottish Protestant theologian and scholar Alesius. I was a grown woman when his epistle arrived and I had been many years a queen, yet the story he told me took me back to my lost infancy.

Alesius had been a great admirer of my mother and he happened to be with her in London during the few short weeks of her downfall. There was nothing planned about this; he was simply unlucky enough to be caught up in events that neither my mother nor her admirer could have anticipated. It took a scant three weeks for my mother to fall from queen to executed traitor.

Alesius's letter was one I delighted in receiving and which I have kept in the little box beside my bed alongside Robin's last letter. The box is beside me now, and after I die no doubt it will be opened and all my secrets rifled through. Only a little while ago such a thought would have horrified me. I have no interest now. Let them think what they think – it is out of my hands.

In his letter, Alesius told me that he had watched as the danger my mother was in slowly dawned upon her. At first, she could not believe what was being said about her and how the rumours of infidelity were being used to blacken the mind of the king. However, Alesius wrote, as the precarious nature of her position began to sink in my mother did all she could to save her own life. Alesius described in great detail how one terrible day he watched my mother desperately appeal to my father using the only lever she had left – me, her infant daughter.

'Alas,' he wrote, 'I shall never forget the sorrow I felt when I saw the sainted queen, your most religious mother, carrying you, still a baby, in her arms, and entreating the most serene king, your father. It happened in Greenwich Palace, where he was looking through an open window onto the courtyard when she brought you to him.'

I wept as I read those words. Although the infant me was too young to have any memory of the event itself – as an adult queen I was transported back in time. I knew exactly which window Alesius was referring to and even remembered seeing my father looking out onto that courtyard whenever we were in residence. I had even looked out of it myself. I could easily imagine my mother scurrying towards it, desperation and hope doing battle in her breast. Had she planned this ambush or had she merely seen my father at the window and grasped her opportunity?

As I read further, I could almost feel what the infant me might have experienced being jolted across the courtyard in my mother's arms. Did she hold me up towards my father as she stood below him outside the window? Did she thrust me towards him as she beseeched him for mercy? I do not know. I do not even know what words were spoken between them, because Alesius could see the interview unfold well enough, but he could not hear what was said. What he could tell for certain was that whatever she said, however urgently she proffered my infant self, her words had no effect.

'The faces and the gestures of the speakers plainly showed the king was angry.'

Alesius could not hear but he could see. Indeed, thanks to his letter, I could see the king and the queen too, the one so high, the other so low, as one beseeched and the other rebuffed. That she tried to use me to soften my father's heart was devastating. Of course, using my existence to plead her cause was to no avail. I was the living evidence of the curse my father believed God had placed upon him and my presence would merely have confirmed his desire to be rid of my mother.

I cried as I read about this desperate conversation all those years ago, but did I cry at the time? It would be strange if I did not. Babies are made anxious by adult anger, understandably so, but my distress would not have helped my mother's cause. The noise I made would no doubt have irritated my father, who never liked to deal with the pain of others.

It breaks my heart to think of my mother, so desperate, so courageous, so determined to try and save her own life. It touches me to think that whatever my father might have thought about my existence she still believed that I had some chance of softening his resolve. She loved me – that is clear. I suspect she even loved him, but all in vain. Maybe he still loved her and that is why he treated her so harshly. His own jealousy and pain were overwhelming his reason.

I cannot bear to think of her after my father closed the windows in her face. I cannot bear to think of her left standing in the courtyard, clasping me to her breast and perhaps sobbing in despair and humiliation as she realised that she could no longer move the man she had once had such power over. I cannot bear to think of all the courtiers who, like Alesius, must have witnessed this exchange. I have seen how quickly former friends disappear when a man falls from royal favour. I hope that at least I was a comfort to her. I hope my existence gave some moments of joy to the little bit of life she had left.

Why do I regret the loss of my coronation ring so much? Why do I feel its loss as an amputation, rather than a liberation? I clasp my hands over the bedclothes once more to worry at the space where my ring once sat.

'The queen is praying!' John Whitgift is kneeling beside my bed and is alert to my every move. He begins to pray with redoubled vigour, but he is wrong. I am not praying. I am beyond prayer. If my experience as an earthly judge is any guide, God has already made His determination about me. I am not so arrogant that I do not tremble at what He may have decided. I have broken many commandments. That is the truth of it. Will He, as wise rulers usually do, take the context of my sins into account? Or does He demand that each of us poor sinners stick to the letter of holy law?

If He forgives me my trespasses and allows me to enter heaven, all I really want is to see my mother. She is the reason I miss my coronation ring so utterly. She is why I grieve its loss almost as if it were an actual person. Inside my ring, in a hidden compartment, with me every moment of every day, was the image of my mother. The ring's broken remains are also in the little box beside my bed. (Odd how my most precious possessions are not the rich jewels or priceless objects and books I have owned. They are letters, broken rings, mementos and fripperies of no value to anyone but me.)

Many people lose their mothers. Many never know their mothers – so many women die in childbirth. But I have never met anyone who lost their mother the way I lost mine. It is something I have tried all my life not to think about and yet the terrible circumstances of my mother's death have dogged me, waking or sleeping. I was the cause of my mother's demise. There, I have said it. When I was born, just a girl, the wrong sex, wrong in just about every possible way, my mother mourned while her enemies celebrated. Had I been a prince, her position as my father's queen would have been unassailable. Because I was a girl, she was suddenly much less secure. Eventually, she gave her life for the sin of creating mine. I have carried this burden with me always.

When I see her, if I see her, will she be proud of me? Will she feel that her sacrifice was worth it? Will she think that I, her daughter, a mere girl, have lived my life in such a way as to do her proud?

Just as I am certain that my father will not be proud of my achievements but blame me for failing to carry on his dynasty, so I hope that my mother will feel the opposite. Some have called me a great queen (even my sworn enemy the Pope confessed his admiration) and I have certainly tried to do my best and choose the wisest course. Always I kept the safety and prosperity of my people at the centre of my decisions. Perhaps it was easier to do so because I had no family of my own, no personal investment in making sure my children ruled after me. I concentrated on the present, doing the best I could while I sat on the throne.

I have remained faithful to my mother's Protestant religion. Those who knew her told me the new faith was very dear to her. I have done what I could to support her beliefs, but without fanaticism and with as little bloodshed as I could manage. When I said I did not want to make windows into men's souls I meant it.

I think also that my long and prosperous reign has vindicated her ambition as well as her sacrifice. After death, through me, she bested her great rival, my father's first queen, Katharine of Aragon. The different legacies of my reign and that of Katharine's daughter, Mary, are profound. Mary sought to see England returned to what she and her fanatical mother called 'the true faith'. She failed. I think that after forty-five years of Protestantism, peace and prosperity, England will never become a Catholic country again.

Moreover, despite all the forces that wanted me to desert my mother and pretend that she never existed, I stayed true to her memory (if memory of her is what I have). Quietly (I could not do it loudly, not even when I was queen) I have maintained my loyalty to the disgraced and despised woman who gave me birth. I may have no memory of her, but I have loved her all the same.

When I was ten years old my father decided to have a painting done of his entire family. We did not sit for this portrait together. After all, we had our own households and although my father's last queen, Catherine Parr, did all she could to bring us to court, she did not always succeed. I was told that I was to be ready for my sitting at a certain time on a certain day. The painting was not done by Master Holbein, but by the artists employed in his studio.

'The artist is here, my lady.'

Kat Ashley poked her head around the door. 'Is that what your father's messenger instructed you to wear?'

I had been sent clothes for the sitting. When I saw

the finished portrait later, I noticed that my sister Mary was wearing the same dress so that the two of us looked like matching bookends on the edge of the central group. The dress was nice enough, with a deep red velvet underskirt and sleeves, slashed to reveal the white linen shirt beneath. A richly embroidered gold and silver surcoat completed the outfit. My hood was also red, trimmed with gold. When Kat stuck her head around the door, Blanche Parry was just securing my headdress.

'Yes, Kat, it is the dress that I was sent.'

'I had to let it out a bit in the back,' grumbled Blanche. 'Your father doesn't realise how much you have grown.'

'What are you to wear around your neck, my lady?'

'My instructions were a double-stranded silver chain with a gold pendant of some kind. And I have just the one.'

When I was informed about the forthcoming portrait, I was not pleased. I had been sent some preliminary sketches so I could see how I must stand to fit the design. Several things displeased me. My sister and I were both placed on either side of the central group and quite some distance from them too, but I was the furthest out of all. A sharp, icy sliver of pain ran through me when I saw how publicly my lowly position in my father's affections was to be displayed. But there was another reason I was dismayed. The woman at the centre of the picture, my father's queen, was not his current Queen Catherine Parr, whom I loved and adored, but the mother of my brother Edward, Queen Jane Seymour, even though she had been dead and buried for more than seven years. I hated the slap in the face that this painting represented to my gentle and learned stepmother. My father made no bones about how he saw his family and who he favoured and who he did not. In one way, this made things easier to deal with; in another it was constantly belittling and humiliating.

I was so angry about the slight to myself and to my stepmother that my first instinct was to refuse to be painted at all. I would plead ill health when the artist arrived and retreat to my bed, but when the initial shock wore off, I realised that this was not possible. Nonetheless I wanted to subvert the painting somehow. It took me days of wondering before I finally hit upon the perfect way to make my point.

'Here, Blanche, can you do this up for me?'

Blanche picked up the necklace I had handed to her, but when she realised which one it was, she hesitated. 'Oh, my lady. You have given me your mother's necklace, the one with the "A" for Anne on it.'

'Yes, I have. Could you please do it up for me?'

'But this painting is by order of your father – of His Majesty – of the king and, forgive me for saying so, my lady, but he will not, he won't—'

'It fits the brief perfectly and it is the necklace I want to wear. If you won't do it up, I will. Give it here!'

I took the bauble from her hands and quickly put it around my neck.

Kat moved away from the door and came closer to me. She spoke quietly and without fluster. 'Are you sure? Your father will not be pleased.'

'No doubt he will have it painted over when he sees it, but at least he will have to see it.'

'You are headstrong. I hope it does not get you into real trouble.'

But Kat did not forbid me and I wore my mother's initial around my neck that day. The artist showed me the finished portrait before he left Hatfield. I was pleased to see he had painted the medallion faithfully.

I calculated roughly how long it would take for the artist to paint my sister and return to London. Then I calculated how long it might take Master Holbein's studio to complete the painting and then for my father to see it. My calculations were, at best, a very rough guess for I had no idea how long a painter takes over finishing a painting, particularly one commissioned by the king.

After three months I began to anticipate the storm that was surely about to break over my head. Every night, before I went to sleep, I imagined my father's reaction when he realised that I was in his official Tudor family portrait wearing a necklace that had not only belonged to the wife he had killed, but bore her famous initial.

I waited, and I waited, and I waited. Every time a messenger came from my father's court – although this was not a frequent occurrence – my heart beat faster and the blood buzzed in my ears, but to no avail. I heard nothing. Half a year passed and finally it was Christmas. As usual, we gathered at my father's court for the celebrations. As we packed to leave, particularly as I watched Blanche pack the red velvet and gold dress I had worn in the portrait, I expected that I would soon be admonished by my father, but even Christmas passed uneventfully enough. My father was distant to me, but no more than usual. However, eagle-eyed though I was, I saw no sign of the portrait.

'Your Grace, has the painting I sat for earlier this year been completed yet? I long to see it.' I was sitting with Queen Catherine, holding a skein of wool for her so that it would not get tangled.

'What painting is that? Oh, the one your father has commissioned of his family. I do not know. I do not think it has been completed for I am sure your father would have shown it to me if it had been.'

'I am sorry you are not in it, Your Grace.' I spoke very low so that no one but the queen could hear me. She looked up and gave a quick, wry smile.

'That is kind of you, Elizabeth, but no need to be sorry. I understand that it is a dynastic portrait and so

Queen Jane as the mother of his son, the future King Edward, is the wife who must appear. I do not take my omission personally.'

I longed to tell her that another wife and mother of one of his children would also be appearing in the portrait. However, despite her kindness and obvious partiality for me (oh, how that warmed my poor starved child's heart) I did not dare.

In fact it was not until the following Christmas that I saw the completed picture. It sat upon an easel in an ante-room near my father's apartments. I saw it as we went in to greet him formally, but I did not dare to stop and examine it more closely. I had a necklace around my neck, I could see that, but which necklace it was I could not tell at such a distance. Later that day I slipped quietly into the ante-room for a closer look.

The necklace was as it was painted at Hatfield. Nothing about it had been changed. For a moment, I was delighted! My silent rebellion had survived. My mother's necklace was in the portrait. Her ghost hovered over that picture. Her memory, much as my father wished it erased forever, would remain.

Then my euphoria subsided. Why had it not been painted over? Why had I not been admonished for my audacity? My father had become short-sighted with age and had to wear spectacles for close work. He did not like people to see him wear his eye-glasses, and whipped them off whenever anyone entered the room, but I knew he would have worn them to examine this important portrait closely. Surely, he would have seen what I was wearing about my neck and recognised it? Surely, he would have understood the message of resentment I was sending him?

Then a terrible explanation occurred to me. He *had* pored over the portrait wearing his spectacles, but he had only looked closely at one part. He had only bothered to examine the central group. He had examined minutely his own image, that of his son, my brother Edward, and Edward's mother, Queen Jane. To the rest of the picture, including the portraits of Mary and me, he had given little more than a cursory glance. To him, his daughters mattered not at all. To him, I would always be just a girl.

My breathing is laboured now and I am drifting in and out of consciousness. When I open my eyes I see very little. Just the glow of the candles through the gloom and some shadowy figures around the walls.

I should be praying to my God. I should be preparing my soul for eternal life, but all I can think of is the life I have lived, here, on this small island. I have done all I can. I hope that it has been enough. I hope my successor finds that my kingdom is in good order. I hope that in the future when people think of me, if they think of me, they remember me with respect.

I think I am ready to die. I certainly have not the

will, the enthusiasm or the energy to live. I am prepared to meet my maker. I will take one last sweet breath and then shall breathe no more. I am impatient to meet my maker and I suddenly know exactly who she is.

Mama.

Cast of Characters

In order of appearance:

ANNE BOLEYN (1507–1536)
Second wife of Henry VIII. Mother of Elizabeth I. Executed for treason and adultery 1536. Queen of England 1533–1536.

KATHARINE OF ARAGON (1485–1536)
Youngest daughter of Ferdinand and Isabella of Spain. Betrothed to Prince Arthur of England. First wife of Henry VIII, divorced in 1533. Mother of Mary I. Queen of England 1509–1533.

ELIZABETH I (1533–1603)
Youngest daughter and second child of Henry VIII. Queen of England 1558–1603.

HENRY VIII (1491–1547)
Younger son of the first Tudor monarch Henry VII (1485–1509) and Elizabeth of York, eldest daughter of the last Plantagenet King Edward V. Father of Mary I, Elizabeth I, Edward VI. King of England 1509–1547.

WILLIAM KINGSTON (1476–1540)
Lord Constable of the Tower of London for the majority of reign of Henry VIII. Also MP for Gloucestershire.

MARY KINGSTON (nee SCROPE) (?–1548)
Third wife of William Kingston, who was her second husband. Attendant to the first four of Henry VIII's wives. Attended Anne Boleyn in the Tower and on the scaffold.

JEAN ROMBAUD (unknown)
Official executioner of St Omer in the 1530s. Believed to be the French swordsman who executed Anne Boleyn.

ROBERT CECIL (1563–1612)
Younger son of William Cecil by his second wife, Mildred Cooke. Secretary of state to both Elizabeth I and James I.

PHILADELPHIA CAREY (1552–1627)
Granddaughter of Elizabeth I's aunt Mary Boleyn. Maid of honour to Elizabeth I 1558–1603. Married Thomas Scrope, 1st Baron of Bolton. Also served Queen Anne, wife of James I.

THOMAS CRANMER (1489–1556)
Archbishop of Canterbury under Henry VIII and Edward VI. Executed for heresy by Mary I.

THOMAS CROMWELL (1485–1540)
Chief minister and principal secretary for Henry VIII 1532–1540. Executed for treason.

BLANCHE PARRY (1507–1590)
Attendant to Princess Elizabeth from 1533, cousin to William Cecil and (possibly) John Dee. Chief gentlewoman of the privy chamber 1565–1590. Like her mistress, she never married.

MARY BOLEYN (1499–1543)
Older sister of Anne Boleyn. One-time mistress of Henry VIII. Married to William Carey (1520) then William Stafford (1534). Mother of Catherine Carey and Henry Carey.

KATHERINE (KAT) ASHLEY (nee CHAMPERNOWNE) (1502–1565)
Governess to Princess Elizabeth from 1537. Married Sir John Ashley, Elizabeth's senior gentleman attendant and cousin to Anne Boleyn. On Queen Elizabeth's accession became chief gentlewoman of the privy chamber until her death.

CATHERINE PARR (1512–1548)
Sixth wife of Henry VIII, who was her third husband. Married Thomas Seymour, Baron Sudeley, Lord High Admiral of England, after the king's death in 1547. Queen of England 1543–1547.

MARY, QUEEN OF SCOTS (1542–1587)
Granddaughter of Henry VIII's older sister, Margaret Tudor. Married King Francis II of France in 1558, Henry Stuart, Lord Darnley in 1556 (by whom she had one son, James Stuart, James VI of Scotland, who followed Elizabeth I to the throne of England as James I in 1603), and James Hepburn, Earl of Bothwell in 1567. Executed for treason by Elizabeth I in 1587.

HENRY CAREY, 1st BARON HUNSDON (1526–1596)
Son of Mary Boleyn, cousin to Elizabeth I, brother to Catherine Carey. Created 1st Baron Hunsdon 1559, MP for Buckingham and courtier.

ROBIN DUDLEY, 1st EARL OF LEICESTER (1532–1588)
Playmates as children, he was Elizabeth's great friend and favourite, becoming her master of horse on her accession.

Many consider he was her one true love; there were rumours they would marry when his first wife died in mysterious circumstances. They never did; he later married Lady Essex. Elizabeth made him Earl of Leicester and he was the most richly rewarded of her courtiers throughout her reign.

EDWARD VI (1537–1553)
Youngest child and only legitimate son of Henry VIII. Inherited the throne aged nine, died aged sixteen. King of England 1547–1553.

GUILDFORD DUDLEY (1535–1554)
Younger brother of Robin Dudley, second-youngest son of John Dudley, 1st Duke of Northumberland. He was the teenage husband to Lady Jane Grey. Executed for treason by Mary I in 1554.

LADY JANE GREY (1537–1554)
Granddaughter of Henry VIII's younger sister Mary Rose Tudor. Married Guildford Dudley, son of John Dudley, Duke of Northumberland, in 1553. Queen of England 10 July 1553–19 July 1553. Executed for treason in 1554.

MARY I (1516–1558)
Eldest daughter of Henry VIII. Married Prince Philip of Spain 1554. Queen of England 1553–1558.

PHILIP II OF SPAIN (1527–1598)
King of Spain, his second wife was Mary I of England. Called Philip the Prudent, he nevertheless launched the ill-fated Armada against England in 1588 and was humiliatingly defeated by Elizabeth I's navy.

WILLIAM CECIL, 1st BARON OF BURLEIGH (1520–1598)
Member of parliament and political advisor, he was first a

servant of Edward VI, then Mary I, finally transferring his allegiance to Elizabeth before she inherited the throne. He then served as her chief councillor until his death. She made him 1st Baron of Burleigh in recognition of his great service and looked on him as a father figure.

SIR FRANCIS DRAKE (1540–1596)

Adventurer, sea captain, slave trader and buccaneer, as vice admiral of the English navy he helped defeat the Spanish Armada in 1588. He was the second person to circumnavigate the world, from 1577 to 1580. Knighted by Elizabeth in 1581.

SIR JOHN HAWKINS (1532–1595)

Admiral Sir John Hawkins was the chief treasurer and comptroller of the Royal Navy during the reign of Elizabeth I and was also a slave-trader, navigator and buccaneer. He served as vice admiral in the battle against the Spanish Armada.

CHARLES HOWARD, 1st EARL OF NOTTINGHAM, 2nd BARON OF EFFINGHAM (1536–1624)

Lord High Admiral under both Elizabeth I and James I. He led the navy against the Spanish Armada. He was a cousin to Anne Boleyn (her mother Elizabeth was half-sister to his father). In 1596 Elizabeth made him 1st Earl of Nottingham and Lord Lieutenant-General of England.

ALEXANDER FARNESE, DUKE OF PARMA (1545–1592)

Formidable Spanish military commander who conquered the Netherlands and Flanders. Commanded the troops who were meant to invade England after being transported across the Channel in the Spanish Armada.

RICHARD III (1452–1485)
King of England 1483–1485. Last Plantaganet king, defeated by Henry Tudor (later Henry VII) at Bosworth Field.

HENRY NORRIS (1525–1601)
Trusted courtier of Elizabeth I, son of the Henry Norris executed for adultery with Anne Boleyn. Ambassador to France, Lord Lieutenant of Berkshire and Oxfordshire.

DR JOHN DEE (1527–1608)
Mathematician, astrologer, magician, tutor. Astrologer to both Mary I and Elizabeth I.

JOHN DUDLEY, 2nd EARL OF WARWICK (1527–1554)
Second son and eventual heir of John Dudley, 1st Duke of Northumberland. Complicit in the plot to put Lady Jane Grey on the throne instead of Mary I, he was sentenced to death but reprieved. Died shortly after he was released from the Tower.

AMBROSE DUDLEY, 3rd EARL OF WARWICK (1528–1590)
Also imprisoned with his brothers in the Tower for complicity in the plot to put Lady Jane Grey on the throne, he was reprieved and went on to enjoy high favour as a courtier and general under Elizabeth I. Made Baron Lisle and 3rd Earl of Warwick in 1564.

HENRY DUDLEY (?–1544)
Eldest son of John Dudley, 1st Duke of Northumberland. Killed during the siege of Boulogne in the reign of Henry VIII.

KATHERINE HOWARD (1521–1542)
Fifth wife of Henry VIII. Niece of the Duke of Norfolk, cousin to Anne Boleyn. Executed for treason and adultery in 1542. Queen of England 1540–1542.

LETTICE KNOLLYS (1543–1634)

Third child of Catherine Carey and Francis Knollys, she was the granddaughter of Mary Boleyn. Her first husband was Walter Devereux, Earl of Essex. Her second husband was Robin Dudley, Earl of Leicester, and her third Sir Christopher Blount. Mother of Robert Devereux, Earl of Essex.

ROBERT DEVEREUX, 2nd EARL OF ESSEX (1565–1601)

Son of Robin Dudley's second wife, Lettice Knollys, grandson of Catherine Carey and great-grandson of Mary Boleyn. A courtier and general who was a favourite of Elizabeth I but was eventually executed for treason.

WILLIAM SHAKESPEARE (1564–1616)

Poet, playwright and actor, he had a successful career in the theatre as a member and part owner of playing company The Chamberlain's Men, later known as The King's Men. Wrote many famous poems and plays, including *Twelfth Night*.

SIR HENRY LEE (1533–1611)

Elizabeth I's queen's champion and master of armouries. He also served under her brother, Edward VI, and sister, Mary I.

JOHN DOWLAND (1563–1626)

English Renaissance composer, lute player and singer.

ANTONIO, PRIOR OF CRATO (1531–1595)

Claimant to the Portuguese throne who sought refuge in France and then England. He tried but failed to claim his throne. He died in Paris, in poverty.

MILDRED CECIL (nee COOKE) (1526–1589)

Second wife of William Cecil, Lord Burgleigh, she was a

highly educated woman and translator who was in charge of educating her son Robert Cecil, later secretary of state under Elizabeth I and Robert Devereux, the Earl of Essex.

SIR FRANCIS WALSINGHAM (1532–1590)
Principal secretary to Elizabeth I from 1573 until his death, he was popularly remembered as her spymaster.

ANTHONY BACON (1558–1601)
Brother to Francis Bacon, son of Sir Nicholas Bacon, nephew of Mildred Cecil, he was a spy for Elizabeth I.

FRANCIS BACON (1561–1626)
Younger brother to Anthony Bacon, son of Sir Nicholas Bacon, nephew of Mildred Cecil, he was a statesman, scientist, juror and orator. First person to be designated Queen's Counsel (QC). Made Viscount of St Albans by James I.

DR RODERIGO LOPEZ (1517–1594)
Physician-in-Chief to Elizabeth I from 1581. A Portuguese Christian convert from Judaism, he is thought to be the inspiration for Shylock in Shakespeare's *Merchant of Venice.* Executed for treason for conspiring to poison the queen.

SIR WILLIAM KNOLLYS (1544–1632)
Son of Francis Knollys and Catherine Carey, grandson of Mary Boleyn. A courtier, soldier and MP, he served both Elizabeth I and James I.

FRANCES DEVEREUX (1567–1633)
Daughter of Sir Francis Walsingham, her first husband was Sir Philip Sydney. On his death she married Robert Devereux, Earl of Essex, by whom she had five children. After his execution she married the 4th Earl of Clanricarde and moved to Ireland.

SIR PHILIP SIDNEY (1554–1586)
A poet, intellectual and soldier, he was the son of Elizabeth's great friend and attendant Mary Sidney and nephew of her favourite Robin Dudley. First husband of Frances Walsingham. He was killed fighting the Spanish in the ill-fated expedition to help the Protestant Dutch.

CATHERINE CAREY (1524–1569)
First cousin to Elizabeth I, she was the daughter of Anne Boleyn's sister, Mary, and her husband, Sir William Carey, although rumours persisted that her father was Henry VIII, which would have made her Elizabeth's half-sister. She was made chief lady of the bedchamber on Elizabeth's accession. She married Sir Francis Knollys.

JOHN WHITGIFT, ARCHBISHOP OF CANTERBURY (1530–1604)
Archbishop of Canterbury from 1583 until his death.

CHARLES BLOUNT, 8th BARON MOUNTJOY (1563–1606)
Lord Deputy of Ireland under Elizabeth I, Lord Lieutenant of Ireland under James I.

HUGH O'NEILL, EARL OF TYRONE (1550–1616)
Called Hugh, The Great O'Neill, he led the Irish rebellion against Elizabeth I during the Nine Years' War.

CHRISTOPHER ST LAWRENCE, 10th BARON HOWTH (1568–1619)
Anglo-Irish statesman and soldier who fought under the Earl of Essex and Baron Mountjoy.

THOMAS EGERTON, 1st VISCOUNT BRACKLEY (1540–1617)
Lord Chancellor and Lord Keeper under Elizabeth I, friend

of the Earl of Essex but required to keep him under house arrest at York House when the earl fell from favour.

FRANCES DEVEREUX, DUCHESS OF SOMERSET (1599–1674)
Youngest child of Robert Devereux, granddaughter of Sir Francis Walsingham. Lived through the reigns of Elizabeth I, James I, Charles I, Oliver Cromwell and Charles II. Second wife of William Seymour, Duke of Somerset.

LOUIS PHILIP, COUNT PALATINE OF GUTTENBERG (1577–1601)
Third surviving son of George John I, Count Palatine. He and his brothers partitioned their territory in 1598 and he received half of Guttenberg.

HENRY GREY, 1st BARON GREY OF GROBY (1547–1614)
Courtier, second cousin to Lady Jane Grey, Lady Katherine Grey and Lady Mary Grey.

PENELOPE RICH (1563–1607)
Sister of the Earl of Essex, daughter of Lettice Knollys, granddaughter of Mary Boleyn.

ANNE RUSSELL (1575–1639)
Daughter of John Russell and Elizabeth Cooke, wife of Henry Somerset, 1st Marquess of Worcester.

HENRY SOMERSET, 1st MARQUESS OF WORCESTER (1577–1646)
Aristocrat who married Anne Russell in 1600. He was a prominent Royalist during the English Civil War.

MARY FITTON (1578–1647)
Maid of honour to Elizabeth I, noted for her scandalous

affair with William Herbert. May have been the 'Dark Lady' of Shakespeare's sonnets.

SIR WALTER RALEIGH (1554–1618)
Poet, explorer, scientist, navigator, courtier, he was famous for many expeditions to the New World. He married Elizabeth (Bess) Throckmorton secretly and was imprisoned in the Tower. He was released and continued his successful career under Elizabeth I. He was imprisoned again by James I, then released to lead an expedition to find 'El Dorado', the mythical city of gold. Executed by James I in 1618.

ROBERT SIDNEY (1563–1626)
Poet and arts patron, he was the son of Mary Sidney (nee Dudley) and nephew to Robin Dudley, whose title he inherited.

HENRY STUART, LORD DARNLEY (1545–1567)
Grandson of Margaret Tudor, Henry VIII's elder sister, he was first cousin to both Elizabeth I and Mary, Queen of Scots. He was Mary's second husband and king consort until his murder. He was the father of Mary's only son, James VI of Scotland and James I of England.

JAMES HEPBURN, 4th EARL OF BOTHWELL (1534–1578)
Widely regarded as an ambitious scoundrel, he had three wives, the last being Mary, Queen of Scots. He is believed to have orchestrated the murder of her second husband, Henry Darnley. He fled Scotland when Mary lost her throne but died insane in a dungeon in Denmark.

HENRY WRIOTHESLEY, 3rd EARL OF SOUTHAMPTON (1573–1624)
Soldier and courtier and patron of the arts, he was a friend and supporter of the Earl of Essex. Received a death sentence

for his part in the Essex rebellion, but it was commuted to life imprisonment. He was released on the accession of James I.

RICHARD II (1367–1400)
Ascended to the throne aged ten, he was deposed by Henry Bolingbroke in 1400, who became Henry IV. Shakespeare wrote a famous play about him.

WILLIAM LAMBARDE (1536–1601)
Writer and antiquarian particularly remembered for writing *A Perambulation of Kent*, the first English county history.

HENRY BOLINGBROKE, HENRY IV (1367–1413)
Son of John of Gaunt, grandson of Edward III, cousin of Richard II, he usurped the throne in 1399, becoming Henry IV.

THOMAS HOWARD, 4th DUKE OF NORFOLK (1536–1572)
The pre-eminent nobleman in Elizabeth's court, he was also her second cousin through her grandmother Elizabeth Boleyn (nee Howard). He held many prominent positions despite his Catholic sympathies until he was suspected of plotting to marry the Queen of Scots. He was eventually executed for treason for his part in the Ridolfi conspiracy.

SAINT EDMUND CAMPION (1540–1581)
An English Jesuit priest who trained at the English College at University of Douai, he was executed for high treason. He was canonised in 1970 as one of the Forty Martyrs of England and Wales.

SIR JOHN CROKE (1553–1620)
A judge by profession, he was Speaker of the House between October and December 1601. He was the last Speaker under Elizabeth I.

LADY KATHERINE GREY (1540–1568)
Younger sister of Lady Jane Grey and granddaughter of Henry VIII's younger sister Mary Tudor, she was touted as a possible successor to Elizabeth I.

EDWARD SEYMOUR, 1ST EARL OF HERTFORD (1539–1621)
Eldest son of Edward Seymour, 1st Duke of Somerset, nephew of Queen Jane Seymour. His first wife was Lady Katherine Grey, granddaughter of Henry VIII's younger sister, Princess Mary Rose.

EDWARD SEYMOUR, LORD BEAUCHAMP (1561–1612)
Eldest son of Lady Katherine Grey and Edward Seymour, born in the Tower.

LADY JANE SEYMOUR (1541–1661)
Daughter of Edward Seymour, 1st Duke of Somerset. A writer and sister to Edward Seymour, she was the only witness to his wedding to Lady Katherine Grey. She died a year later, probably of tuberculosis.

THOMAS SEYMOUR (1563–1600)
Youngest son of Lady Katherine Grey and Edward Seymour, also born in the Tower.

LADY MARY GREY (1545–1578)
Third and youngest daughter of Henry Grey, 1st Duke of Suffolk, and Lady Frances Brandon, daughter of Henry VIII's younger sister Mary. Married Thomas Keyes.

THOMAS KEYES (1524–1571)
Sergeant-at-arms for Elizabeth I, secretly married Lady Mary Grey, imprisoned for treason in the Fleet.

JANE SEYMOUR (1507–1537)
Third wife of Henry VIII. Mother of Edward VI. Sister of Edward Seymour, 1st Duke of Somerset, first Lord Protector of Edward VI, and Thomas Seymour, 1st Baron of Sudeley, Lord High Admiral and fourth husband of Catherine Parr. Queen of England 1536–1537.

NICHOLAS THROCKMORTON (1515–1571)
Elizabeth I's ambassador to both France and then Scotland, he was always suspected of being too close to Mary, Queen of Scots. He was also implicated in the Duke of Norfolk's plot to marry the Scots Queen. He was the father of Bess Throckmorton.

BESS THROCKMORTON (1565–1647)
Daughter of Nicholas Throckmorton, she was lady-in-waiting to Elizabeth I from 1584. In 1591 she married Sir Walter Raleigh in secret, gaining Elizabeth's lasting displeasure.

JOHN AYLMER, BISHOP OF LONDON (1521–1594)
Famously hard-line, Aylmer was the bishop from 1576 until his death.

MARGARET (MARGUERITE) OF NAVARRE (1492–1549)
Princess of France, married to Henri II of Navarre.

CATHERINE BRANDON, LADY SUFFOLK (1519–1580)
Fourth wife of Charles Brandon, 1st Duke of Suffolk. Close friend of Catherine Parr.

HENRI II (1519–1559)
Inherited his throne when his elder brother François died, he was a staunch Catholic and persecuted heretics throughout his reign. He married Catherine de Medici by whom he had

ten children, but was famous for his long-term relationship with Diane de Poitiers to whom he gave Chenonceau.

SIR (SAINT) THOMAS MORE (1478–1535)
Statesman, educator, writer and Lord High Chancellor of England under Henry VIII. He was a devout Catholic and refused to acknowledge Henry as Supreme Head of the Church. Executed for treason.

ALEXANDER ALESIUS (1500–1565)
Scottish Protestant theologian, friend and admirer of Anne Boleyn.

HANS HOLBEIN THE YOUNGER (1497–1543)
Famous German humanist and artist working in the court of Henry VIII.

Bibliography

Ackroyd, Peter, 2012, *Tudors: The history of England volume II*, Pan Macmillan, London.

Borman, Tracy, 2009, *Elizabeth's Women: The hidden story of the Virgin Queen*, Vintage, London.

Gristwood, Sarah, 2007, *Elizabeth and Leicester*, Bantam Books, London.

Hutchinson, Robert, 2006, *The Last Days of Henry VIII*, Phoenix, Great Britain.

Hutchinson, Robert, 2009, *House of Treason: The rise and fall of a Tudor dynasty*, Phoenix, London.

Jenkins, Elizabeth, 2000, *Elizabeth the Great*, Phoenix Press, London.

Johnson, Paul, 1974, *Elizabeth I: A study in power and intellect*, Weidenfeld & Nicholson, London.

De Lisle, Leanda, 2014, *Tudor: The family story*, Vintage, London.

Martyn, Trea, 2008, *Elizabeth in the Garden*, Faber and Faber, London.

Plowden, Alison, 2004, *Elizabeth I*, Sutton Publishing Ltd, Great Britain.

Porter, Linda, 2013, *Crown of Thistles*, Pan Books, London.

Shapiro, James, 2005, *1599: A year in the life of William Shakespeare*, Faber and Faber, London.

Soberton, Sylvia Barbara, 2015, *The Forgotten Tudor Women: Margaret Douglas, Mary Howard and Mary Shelton*, Createspace Independent Publishing Platform, USA.

Tillyard, E.M.W., 1943, *The Elizabethan World Picture*, Chatto and Windus, London

Watkins, Sarah-Beth, 2015, *Lady Katherine Knollys: The unacknowledged daughter of King Henry VIII*, John Hunt Publishing, UK.

Weir, Alison, 2009, *The Lady in the Tower: The fall of Anne Boleyn*, Jonathon Cape, Great Britain.

Weir, Alison, 2009, *Elizabeth the Queen*, Vintage Books, London.

Acknowledgements

It is with regret that I leave the world of Elizabeth Tudor for the final time. I am, of course, both delighted and relieved to have completed the task I set myself a decade ago; namely to write a trilogy of novels about the remarkable life of Elizabeth Tudor, written in her voice. But I will miss her. The Elizabeth I have created is a product of my imagination, but the life she lived is not. I have followed the known facts about her remarkable history and times as closely and accurately as I could. Most of what happens to her – in all three volumes – really did happen to her. My aim from the first words of volume one, *Just a Girl*, was to discover what it must have felt like to be her – this famous woman who is most often seen both as an anomaly and from the outside. I have tried to turn the girl, the queen and the ageing Gloriana into a flesh-and-blood human being. Which, of course, she was.

I have been immeasurably aided in this task by my

wonderful publisher Kristina Schulz and editor Mark Macleod. They have been with me every step of the way on this journey and I simply could not have completed this project without them.

Kristina had the guts to publish *Just a Girl* and stick with me as I wrote each of the others. Her warm, wise and thoughtful suggestions have always helped me whenever I got bogged down in my own research – an occupational hazard for any historical novelist. We fall in love with what we discover, sometimes to the detriment of the story. Kristina has always been brilliant at pointing out whenever I have allowed the history to overwhelm the tale.

Mark Macleod has edited all three books with enthusiasm, understanding, encouragement and love. He has taken each manuscript and deftly turned it into something that came alive on the page. My debt to him is unpayable.

There are many other people who have been instrumental in helping me with each of the books over the last ten years and they have been thanked in the acknowledgements section of the other volumes. For *Just Flesh & Blood* I owe Cathy Vallance a particular debt. It was Cathy who suggested I turn the Anne Boleyn section into a prologue. A stroke of genius, to my mind.

I also want to thank everyone at UQP for their help and support over the years. I also want to thank every single reader; without them, none of these books would matter.

But most of all I want to express my gratitude and admiration to Elizabeth Tudor herself. Her existence and commanding presence in history has always mattered to me. Whatever her mistakes and cruelties – and she was a monarch of her times so they were many – she proved to me when I most needed the proof that women could lead, they could wield power at least as well as any man, and they could do so on their own. I hope she helps young readers new to her story in the way she helped me when I was a girl in search of a hero.

After the publication of *Just a Girl*, at a schools session at the Melbourne Writers Festival, a girl – I'd say she was about eleven – revealed to me why I fell in love with Elizabeth Tudor all those years ago. She asked me if I had realised while I was writing that first book that I was rewriting the Cinderella myth. I answered her truthfully that I had not but that she was quite right. I thanked her for her remarkable insight and then I had an epiphany. I knew why it was I loved the long dead Virgin Queen. Cinderella was rescued by a prince. The truly remarkable thing about the neglected, unloved second daughter of the tyrannical Henry VIII was that she grew up, became her own prince and rescued herself.

JUST A GIRL
Jane Caro

I do not remember when I discovered how my mother died, it seems to be something I always knew, a horror I absorbed through my skin.

Determined, passionate, privileged and headstrong, Elizabeth was born into a world where she felt she didn't belong and had to fight to survive.

Her mother, Anne Boleyn, was executed by her father Henry VIII. From that moment on, Elizabeth competed with her two half-siblings for love and for Britain's throne. In the gilded corridors of the royal palace, enemies she couldn't see – as well as those bound to her by blood – plotted to destroy her.

How do you find the courage to become queen even though you are just a girl?

'This is elegant historical fiction.' ***Weekend Australian***

'This confident and well-structured novel draws the reader in.' ***Sydney Morning Herald***

'This is a fine novel, thoroughly engaging and written with passion.' ***Reading Time***

ISBN 978 0 7022 3880 2

JUST A QUEEN
Jane Caro

The Queen of Scots is dead and they say I killed her. They lie!

Just a girl to those around her, Elizabeth is now the Queen of England. She has outsmarted her enemies and risen above a lifetime of hurt and betrayal – a mother executed by her father, a beloved brother who died too young and an enemy sister whose death made her queen.

Not knowing whom she can trust, Elizabeth is surrounded by men who give her compliments and advice but may be hiding daggers and poison behind their backs. Elizabeth must use her head and ignore her heart to be the queen her people need. But what if that leads to doing the one thing she swore she would never do?

'*Just a Queen* takes us right into the heart and mind of Queen Elizabeth I. This is a vivid and true insight into one of England's most fascinating rulers – a powerful retelling of history that is sure to speak to readers today.' **Georgia Blain, author of the acclaimed *Closed for Winter* and *Dark Water***

ISBN 978 0 7022 5362 1